STUART WOODS

UNDER

THE LAKE

SIMON AND SCHUSTER NEW YORK

This novel is a work of fiction. Names, characters, places and incidents either are the product of the author's imagination or are used fictitiously. Any resemblance to actual events or locales or persons, living or dead, is entirely coincidental.

This book is for Mark Sutherland

PROLOGUE

Benny Pope stole the boat because he had never been fishing. He had lived right next to the lake forever, but he had never been fishing. It didn't seem right. The more beer he drank the more apparent this injustice became, and, at two o'clock in the morning, after two quick six-packs, he determined to right the wrong.

He shuffled from his room at the back of Ed Parker's Sinclair station, clutching the other two six-packs of the case of beer, and made his way past the wrecked cars and piles of old tires, through the trees and down to the little dock where Ed rented space to locals. He cast a slightly-out-of-focus eye on the array of small boats tied there and chose the aluminum skiff belonging to the lawyer, McAuliffe, because there was a fishing rod lying in it and because it had two motors. Two motors seemed like a good idea to Benny; you never could tell when one would conk out. Folks were always bringing them up to the station to get fixed.

Benny got the outboard started easily enough, though he nearly fell overboard doing it, then he pointed the skiff toward the middle of the lake, steering an erratic course. The night was clear and warm and still, and the noise the outboard made soon began to intrude upon Benny's appreciation of the nature around him, so he switched it off and changed to the little electric trolling motor which ran off a car battery. Its dim hum was more in harmony with the surroundings, and soon Benny had some line played out behind the boat and was happily trolling aimlessly across the lake, unconcerned with whatever kind of lure he was towing. He was fishing, by God. He glanced back toward the town; the only electric lights to be seen were at Bubba's, where a low-stakes pool game was still going on. The old-timey gaslights along Main Street cast a warm glow over the brick storefronts, giving the white trim a honey tint. It was all very pretty, Benny thought, a pretty town. He was glad he lived there. During the week, he did his work, stayed sober and said hey to folks, helped Ed bring in the business to the filling station. On Saturday nights, he cashed his paycheck, bought a case of beer, and drank it by himself. Sundays, he slept late. He didn't go to Mass anymore. Nobody did. He cracked another cold beer and settled in the bottom of the boat, his head resting against a seat cushion, and gazed, awestruck, at the wild array of stars twinkling at him in the moonless night.

Benny wasn't sure what time it was when he woke up. He was closer to shore, and the little electric motor was draining the last of the battery's juice, barely moving the boat. A moment later it stopped altogether, and the boat drifted. The night and the water were absolutely still. The stars were reflected in the lake, and for a moment Benny felt he was floating in space, with stars both over and under him. He was so enchanted with the beauty of the moment that he didn't even want another beer. Then he saw the lights in the water.

They were obviously not stars; they were too bright and too well arranged. Benny froze just for a moment. The faint memory of an old movie came to him, something about space invaders. If the lights were reflected in the water, then they had to be over his head, but he heard nothing. Jesus God, it was a flying saucer! Those things didn't make any noise, did they? He got slowly to his knees, unable to take his eyes from the reflection in the water. The lights weren't moving; the goddamned thing was hovering right over him! He forced himself to slowly swivel his neck and look up. There was nothing there. It was gone. It had flown off in an instant, without a sound, before he could see it.

Benny's breath rushed out of him in a huge sigh of relief. He sank back into the boat. Now he needed another beer; he drank deeply from it. He was too sober for this sort of experience. He set the beer down on a thwart and reached into the back pocket of his overalls for the half-pint of Early Times he had stashed there in case the beer didn't do the job. It wasn't doing the job now, and he knocked back a bunch of the bourbon and chased it with the beer. His heart was thumping against his chest, accelerated by his close call with being kidnapped into space. Benny had read something in *Reader's Digest* about some folks that had got kidnapped by a flying saucer, and while it sounded like they had had an interesting experience, it sure had screwed up their lives good. Nobody had believed them or anything, and sure as hell, nobody would believe him if he got kidnapped into space and came back to tell about it. Shoot, they didn't believe him about his other experiences, the ones he'd had right here at home, so he could imagine the grief he'd have to take if he told them he'd been off in a flying saucer, even if he really had been. As the bourbon found its way to the right places, he began to chuckle at himself, at his foolishness. He laughed out loud. He began to feel cold, and he pulled at the bourbon again. It was time to be getting back. As he struggled up to the seat to start the outboard, he glanced at the lake. The lights in the water were back, winking at him in the ripples his movements in the boat had made.

He looked quickly above him, determined to catch it this time, then back at the reflection. He did this three or four times before he was sure there was nothing above him. He looked back at the lights. They were still there, but they weren't reflections in the lake. They were *under* the lake.

Benny stared dumbly at the lights for a moment, tried to get his brain to think through the bourbon. The lights didn't seem close to the surface, but far below. And there was a pattern, a familiar pattern. A house. They were the lights of a house. And all of a sudden Benny knew; he remembered. He had seen this place before, and he had never expected to see it again. He looked quickly up at the shoreline for evidence that this wasn't happening. Trees; up yonder a cabin. He turned and looked for the water tower in the town, found its string of red lights in the distance over a promontory. His mind triangulated his position as if it were a big radio. He was in the cove. Oh, sweet Jesus, he was back in the cove.

In terror, he looked back at the lights; now he could see more. He was looking at fields and trees under the lake. He could see the house and the road from above, as if he were floating in some silent dirigible. As he looked, a car, its headlights burning, pulled away from the house and moved rapidly up the road. He had, he knew, seen all this before. Benny Pope lost his fight with panic. He grabbed the starter cord on the outboard and yanked, and thank God, the engine started immediately. Then, as he reached for the gear lever, a soundless explosion of light came from the lake, illuminating the water about him. For an instant the little boat seemed afloat on a sea of pulsating light.

Benny slammed the motor into gear and twisted the throttle wide open. The boat shot forward, dumping him into the bilges, screaming. He kept screaming as he somehow found his knees and got the wobbling, yawing boat pointed toward the distant water tower. His screams mingled with the roar of the motor and echoed off the hills.

• • •

Bubba Brown had finished mopping the floor at Bubba's Central Café and Recreation Parlor and was fishing for his keys to lock up when Benny Pope exploded through the front doors, damn near shattering the plate glass.

"I seen it, Bubba, I seen it!" Benny was shouting. "Over to the cove! I seen it again!"

"Hey! Come on, Benny!" Bubba yelled back at him, holding his wrists and guiding him toward a seat in a booth. "Just sit down here and take it easy for a minute." He got a bottle of his own stuff from behind the counter and poured a stiff one into a water glass. "Here, now get that down and relax."

Benny knocked back the whiskey and held on to the table edges while it did its work. "I seen it, Bubba," he said, and he seemed to be calming down a bit.

Bubba poured him another drink. "Now look, Benny, you been doing real good lately. You been going easy on the booze, and you haven't seen anything for a couple of years now, have you?"

Benny yanked off his Caterpillar cap and wiped his sweaty brow with a sleeve. "I seen under the lake," he gasped.

"What do you mean, you seen under . . ." Bubba stopped and stared at the little man. "Jesus, Benny," he said. "Your hair's done turned all white."

1

John Howell stirred to the sound of a familiar voice. Elisha Cook, Jr., he registered immediately. He kept his eyes shut and listened to the next voice. Sidney Greenstreet. He had the scene before Bogart even spoke: *The Maltese Falcon* and Bogart had just been drugged. Howell sat up and, throwing up a hand against the morning sunlight, stared at the television set in disgust. *The Maltese Falcon* was a midnight, not a mid-morning movie. Where did these people come off putting a black movie like that on at ten o'clock in the morning? Probably some postgrad Bogart freak of a programmer at the station. He should be waking up to *I Love Lucy* reruns, not *The Maltese Falcon*. What was the world coming to? There was no sense of fitness, of propriety, anymore.

He looked about him at the seedy room above the garage. It was a mess, as usual; manuscript paper scattered over the desk and floor; the typewriter, its keys dusty from disuse, waiting. The sight of it filled him with the nameless dread that seemed to start most of his days lately. The inside of his mouth felt like the inside of his head; swollen, in-flamed, dirty. There was an empty Jack Daniel's bottle and a second, one-third empty, on the desk next to the typewriter, silent evidence of the origin of his condition. No, not the origin, just a symptom. The origin was harder to pin down, required more thought than Howell felt able to muster. He fixed his mind on the only thing that would move him off the old leather sofa and get him into the house: a toothbrush. He would kill for a toothbrush.

He squinted to bring his wristwatch into focus: eleven fifteen. Shit, he had an appointment at noon. He struggled upright, slipped his feet into his sneakers, grabbed the empty bourbon bottle and headed for the house, dropping the bottle into a trash can next to the back door. He didn't want the maid picking up empties.

"Afternoon, Mr. Howell," the maid said dryly as he passed through the kitchen. Bitch. He didn't need that from her. He ran up the stairs to the bedroom. She had left it pin neat; the maid wouldn't have to lift a finger. He dug a suit out of his dressing room, flung it on the bed, brushed his teeth violently for two minutes, then dove into a hot shower.

Forty-five minutes later, miraculously on time, he sat flipping idly through the pages of *Poultry Month* magazine and wondering what the hell he was doing there. The reception room was a perfectly normal, even tasteful one, with plush carpets, leather furniture and decent art. Only the seven-foot-high fiberglass chicken seemed out of place.

The phone on the reception desk buzzed, and the young woman lifted it and turned toward Howell. "Mr. Pitts will see you now," she said. She rose and opened the office door for him.

Lurton Pitts came at him from behind the huge desk like a baseball manager comes at an umpire after a questionable call. Only at the moment his hand shot out did the man smile. "John . . . can I call you John? I'm awful glad to meet you. I've admired your work for an awful long time, I can tell you. I've been reading your stuff ever since you won the Pulitzer Prize for the stories about those murders. I read your book about it, too. Fine stuff, that was."

"Well, thanks, Mr. Pitts."

"Call me Lurton, son, everybody does. Can we get you a glass of ice tea or something?"

Howell supposed that a man who had on his office wall a warmly autographed photograph of himself with the Reverend Jerry Falwell would not have a bar in the same office. "No thanks, I'm just fine, uh . . . Lurton."

"Good, good," Pitts said, directing him toward a chair and circling the desk to find his own. "I'm grateful to Denham White for arranging this meeting. I know how valuable your time is, and I'll get right to the point. What do you know about me, John?"

"Well, only what I read in the papers, I guess." Howell knew that the man had over a thousand Little Chickie fried chicken parlors all over the country, that he was the quintessential self-made man, and that he espoused causes and gave money to charities and officeholders that were all over the political ball park, from far right to far left field. It was hard to get a fix on Lurton Pitts.

"I've had a rewarding life," Pitts said, leaning back in his high-backed leather chair and gazing out over the Atlanta skyline. "My daddy was a one-mule farmer until I showed him how to get in the chicken-raising business. I was fourteen when I figured that out. By the time I was twenty-one I was the biggest chicken farmer in the state. I opened my first Little Chickie that year, too. It's grown by leaps and bounds, and I don't mind telling you we're snapping at Colonel Sanders' ass, if you'll pardon the expression."

"Mmmm," Howell said. He couldn't think of anything else to say. Why was he here?

"But my interests have always been broader than the chicken business," Pitts continued. "I'm interested in foreign relations; bet you didn't know that."

"Nope," Howell replied, trying not to giggle.

Pitts leaned forward and fixed Howell with an intense gaze. "John, can I confide in you?"

"Oh, sure." This was some bizarre joke of Denham White's. He would arrive at lunch and there would be six guys around a table, drinking martinis and speechless with laughter. He tried to think of some graceful way just to leave, but failed.

"This is strictly off the record, now."

"Don't worry, Lurton, I'm not a newspaperman anymore."

"This is August first, the year of our Lord 1976," Pitts said. "In November, Gerald Ford is going to be elected President of the United States."

"Could be," Howell said.

"The American people are not going to elect a peanut farmer to the presidency," Pitts said, in a voice that brooked no argument.

Howell agreed with the man but said nothing.

"Four years from November I'm going to be elected the next President of the United States of America," Pitts said, with absolute confidence.

Howell let his breath out as slowly as possible to keep from bursting out laughing and worked at fixing his face in an interested expression.

"I guess that's left you pretty much speechless," Pitts said after a moment.

"Pretty much," Howell agreed. Pitts was not only eccentric, he was crazy. If the American people wouldn't elect a peanut farmer President, why a chicken farmer?

"Well, let me tell you, I'm not going about fulfilling this ambition haphazardly. Some of the finest minds in this country are signing on to help me realize it."

"Anybody I know?"

Pitts held up a hand. "Too soon to talk about that right now. What I want to talk about right now is you."

"Me?" Here it comes, he thought. He wondered how long Denham White had been planning this.

"I want you to write my autobiography."

Howell was so entertained by the contradiction in that statement that he forgot to reply.

"What do you think of that?" Pitts asked.

"Well, it's very kind of you to think of me for something as . . . important as that, Mr. Pitts . . ."

"Lurton."

"Lurton. But I'm pretty wrapped up in my own work at the moment." That was a bald-faced lie; half a dozen publishers had already rejected his attempt at a novel, and he didn't have an idea in his head.

"Yes, Denham White told me that you were writing for yourself at the moment. Of course, you understand that I would expect to meet your usual fee for writing a book. Excuse me if I get personal for just a minute, John, but how much did the Pulitzer Prize pay you?"

"A thousand dollars."

"And how much did you make on the book when that came out?"

"About sixty thousand, I guess."

"Then I would expect to pay you sixty thousand dollars to write my book."

Howell was speechless again, but not in danger of laughing. He was astonished at what the mention of that sum was doing to his insides.

Pitts rose, walked to a credenza, and picked up a cheap plastic briefcase. He set it down in front of Howell. "Tell you what," he said. "This contains twelve reels of recording tape. I've spoken everything I can remember about my life onto those tapes. You take them home and listen to some of them, then call me back and tell me if you think you can make a book out of them."

Howell got to his feet. "Well, I'll be happy to give you my opinion, Lurton, but I don't know . . ."

"Just listen to them, John. I think you'll realize what a story my life has been. Call me in a few days."

"All right." Howell picked up the briefcase and held out his hand.

"There's just two things I ask of you," Pitts said. "First, nobody must ever know that I didn't write the book myself. Wouldn't look good."

That suited Howell. He would never be able to hold up his head again if anybody he knew thought he had even considered ghostwriting a book for Lurton Pitts.

"Second, I'd ask you to do it in three months."

"I'll listen to the tapes first, Lurton, then we'll talk."

"We mustn't meet again, John. Security, you know."

That suited Howell too. He walked the two blocks to his lunch date, sweating in the August Atlanta heat, trying not to think about this. He wanted to hear what Denham White had to say first.

He stepped gratefully into the air-conditioned lobby, took the elevator to the fourteenth floor, and stepped out into the foyer of the Commerce Club. As he entered the large dining room, he could see his brother-in-law across the room at his usual table. Howell picked his way through the elegant room full of Atlanta's most important bankers, businessmen, and lawyers, shaking a hand or tossing a wave here and there. He had known these people from a distance as a journalist, and now he knew them closer up because of whom he had married. He reached the table, and a black waiter was there to hold his chair.

Denham White was dressed in a gray three-piece suit that said "successful lawyer." Howell knew that Denham was dressed by Ham Stockton, the city's premier clothier, who each year chose for him a range of suits, shirts, and ties in basic hues of blue and gray that were entirely compatible. All Denham had to do was to choose any suit, any shirt, and any necktie, in the certain knowledge that they would complement each other beautifully. He could do it with his eyes closed, and he probably did. Denham had already started on the bread. "Well?" he asked, his mouth full.

"Well, what?"

Denham waved at a waiter and ordered them both a martini. "Are you going to do it?"

"You mean you knew what Pitts wanted? And you set me up for that?"

"I only had an inkling. Did he offer you sixty grand?"

"How did you know that?"

"It's what you made on the book, isn't it?"

"You sonofabitch. If you knew he was going to offer me what I made on the book, why didn't you tell me? I would have told him I made a hundred thousand on the book."

Denham spread his hands. "John, the man is my client, after all. He pays me a hundred and fifty bucks an hour to look after his interests."

"I'm your client too."

"Yeah, but you're family; you don't pay. Anyway, where else are you going to make sixty grand in three months? Since this is on the quiet, I can probably get him to pay you in cash. He deals a lot in cash."

"So now my lawyer is advising me to evade income tax?"

"I'm giving you no such advice, boy, I just thought you might find cash more . . . convenient."

A waiter brought menus. "How come you're being so nice to me, Denham?" Howell asked. "I'm not exactly your favorite brother-in-law."

"Sure you are. You're my only brother-in-law. Oh, come on, John, you know I've always liked you. It's made me sad to see you screwing up your life the way you have. You had such a flying start."

"Screwing up my life, huh? I'm doing what I want to do, buddy. How many people you know do that?"

"Almost none, granted, but you're making my sister unhappy, sport, and I can't have that, not if I can help it." Denham was looking serious now.

"And you think my earning a few bucks might fix things up at home, huh?"

Denham looked away from him. "I think your earning a few bucks somewhere else might give you both a breathing spell to figure things out," he said uncomfortably.

Howell looked at him, surprised. "Somewhere else?"

"Well, you don't seem to get a hell of a lot done over that garage, do you? What you need is someplace quiet, out of the way, a place with no distractions." Lunch arrived.

Howell swallowed an oyster. "I have a feeling you have some place in mind."

Denham fished a key out of a vest pocket and slid it across the tablecloth. "How about a cabin in the mountains? Nice view over the lake, total privacy, a writer's paradise."

"I didn't know you had a cabin in the mountains."

"Well, 'cabin' may be stretching it a bit. 'Shack' might fit better." Denham leaned back from his oysters and assumed a faraway expression. "It's up on Lake Sutherland; you know it?"

"No."

"Up in the very prettiest part of the north Georgia mountains. A local power company built it after World War Two; they didn't sell any of the lakefront lots. Instead, they leased them out to friends and other suitables, cheap, on long leases. Kept out the riffraff. I got a lot for a hundred years at ten bucks a year back when I was in law school. My old man knew Eric Sutherland, who built the dam and modestly named both the lake and the town next to it after himself."

"Ten bucks a year? Not bad."

"You know it. I'd go up there on weekends and buy a load of green lumber at a sawmill and have it delivered to a fishing camp at the opposite end. There wasn't even a road around the lake in those days, so I'd nail it into a raft and tow it down the lake with a canoe, then pull it apart. I built a one-room shack, then eventually expanded it into a three-room shack. There's power, plumbing, a fireplace, a phone that sometimes works, and a little runabout with a big outboard. Terribly romantic."

"Terribly primitive, from the sound of it." Howell gazed out over the crowded dining room for a moment. "I'll think about it."

"I hope you'll do more than think about it, boy. You need a change."

Denham was pushing all the right buttons, Howell thought. God knew he needed a change. On the way out of the building, Howell stopped at a phone booth, rang Lurton Pitts and told him he would be his autobiographer—a wonderful word, Howell thought.

"That's fine, fine," Pitts said. Howell could hear him grinning. "I'll see that you get an advance to meet your expenses, and, I'll tell you what, I've got a piece of a company that makes those new word processors. I'll send you one of those over, too. You let me know how you like it."

Howell hung up the phone and pressed his forehead against the cool glass of the booth. The world was suddenly a different place. He wasn't sure he liked it.

It would have been easier if she had been a shrew, Howell thought. He looked at Elizabeth across the breakfast table and, as always, was moved by her pert, wholesome, all-American beauty. She looked the part of the well-brought-up young matron, so attractive in tennis clothes, so active on so many committees. It would have been easier if that were all she was. But from a basement jewelry-design workshop, she had built a mail-order business that employed sixty people, grossed millions of dollars a year, and provided the Howells with a life-style that his own income, even in his best year as a newspaperman and author, could never have made possible. The house was large, comfortable, with a tennis court and pool. There were a Mercedes and a Porsche in the garage, and a giant station wagon for the cook to do the shopping.

It was not as if he was unemployed. He was on the board of her company and was in charge of public relations. He had even tried to do the damned job, but he wasn't cut out to be a flack, especially for his wife. She constantly consulted him about the business, sought his opinion, often took the advice he gave, but he knew she would have done just as well if she had never met him—better, probably.

Howell had tried once to figure out at what time of his life he had been happiest, and he reckoned it was before the Pulitzer, when he was out there on the ground—chasing Klansmen in Mississippi; following waning presidential candidates through the hell of grange meetings and barbecues and rubber-chicken dinners in smoke-filled hotel banquet rooms; living in rented cars and Holiday Inns and screwing campaign aides and girl reporters for lack of anything better to do; impaling some grafting state politician on his long-distance records and credit-card stubs; flying through thunderstorms in light airplanes toward hot stories that turned cold before the plane touched down; needling nervous governors with embarrassing questions about their relatives and political appointments; and finally, helping a black police chief in a small Georgia town nail a politically protected maniac who had been burying teenaged boys in his backyard for more than forty years. On reflection, that had been the one that finished him as a reporter. It had brought him the Pulitzer, it had brought him the book, and it had brought him the most horrible thing of all, the daily column.

There was a moment when it might all have been avoided. He knew that moment well; it came back to haunt him whenever he began to reminisce like this. The two things had come at once. He had been Atlanta bureau chief for the *New York Times* when the call came. It was Vietnam, the executive editor had said, in tones conveying that something rare was being bestowed. As it was every professional soldier's dream, it was every newspaperman's: a war. Nearing the end, to be sure, but ahead loomed a glory never before imagined by a journalist: the opportunity to report the chaos accompanying a final American defeat. Reporters had been scrambling for the war correspondent's mantle since the mid-sixties, but not Howell. There were other, even more important things happening at home, he said, whenever the subject had come up. And now he was being handed the thing on a platter.

He didn't want it. He had a comfortable life, and he didn't want to live in tents and bathe biweekly; he didn't want to spend his evenings in Saigon bars with tiny whores draped all over him; he didn't want to get *dirty.* But there was more: at the bottom of him, undermining all the ambition and aggressiveness, he was, he knew, flat scared. He'd been brave and foolish too often already, and he felt he'd used up whatever luck he might have coming to him. He didn't want to get shot at, and especially, he didn't want to get shot. He didn't want to die in the mud with his belly full of grenade fragments; he didn't want to scream his way to the ground in a burning helicopter; he didn't want to turn to jelly, as he knew he would, when the shooting started. He didn't want to go, and he couldn't turn it down. That would have finished him; he would never have lived it down.

And then, when he had said he would go, salvation came. The *Atlanta Constitution* called. They needed a name, and he filled the bill. He could do pretty much what he wanted; he told them he wanted a column, and, somewhat to his surprise, he got it. The money was great; he was leaving the *Times* for something better; and he wouldn't die in a jungle.

But he hadn't counted on what the column would do to him. Shoveling a thousand words a day into the omniverous maw of that page-two killer, five days a week, fifty weeks a year, while all the time eating rich lunches, wearing Ralph Lauren suits and trooping from Kiwanis to Rotary to Lions Club for after-dinner speeches at five hundred bucks a pop—all that had wrung him dry in just under three years, had left him ripe for the editorial arguments and final fistfight that had blown him out of newspapers for good. At least he'd got out with his reputation, before the column had lost its bite. In between the humor pieces and the human interest stuff, there had been enough hard-hitting investigative stories to stamp him firmly in his readers' minds as a first-rate reporter. Since then, though, in spite of the crutch of novel writing, he had been good for nothing but lunch and tennis every day at the club with rich men's sons who couldn't make it in even their fathers' businesses.

"Look," he said. "It's only three months."

"Can't you do it here?" she asked, knowing he had already decided he wouldn't.

"I think it would do me . . . do us both good if I just lock myself in up there and get this out of the way."

"I'll miss you so, Johnny." She meant it, too.

He shook his head. "I haven't been much use to you around here," he said.

"I don't mind about the sex, really I don't. You'll get over it. Maybe if you saw a doctor . . ."

He flushed, felt cornered. He hadn't meant to open that particular subject.

"You don't *have* to sleep over the garage, you know. I know I may not be the greatest thing in the world in bed, but . . ."

"Oh, it's not your fault, Liz, really it's not. Look, it was fine as long as I had work of my own. We had some good years when I was still on the paper, and a good year when I was working on the novel. It's just been the past year, when nobody wanted the book, when I couldn't come up with something else. Well, now there's something else. I just want to go away and get this job done, then I can come back fresh and . . ."

"You're not coming back, are you, Johnny?" Tears welled up and rolled down her face.

He put a hand on her cheek. "Don't do that, please, Lizzie. I'm not running out, really I'm not." He hoped he sounded more convinced of that than he felt. "I'm just no good to you the way things are now, and maybe the time away will put things into some sort of perspective for both of us. We both need the time." How many times had that line ended a marriage, he wondered.

"I love you, Johnny."

"I know, I know." He didn't return the sentiment; he didn't know whether it would be a lie, and he didn't want to lie to her.

"I wish there were something else I could have done, Johnny." She meant it, she really did, and that made it hurt all the more. "I wish you could have found a way not to feel such guilt about the money."

Picking his way through the lovely suburban streets, he wondered how different things might have been if he had gone to Vietnam and survived; if he had married a girl who would have been content to live on a reporter's salary. But after a Pulitzer and a book, who could have resisted the chance to editorialize, to pontificate in a daily column? And who could have resisted the poised and beautiful girl who had been so drawn to the newspaperman? Not many, perhaps, but a wiser man would have been a better politician in a newspaper empire, would have said less of what he thought, would have been less of a pain in the ass to management. A more temperate man would have thought before chucking it all for the risky game of writing fiction. A less volatile man wouldn't have burned so many bridges. Downtown in an office building there was still an executive editor with three capped teeth and a permanently bruised ego.

He drove north on the interstate and watched the hills rise around him. After two hours he turned onto a state road that climbed even higher and turned more sharply. The big station wagon, overloaded with the remnants of his life and the shiny new word processor, swayed horribly on the bends. God, he missed the Porsche. Three hours from Atlanta he found the southern shore of the lake and, following Denham White's directions, wound along it toward the town of Sutherland. The lake glistened in the midday sun. It didn't look man-made, he thought; it was too beautiful. He would have thought a finger of some ancient glacier had scratched it out. Suddenly, looking out over the water as he drove, he felt a tiny knot of dread forming inside him. Three months here pounding out garbage, and then what? Sixty grand in the bank and nowhere to go with it but down. He had the peculiar and very real feeling that he might never leave this place.

• • •

In Sutherland, a man answered a telephone.

"Yes?"

"You know who this is?"

"Yes."

"I have some information for you."

"I'm listening."

"They've sent a reporter up there to do some digging."

A pause. "When?"

"I don't know. From the conversation I heard, he could already be there."

"Well, I'll waltz him around a little and send him on his way."

"You don't understand. My impression is that he's not going to introduce himself."

"I'm not sure I get your drift."

"Well, I only heard a part of a conversation between two editors, but it sounded to me like they were sending a man up there undercover."

A snort. "He'll have to go under*ground*. There's no cover up here. I know who comes and goes."

"Well, I just thought I'd tell you what I heard."

"Thanks, I'll keep an eye open. You calling from a pay phone?"

"Of course. If this comes to anything, just remember where you heard it."

"Don't worry about that. Thanks again."

3

As Howell drove into Sutherland a red-brick, white-columned colonial house appeared on the lake side of the road, its back garden rolling down to the water. Near the road a black gardener was being supervised by a tall, elderly man with a fringe of white hair. This had to be Eric Sutherland, the power company owner and, from what Denham White had said, de facto ruler of the town which bore his name. "Better call on the old man and pay your respects," Denham had advised. "He'll be your landlord, in a manner of speaking, and he likes to know who's treading on his turf." On impulse, Howell stopped the station wagon and got out. Might as well get it over with.

"Mr. Sutherland?" He approached and offered his hand. The man grunted and took the hand gingerly. "My name is John Howell. My brother-in-law, Denham White, has offered me his cabin up here for a while, and he suggested I drop by and say hello."

Sutherland glanced at the heavily loaded station wagon. "Looks like you could be homesteading, Mr. Howell."

"Well, yes, I suppose it does. I should be here for about three months, and I didn't want to make any unnecessary trips back to Atlanta." Howell nodded toward the lake. "What a beautiful setting. I understand this is all your handiwork."

"Yes, it is," Sutherland replied, without modesty, "and God couldn't have done a better job." He didn't seem to take much pleasure in his achievement, Howell thought. "I like the folks who come up here to do their part in keeping it as it is."

Howell smiled. "Well, I've no plans to change anything."

"Yankee, are you?" asked Sutherland.

"No, sir, North Carolina originally. Chapel Hill. Guess my accent

has gotten a little scrambled with my travels." Shit, the old bastard had
him on the defensive already.

"I knew your father-in-law. Damned good man."

Howell nodded. "So I hear. He died before I met my wife." Howell
had heard nothing of the kind. Denham White Senior had been a ruth-
less buccaneer of a businessman; not even his own children had a kind
word to say about him. Howell figured anybody who remembered him
as a "damned good man" bore watching himself. "Well, it's nice to have
met you, sir," he said, starting to turn toward the car. But he had not
yet been dismissed.

"I believe you're a newspaper reporter," Sutherland said, staring
right through him. "What do you think you might have to report on in
these parts?"

"No, sir, I've been out of the newspaper business for a couple of years
now. I'm writing free lance; that's why I'm up here. I'm working on a
book."

"And what is the subject of your book? Wouldn't be anything local,
would it?"

Howell was a bit taken aback by Sutherland's increasing hostility.
"Oh, no, sir. It's a novel. I'm . . . not quite ready to talk about it just
yet. Superstitious, I guess."

Sutherland gazed at him in silence for a moment. "We've already got
too much superstition around here," the old man said. "Good day."
Abruptly, he turned and walked toward his house.

As the man walked away, Howell reflected that, in his experience,
people who didn't like reporters usually had something to hide. He tried
to shake off the thought. He wasn't up here to report on anything; he
had other work to do.

He drove slowly through the little town, a neat, prosperous-looking
place with the usual assortment of stores and businesses for a small
north Georgia town, but with a difference. The business districts of
Georgia towns were not, in general, very pretty. The shops and offices
grew up out of necessity rather than by plan, and if one merchant had
some sense of taste and style, his next-door neighbor usually didn't,
creating a hodge-podge that averaged out as plain, or sometimes, plain
ugly. But Sutherland looked as though someone had worked out a uniform architectural plan on Main Street. The buildings were all consis-
tent in style, and there were no neon or other garish signs. Instead, the
name of each business was lettered in the same typeface. There were
old-fashioned gaslights here and there and park benches scattered along

the street where elderly people took the sun. The effect was pleasing, Howell thought, if a little artificial, and it seemed to have grown out of one mind. He had not much doubt that the mind was Eric Sutherland's. Still, if Sutherland the man didn't radiate much charm, Sutherland the town did, and he liked it.

Following Denham White's instructions, he continued through the town and along the mountainous north shore of the lake until he came to a crossroads with a mailbox marked WHITE. He turned left and drove downhill through dense woods toward the water. Suddenly, after a few hundred yards, he came around a sharp bend and had to brake hard. The road simply disappeared into the lake. He sat, bemused by this circumstance, thinking it was Denham's idea of a joke. Then he looked to his right, and there, at the end of a few yards of overgrown drive, was the cabin.

It sat right at the lake's edge, seeming to lean into the steep slope of the hillside. A deck reached out over the water, supported by piles; a motorboat covered with canvas rested under it. An open woodshed next to the front door contained three logs. Howell groaned at the thought of chopping wood. He backed the wagon into the drive and got out. The place was certainly ramshackle, but not as bad as he had imagined. He climbed the steps, testing each with his weight. Sturdy enough. The key worked smoothly in the lock. He stepped into a room which ran the length of the cabin, perhaps twenty feet, and was half as wide. A large fieldstone fireplace dominated the wall facing the lake. Light poured in through windows which ran the length of the room, overlooking the deck and the lake. On either side of the fireplace was a door. The first opened into a decently equipped kitchen, the second into a bedroom.

The whole place was furnished with what looked like remnants of various White households. There was an old leather Chesterfield couch and a couple of beat-up armchairs in front of the fireplace. A large round table sat near the kitchen door, surrounded by eight chairs, three of which matched. At the far end of the room there was a small rolltop desk and an office chair. Next to the desk was an old-fashioned player piano with a stack of dusty rolls on top. The bedroom contained a double bed, a bureau, and, along one wall, a length of iron pipe concealed by a curtain, making an ample closet. A bathroom led off the bedroom.

He tried the bed. Not bad. In fact, the whole place was not bad. Denham White had been too modest about his building skills. Oh, there probably wasn't a square angle in the place, Howell thought, but it was snug and comfortable. Everything he needed. For a moment he felt uprooted, forlorn. Quickly, he gathered himself up and went about getting settled. An hour later the wagon was unloaded, his clothing put away, and the word processor sat in its boxes next to the desk. Tomorrow would be soon enough for that. He sat down at the piano and played a few chords. Needed tuning. He had played in a dance band in college, but since then, only at the occasional party. He pumped the pedals. Nothing happened.

He went into the kitchen and opened cupboards. Dishes, jelly glasses, the usual for this sort of place. There was a curtained-off pantry at the end of a counter. Howell brushed it open and found a dismantled outdoor grill, half a sack of charcoal, and a double-barreled shotgun. He stood looking at the weapon as if it were a deadly snake. There was a sourness in his stomach, a weakness in his knees. He would have to share this place with that thing, that black, shiny, tempting instrument, that key to the Big Door, that way out. He had owned a pistol until recently; he had thrown it off a bridge into the Chattahoochee River, afraid to have it handy. He jerked the curtain back into place and resolved to forget that it was there.

There was no food in the place, but he needed to go into Sutherland anyway. In town, he found an attractive little shopping center with a large supermarket. He was puzzled by an extremely large display of electric heaters in the hardware department. Ten bags of groceries in the car, he stopped at the post office to tell them who and where he was, then at the telephone exchange to ask them to turn on the phone in the cabin. On his way back he stopped at a Sinclair station for gas.

A wizened little man with snowy hair stopped fixing an inner tube and shuffled out to the car. "Fill 'er up with the high-test and check the oil and water, please," Howell said, as he got out of the car to stretch. There was another man tilted back in a chair against the building, whittling.

"Lotsa groceries there," the white-haired man said as he started the gasoline pump. "You staying around?"

"Yep, up at Denham White's place on the lake, near the crossroads."

The man's brow furrowed and he shook his head. "Better you than me, friend," he said.

"Huh?"

"I know young Denham," the man said, seeming not to want to pursue his first remark. "His daddy used to come up here and hunt with

Mr. Sutherland. I used to run dogs for 'em. He's under the lake now, Mr. White."

"Beg pardon?"

"Under the lake."

The other man got up and walked over. "Passed on," he said. "Local expression. I'm Ed Parker. You staying with us for a while, then?"

"A few weeks."

"I'm Benny Pope," the little man said. "Hope we'll have your business while you're here." He looked at Ed Parker to see if he'd said the right thing.

Parker smiled at him. "Benny's my number one salesman," he said.

As Parker spoke, another car pulled into the station, and a man wearing a tan gabardine suit and a Stetson hat got out. "Fill 'er up, Benny," he said, then turned and looked at Howell.

"Aren't you John Howell?" he asked.

"That's right."

"Recognized you from your picture in the paper. I'm Bo Scully. I used to read your stuff in the *Constitution.*" He stuck out his hand. "I liked it," he grinned, "most of the time."

"Most of the time ain't bad," Howell laughed, taking the man's hand. "That's more often than my editors liked it."

"How come I don't see your column anymore?"

"Oh, I left the paper a couple of years ago. I'm staying out at Denham White's place for a while, working on a book."

"Well, that's a right nice place out there; nice view," Scully said. "Say, I was just going across the street to Bubba's for a cup of coffee. Join me? Benny'll park the car for you."

Howell shrugged. "Sure. I could use a sandwich, too. Missed lunch."

"Bubba will feed you," Scully said, starting across the street. He was a big man, six three or four, Howell reckoned, with the musculature of an ex-athlete, fading red hair with a touch of gray, and an open, freckled, Irish-looking face; probably in his mid-forties. Howell came up to his shoulder. Scully ushered him into the café. "Bubba, this is John Howell. You remember, the columnist for the *Constitution?*" Bubba waved from behind the counter. "Fix him one of your best cheeseburgers. How you like it, John?"

"Medium is fine." Howell heard a loud click and looked toward the back of the place where a couple of men were moving around a pool table. Howell had followed up stories in a hundred places like this in little towns across the South. It smelled of chili and stale cigarette smoke. The churchgoing people of the town would think it was a fairly disreputable place, but a man could get a cold beer here, and Howell liked it.

"Medium, Bubba, and two cups . . . could you use a beer, John?"

"Sure."

"A beer and a cup of coffee. I'm working this afternoon." He showed Howell to a booth. "So, what sort of book brings you up this way?"

Howell told him what he had told Sutherland.

"A novel, huh? Guess you don't want to talk about what it's about."

"Not yet, I guess. Tell me, how many people live in Sutherland?"

"Oh, round about four thousand now, I guess, what with the new hair curler factory that opened up this spring."

"Much industry?"

"Much as Mr. Sutherland wants."

"He decides that sort of thing?"

"He decides pretty much what he wants to. Mr. Sutherland is responsible for the prosperity we've got here."

"You mean the lake, the tourists it brings?"

Bo Scully chuckled. "Tourists are just about the last thing Mr. Sutherland wants. They're noisy, dirty. There's a public beach way down the other end by the fish camp, but that's it. The power company owns the whole lakeshore and leases lots to those folks Mr. Sutherland feels are all right."

"Then what's the source of the prosperity?"

"The dam. That was built with Sutherland family money, and it's owned by Sutherland Power. They wholesale the electricity to the Georgia Power Company, which brings in a bunch of money, you can bet your ass."

"I can see how it would," Howell replied.

"The nice part for the town is that Sutherland Power sells electricity dirt cheap, locally. With what's happened to fuel prices since the Arabs got mean, you can imagine what a magnet that would be for industry to come in here."

"That must be why the supermarket sells so many electric heaters."

"You bet. There's not a gas stove or furnace in the town. Most folks have got electric heat pumps and furnaces, and those who don't use electric room heaters. It wouldn't even pay to chop your own wood around here, unless you're just a romantic who likes to gaze into a fire."

"Speaking of chopping wood, you know anybody I could get to stock up the cabin?"

"Sure, ol' Benny across at the gas station'll do it. He's got a chain saw, picks up a few bucks cutting wood for the summer folks. Up here, it can get pretty chilly at night, even in July."

"Great. So what industries do you have locally?"

"Well, like I said, there's the new hair curler factory, and there's a brassiere factory, and we've got a big plant that manufactures plywood, too."

"That's it? With the cheap power, I'd have thought you'd be crawling with industry."

"Like I said, Mr. Sutherland makes those decisions. He only lets new business in when he's ready to develop a new section of town, and he's pretty choosy about what he lets in. Last year one of the girlie magazines wanted to open up a big printing plant down here, but Mr. Sutherland wouldn't have it. He's got a puritan streak, he has, although he'll take a drink. Throws a big party out at his place every fall and serves booze. We're a wet town, too; a man can get a drink—not a mixed drink, mind you, but a bottle."

Thank God for small mercies, Howell thought. "How long has the lake been here?" he asked.

"They started the dam after World War Two, as soon as they could get materials again. Filled it up in '52."

"Looks older than that."

"It does, doesn't it? But we've got clear mountain water feeding it, you know, not your muddy Chattahoochee. I think the mountains help, too. It was a deep little valley before the lake."

"What was in the valley before?"

"Just farms, a few houses, a country school, a church. The town of Sutherland hardly existed. It's mostly been built since, because of the lake. The lake has been a grand thing for us. We're grateful to it every day, I can tell you."

"Did Sutherland have any problems putting the land together when he built the dam?" Scully's reaction made Howell think he had hit a nerve.

Scully looked down into his coffee and took a deep breath. "Oh, there's always a few malcontents in a case like that, I guess. Folks were well compensated for their land, though. Got better'n market value." He looked up at Howell. "Don't let anybody tell you different."

Howell wondered if they had been compensated at anything like the rate Eric Sutherland had been for the use to which he put their land.

Since Scully seemed uncomfortable with the subject, Howell changed it. "You look like you might have played some football, Bo."

"Oh, yeah," Scully replied, smiling again. "I played in high school, and I played two years down at Georgia for old Wally Butts. Made all-conference my sophomore year."

"What happened? Get hurt?"

"Flunked out." He grinned ruefully. "Not even Wally Butts could save me. That was in '50. Korea was happening. They were about to draft me anyway, so I joined the Marines."

"Action?"

"Oh, sure. There was plenty of that to go around."

"You seem to have come out in one piece."

"Well, I got my Purple Heart. Didn't pay too dearly for it, though. I'll tell you the truth, it was worth it to get out of there. Police action, my ass. They should've sent cops." Scully glanced at his watch and made to get up.

Howell suddenly didn't want him to go. He needed the company, the conversation; he didn't want to go back to that cabin and be alone. "What do you do with yourself, Bo?" he asked, willing the man to stay a little longer.

"Oh, I'm the sheriff," Bo Scully said, laughing and getting to his feet. "Better keep your nose clean, boy, or I'll put you *under* the jail." He punched Howell playfully on the shoulder. "Well, I've got half the county to cover. I'll see you around, I 'spect. Bubba, put John's lunch on my tab." Then he was gone.

Howell sat there, trying to raise enough energy to move. He wondered if Eric Sutherland ran the sheriff like he ran everything else. Sutherland seemed like the sort of man who, if you got in his way, would put you not just under the jail, but, as Benny Pope would have put it, under the lake.

Howell went back to collect his car. As he paid for the gas, he asked Benny Pope about the firewood.

"Sure," Benny said. "I'll run out there on Sunday, if that's soon enough. I don't get off here until seven on weekdays, and I ain't about to get caught out at the cove after dark."

Howell was about to ask why not, when Benny almost snapped to attention. "Afternoon to you, Father," he said over Howell's shoulder. Howell turned to see a peculiar sight in a small Georgia town: a Catholic priest, and a very old one at that.

"God bless you, my son," the priest said to Benny, making the sign of the cross, then continued walking down the street—a little unsteadily, Howell thought. Surely there couldn't be enough Catholics in Sutherland to warrant a full-time priest, or enough for him to worry about to get him looped this early in the day, he thought as he got back into the car.

It had been clouding up all afternoon, and before he could get back to the cabin it began to rain heavily. He got soaked trying to unload the groceries during a lull in the thunderstorm. That night he ate a can of spaghetti, staring disconsolately into a fire of his only three logs, and washed his dinner down with a bottle of California burgundy. He sat listening to the rain on the roof. He felt not just cold, but as if he would never be warm again. He had relentlessly painted himself into this corner, leaving first his work, then his wife and home. He had used up what life had given him, spent his good fortune in a profligate way. He had not been able to preserve anything that was important to him, not even his self-respect; he had sold that cheap to Lurton Pitts. Now he had imprisoned himself here in this shabby place, and he knew no one was coming to get him out. He got well into a bottle of Jack Daniel's before passing out on the sofa, alone with his terrible self-pity.

In the middle of the night Howell jerked awake, ran to the bathroom, and retched until he was too weak to rise from his knees. He sprawled on the linoleum floor, his cheek pressed against the cold porcelain of the toilet, still drunk, still sick, and shivering with cold. He tried not to think. That was the trick, he said to himself, struggling to his feet and leaning heavily against the wall; no thinking.

He shuffled out of the bathroom, through the living room, toward the kitchen. Don't think about the girls you've screwed, don't think about your wife; don't think about the work and the glory; don't think back, don't think forward; don't think about God or what's waiting; don't think at all. He noticed vaguely that it was still raining outside. Don't think about the rain. He made it to the kitchen and flipped the light switch. Nothing happened. Power failure. He ripped back the curtain and found the cold steel, found the box of fire and lead. He bruised a shoulder on the kitchen doorway in the darkness, dropped the shotgun, picked it up again, got to the living room.

He sat down on the back of the sofa, facing the lake, and fumbled for the shells. Don't hesitate, don't think; one move after the other, no pauses. He got two shells into their chambers. Would it take two? Don't think about it, keep moving right along. He turned the gun around, rested the stock on the floor, and put the barrels into his mouth. Steely, oily taste. He couldn't reach the triggers and still keep the barrels where they would do the most good. He kicked off a shoe, ripped off a sock, and felt for the triggers with his big toe, trying twice and failing. His legs were too weak; his foot trembled uncontrollably whenever he lifted it from the floor.

He went to the desk and got a pencil, good old No. 2, yellow job, schoolboy's friend. Don't think about school, childhood; he wedged the pencil between his toes, put the barrels back into his mouth, got the toe-held pencil through the trigger guard, and pushed. The pencil slipped sideways, couldn't be held by the toes. There was a flash of lightning, illuminating everything, making the barrels gleam, huge sticks of licorice protruding from his mouth. Finally, he got the pencil back into the trigger guard, froze it there for a moment, lifted his other foot to the pencil, and pushed it against the triggers, hard, with both feet.

Howell thought he wouldn't hear anything, but it was the loudest noise he had ever heard. He let go of the shotgun, fell over the back of the sofa, and sprawled on the floor, the noise still in his ears. The windows and French doors rattled violently. Thunder, unbelievable thunder, and he was still alive. Why hadn't the shotgun gone off?

He struggled to his feet and started around the sofa to find the shotgun; then he stopped. It had gone very quiet. It was pitch dark, but he knew absolutely. There was someone else in the room.

He stood perfectly still, held his breath, and listened. He could hear breathing, and it wasn't his. He let out his breath as slowly as possible. He opened his mouth and breathed in again. "I know there's somebody . . ."

His words turned into an involuntary shout as a blinding-white flash of lightning lit the room for a tiny moment, fixing everything in it in his mind's eye before winking silently out, leaving him cringing, blinded. He saw it all against the insides of his tightly closed eyelids, the room, the rug, the furniture, and—standing with back not quite turned to him —a child of eleven or twelve, a farm child, in overalls and a blue work-shirt, pigtails, a girl, standing at the window, nearly in front of him, eight or ten feet away, ignoring him, gazing out over the lake.

Howell opened his eyes to blind blackness, then jammed them shut again as a second roaring explosion of thunder assaulted the cabin, violently rattling the windows and the French doors, making him think the glass would shatter. As he opened his eyes again, another, steadier roar filled the cabin and, as suddenly as the lightning, the lights came on, causing him to jump and cry out. The child was gone. One of the

French doors was open and banging, and rain was coming through it. He ran to close it, and was instantly soaked by the downpour. He put his hands to the glass and looked out over the lake, or where the lake should have been. All he could see was a solid wall of rain, coming down vertically, no wind, the heaviest rain he could remember.

No child should be out in that, he thought, and he started to open the door and look for her, but the intensity of the rain frightened him, and he hesitated. He backed away and stood in the middle of the room, wondering whether the roof could take it. For two or three long minutes the rain came down, the sound of it riveting him to the spot. Then it seemed to slacken, and half a minute later it was no more than an ordinary thundershower.

Howell opened the door and stepped onto the deck, unmindful now of a rain that seemed gentle compared to what had just passed. Brief flashes of lightning illuminated the deck, the lake, and the woods around it. He could not see the girl, and he hoped she was all right. He felt ashamed that he had not gone after her.

He went back into the cabin, took a towel from the still-unpacked linen box, and rubbed his face and hair. He cautiously looked into the bedroom and kitchen to be sure he was alone. Every light in the cabin was on, lights he was sure were not burning when he had fallen asleep on the sofa. He picked up the bottle of bourbon and drank directly from it. His heart was still thumping against his chest, and he was breathing so rapidly that he nearly choked on the whiskey. He sat down heavily on the sofa and waited for the warmth of the bourbon. Gradually, his vital signs regained some sort of normality, but he still felt stunned, unable to cope with the image of the child, unwilling to wonder whether he had truly seen her there.

Then he remembered what he had been about before the thunder had interrupted him. He got up and walked around the sofa. The shotgun was gone; so was the box of shells. Had the child taken them? Had she been watching the whole thing, wanting to stop him? He was embarrassed to think that someone had seen him in those circumstances. But why hadn't the shotgun fired? He remembered the triggers giving way under the weight of his feet on the pencil. The pencil lay at his feet, broken in two. He was sure the triggers had moved.

Somehow, he didn't feel cheated; he didn't want the shotgun back. Something had saved him from that one, mad moment, and he was glad. He got a blanket and a pillow from the linen box, then went about the cabin, turning off lights. He went into the bedroom, stripped off his wet clothes, and threw himself onto the bed, exhausted. In his last moment of wakefulness, he reflected that, a few minutes before, he had hit bottom, and he had bounced.

Howell's response to the hammering was panic; he didn't know where he was, and when he remembered, he wasn't sure what had happened during the night. The events seemed curiously remote, and he would have thought he had been dreaming, if he had not remembered everything so clearly. Finally, his muddled brain focused on the front door as the source of the noise, and, cursing, he struggled into a bathrobe and got going, shivering in the damp chill of the uninsulated cabin. It was still raining. He yanked open the door.

A young man stood on the landing, rain dripping from his slicker and from his hair. It seemed immediately obvious to Howell that he was probably retarded. His eyes were not coordinated, and he seemed to be looking out across the lake as he spoke to Howell.

"You want some wood?"

The fellow was oddly handsome, Howell thought. His features were regular, chiseled, almost patrician; he had excellent teeth. Only the eyes and a slackness of the jaw made him seem other than normal.

"You want some wood?" he asked again, smiling a little this time, revealing the beautiful teeth. "Mama said you needed some wood."

Howell looked over the man's shoulder and saw a battered pickup truck with a tarpaulin covering its bed. He finally got the picture; the fellow was selling firewood. Benny Pope had said he couldn't come until Sunday, and it was only Tuesday. "Yeah, sure," Howell managed to say finally. "Just put it right there." He pointed to the shed next to the steps.

"Yessir," the fellow said. He ran to the truck, pulled back the tarp, revealing a random pile of split logs, and began bringing four or five at a time to the shed. It occurred to Howell that he hadn't asked a price, and he wondered if he would get bitten, but what the hell, he'd burned all the wood he had the night before. When the truck was empty and the shed full, the man tossed a burlap bag of kindling into the shed, waved, and started for the truck again.

"How much do I owe you?" Howell shouted after him.

"Oh, that's all right," he yelled back. He got into the truck on the passenger side, and Howell realized that someone else was driving.

Howell was too surprised to shout his thanks until the truck had turned around and was headed up the hill toward the crossroads. A woman was driving, but the truck window was too misted over to get a good look at her. He dashed down to the shed in the rain, grabbed the gunny sack of kindling and a couple of logs and, stepping gingerly in his bare feet, ran back up the steps. He had a fire going and was halfway through his first cup of coffee before he remembered what the fellow had said. "Mama said you needed some wood." Who the hell were the young man, the woman driving him, and, above all, Mama? And how did she know he needed wood? Some friend of Denham White's, he supposed, who had seen the empty woodshed and was being neighborly. That was all right with him, Howell thought, basking in the glow of the fire. He'd have to call Denham and ask him who the people were so he could thank them. Then, as he warmed his hands, a thought struck him. A few minutes before, when he'd been waked by the fellow at the door, he'd felt terminally hung over; certainly he'd had enough to drink the night before. Now, oddly, he felt perfectly well—no headache, no fuzziness.

The phone rang. As he picked it up, he hoped it wasn't Elizabeth. It was Denham White. "How you doing, sport?"

"Okay, I guess. The place is nice, Denham. You made it sound like the pits."

"It'll do, I guess. You'll have to lay in some firewood. It can get chilly at night up there."

"Funny you should mention that." He told his brother-in-law about the arrival of the wood. "Who are your friends?"

"Beats me. Nobody ever gave me anything up there. I never had much truck with the locals. Weird bunch. They know how to make a buck out of the summer folks, believe me."

Howell knew how aloof Denham could be with people he considered his social inferiors. He was perfectly capable of not knowing who his neighbors were.

"You meet old man Sutherland yet?" Denham asked.

"Yeah, right off the bat. Something of a shit, I'd say. He seemed to take an instant dislike to me."

Denham laughed. "Keen judge of character, Mr. Sutherland. Now listen, John, I've got to go on living with the guy, so don't piss him off if you can help it, okay? Just stay out of his way."

"I'm out of *everybody's* way up here. You seen Elizabeth?"

"We had dinner last night. She's okay; in the middle of getting out the Christmas catalogue. That'll keep her busy for a few weeks."

"Listen, Denham, something strange happened here last night."

"Yeah?"

"Yeah. I . . . uh, woke up in the middle of a thunderstorm and there was a girl in the living room."

"Some people have all the luck."

"No, listen. It was a young girl, a kid, really. Maybe eleven or twelve." Howell told Denham everything he could remember. He didn't mention the shotgun.

Denham didn't say anything for a moment. "John," he said finally, "how much did you have to drink last night?"

"Well," Howell replied sheepishly, "I had some wine with dinner and a couple of bourbons, I guess."

"I guess you had a lot more than a couple, the way you're talking. Look, why don't you try to lay off the sauce completely while you're up there? I expect the work would go a lot faster without bad dreams and hangovers."

"Yeah, all right, Denham. I don't need any lectures." Howell couldn't think of anything else to say.

"Take care, sport, and work hard. Lurton Pitts is used to getting good value for his money."

They hung up. Howell wondered again who Mama was. Then he had it. It must have been the sheriff, Bo Scully, who sent the wood. He was the only person besides Benny Pope who knew he needed it. Not a bad fellow, Bo Scully. He'd have to buy him a bottle, or something. Maybe Scully would have some idea who the girl was, too.

It rained for four days. Howell ranged about the cabin like a caged cat. He got up late, ate canned and frozen food, read everything he had brought with him, drank too much, got to bed late, and dreamed a dream, always the same dream. Then, when morning came, it was gone. He could not recapture it, but he didn't think the girl was in it.

He unpacked Pitts's vaunted word processor and played with it.

Howell had never been much for following directions, but after a day or two of snarling at the thing, he had it up and running. After poring through the manual and going through the drills of commands over and over, he began to get the feeling the machine was training him. By the fourth day, all was in readiness. The machine sat, waiting, just as his typewriter had before it. A box of continuous-form paper was fed into the printer; a stack of floppy diskettes waited to record his output; the twelve boxes of recording tape waited next to the tape recorder. Howell threaded the first tape into the machine and pressed a button. The voice of Lurton Pitts came at him just the way Pitts himself had from behind his desk. "Chapter One," Pitts boomed out. "How I Found God."

Howell stopped the machine and buried his face in his hands. "Oh, shit," he muttered. It was the first time in his working life that he had not been able to convince himself that what he was doing was worthwhile, the first time he had tried to write something just for the money. He didn't like it. He didn't know if he could do it. He felt the weight of the old depression, the one that came with feeling useless, burnt out. It lay upon him like some heavy, stinking garment whenever he was unexpectedly faced with the prospect that he might really be used up, worthless to anyone. It held his shoulders slumped, his hands pinned to the arms of his chair; it made him immobile for long minutes, caused nausea to eat at him and sap his energy.

He sat that way for a few moments, and then he felt a sudden warmth. He looked up to see the desk dappled with sunlight. The rain had stopped, and he could see patches of blue between the scudding clouds. His depression lightened a bit; he pushed back from the desk and walked over to the piano. He pushed the pedals, but got no response; he played a few blues chords, wincing at the sour sound. He jumped about a foot as a loud knock came at the door.

Howell leaped to his feet. There had been no visitor to the cabin except the man who had brought the wood, not even any mail. He would be happy to see absolutely anybody. He walked across the room to the door and opened it. A man and a dog stood on the porch, both wet. The man took off his hat to reveal a shock of perfectly white hair; his skin was a bright pink. Howell knew that behind his dark glasses there would be pink eyes; he was an albino. "Good morning to you," the man said. There was something strangely, strikingly familiar about him, but Howell didn't know any albinos. And there was something peculiar about the dog. He sat patiently next to his master, panting, his eyes closed. "I've come about the piano," the man said, looking out across the lake. He didn't seem to want to look at Howell.

"The piano?"

"Don't you need a piano tuned?" the man asked, still not looking at Howell.

Howell noticed a leather case at the man's feet. "You're a piano tuner?"

"That's right." The man stood, waiting.

Howell stood gaping at the man. He had been thinking about asking around for a piano tuner in the town, but he hadn't done anything about it. Or had he? Had he been that drunk in the afternoons? "Oh," he said, recovering, "come on in."

The man picked up his case and stepped into the room, stubbing his toe lightly on the sill. The dog got up, walked straight past him a few feet, bumped head-on into the sofa, retreated, turned right, knocked over a small pedestal table, reached the hearth, sniffing, flopped down in front of the fire, fell over onto his side, then turned on his back, all four feet in the air, and emitted a long sigh. He seemed to be instantly asleep. Howell stared at him. The dog was blind.

"Didn't do any damage, did he?" the man asked.

"No," Howell replied, righting the table.

"Riley will remember where things are. Where's the piano?"

"Right over there," Howell replied, pointing. The man didn't move. Suddenly, Howell realized that he, too, was blind. "Oh, sorry. Straight ahead." He took the man's elbow, guided him across the room, and placed his hand on the piano.

The albino shucked off his raincoat, put his hat on the piano, sat down, and ran loudly up a C scale with both hands. "Whew! I didn't come a moment too soon, did I?"

Howell laughed. "No, I guess you didn't. The player mechanism isn't working either. Can you do anything about that?"

The man slid back the doors that covered the player roll and felt around with his hands. "Look behind the piano," he said.

Howell looked between the piano and the wall and saw an electrical cord. He squeezed his hand behind the instrument and plugged it in. Instantly, the ghost of George Gershwin began to play a wildly-out-of-tune "Strike Up the Band." The albino switched the piano off. "Fixed that in a hurry, didn't we? That'll be two hundred dollars." He laughed.

"Well, I'll leave you to it," Howell said.

"Right."

Howell walked out onto the deck, the first time the weather had permitted. The woods around him were heavy with moisture from the days of rain. The lake flashed moments of blue at him as the new sun struck its surface in places. The light was warm on his face. The sounds of sour piano notes turning sweet drifted out from the living room as the albino tightened strings. Occasionally, a whole chord sang out. Howell felt his spirits lifting with the changing weather. It was as if he were being tuned, like the piano. He took a folding canvas deck chair from under the deep eaves and flopped down in it. He felt good for the first time in weeks, maybe months.

As he tuned the piano, the albino began to play little fragments, a few chords, of a tune Howell couldn't quite pin down and was too drowsy to care much about. It was mixed in with runs and other chords and octaves. Three quarters of an hour later, Howell was stirred from a doze by the sound of tools striking other tools and the clasps of the toolcase being closed. Then, unexpectedly, the albino played a few chords and began to sing, in a high, clear tenor:

> *I'll take you home again, Kathleen,*
> *Across the ocean wild and wide.*
> *To where your heart has ever been,*
> *Since first you were my bonnie bride.*
> *The roses all have left your cheek,*
> *I've watched them fade away and die.*
> *Your voice is sad whene'er you speak,*
> *And tears bedim your loving eyes.*
> *Oh, I will take you back again,*
> *To where your heart will feel no pain.*
> *And when the fields are fresh and green,*
> *I'll take you to your home again.*

By the time the albino finished, Howell was practically in tears from the beauty and sadness of it.

"Your piano's tuned," the man called out.

Howell roused himself from the deck chair and returned to the living room. The dog, Riley, was still lying on his back in front of the dying fire, snoring softly. "You sing and play very well," Howell said to the albino.

"Oh, God gives everybody some sort of talent, I guess. Mine's making music. I play the guitar and the mandolin and the accordion, and fiddle a bit, too. You ought to come down to one of the Saturday night dances at the community center sometime. Want to try the piano?"

Howell sat down at the keyboard and played a few bars of "Lush Life." "You like Duke Ellington?" he asked.

"Oh, yeah," the albino replied. "That's Billy Strayhorn's tune, though. It's hard to separate Ellington and Strayhorn; seems like one takes up where the other leaves off."

"Right. Say, I didn't call you about tuning the piano, did I? I mean, my memory has been a little spotty lately, but . . ."

The albino laughed. "Oh, no. Mama sent me. She said you needed the piano."

Now Howell knew why the albino looked familiar. "That was your brother who brought the firewood, wasn't it?"

The albino nodded. "That was Brian. Brian's a little . . ." He made a gesture. "But he's a good lad. He liked bringing you the wood."

"He wouldn't let me pay him for it. I wanted to . . ."

"Oh, no, Mama wouldn't have that."

"Now look, I want to pay you for the piano tuning. You do that for a living, don't you?"

"Yes, that and playing at the dances. Well, all right. I usually get twenty dollars for a tuning."

Howell pressed the money into his hand. "Listen, I don't quite understand about 'Mama.' Who is she?"

"My mother." He stuck out his hand. "I'm Dermot Kelly."

Howell shook the hand. "Glad to meet you, Dermot. I'm John Howell. But how did she know I needed firewood and the piano tuned? Did Bo Scully tell her about me?"

Dermot Kelly picked up his case and began to move toward the door. He didn't seem to need assistance finding his way. "Mama and Bo Scully don't have much to do with each other," he said. "No, Mama just knows things other people don't know. She's been sick for a while now, but she still has her moments."

Howell walked with Dermot to the door. "I'm afraid I don't really understand this, but I'm grateful to her for sending you and Brian around. Will you thank her for me?"

"Thank her yourself," Dermot replied. "She wants to meet you, anyway. She says she's been waiting for you for a long time."

Gooseflesh rose on Howell's skin. "Well, I'll drop by and see her if she's well enough. You said she has been sick?"

"Yes, but she'll be well enough when you come. We're just a ways up the hill from the crossroads," he said, pointing. "You'll see the mailbox. Come any time."

"Thanks, I will. And thanks again for the tuning."

"Don't mention it. Riley!"

The dog, who had never stopped snoring, was instantly on his feet. He walked quickly to Dermot's side, neatly avoiding the furniture. Together, the two of them walked down the steps, down the short drive, and started up the road. Dermot moved slowly, but with some confidence.

Howell watched them for a moment. Before they went into the trees, Dermot Kelly raised a hand and waved, as if he knew Howell was watching them. When they were gone, Howell went back into the house, still amazed at the pair. "Talk about the blind leading the blind!" he said aloud to himself.

5

As Howell turned right at the crossroads and headed for town, he looked up the hill and saw the Kelly mailbox at the roadside. Somehow, he wasn't ready to meet a sick old lady who knew when he needed firewood and piano tuning. Too bad she didn't know that he was out of beer and booze, too, and send somebody around with that. There was ample reason for a trip to town. He could always work over the weekend to make up for lost time.

He found a parking space on Main Street; he could use one of Bubba's cheeseburgers and a beer. The place was fairly crowded. "Sit over yonder with McAuliffe," Bubba said, motioning toward a booth where a man ate alone.

"You mind?" Howell asked the man, pointing to the empty seat.

"Glad for the company," the man said, sticking out his hand. "Enda McAuliffe, known to one and all as Mac. Sit yourself down." McAuliffe was a slender, rumpled-looking man somewhere in his forties, dressed in a blue wash-and-wear seersucker suit that had been washed too many times.

Howell introduced himself. "How's the, ah . . . ?" He indicated the food on McAuliffe's plate.

"Stuffed cabbage," McAuliffe replied. "No worse than the pork chops, and a damn sight better than the chicken-fried steak. In fact," he said loudly, glancing sideways at the approaching Bubba, "we've never been too sure around here from which animal the chicken-fried steak derives. It ain't chicken, and it sure ain't steak."

"Now, Mac," Bubba cautioned, "don't go knocking my cooking; you eat it most every day."

McAuliffe nodded. "The voice of experience. Bubba came to us from

Texas," McAuliffe said to Howell, "which will explain a lot as you get to know him, but not the origins of the chicken-fried steak—or, for that matter, one or two other bits of Western exotica which occasionally pop up on the menu."

McAuliffe had the characteristic mountain drawl of the local residents but spoke in different cadences, somehow. Howell ordered a cheeseburger and a beer.

"Well chosen," McAuliffe said. "Not even Bubba can do much harm to a cheeseburger. What brings you to our parts, Mr. Howell? I know you from your journalistic endeavors, of course."

Howell gave what was becoming his standard explanation of his presence, one which everybody seemed to accept with a grain of salt. Nobody seemed willing to believe that he had actually come to Lake Sutherland to write a book. "Enda . . . that's an Irish name, isn't it?"

"It is indeed. So's McAuliffe."

"Seems like I've run into a lot of Irish names around here—for Georgia, anyway."

"I expect you have. There are still a number of us scattered hereabouts."

"Still? Were there once more?"

"There was a little community of us in the valley before it became the lake. A group that somehow ended up in Savannah instead of New York or Boston during the potato famine of the last century. They were hired right off the boat to work on the railroad up here, and eventually they bought some land in the valley and settled in. Their descendants lived in the valley for nearly a hundred years before the lake came. A very tight little community, they were."

"I saw a priest on Main Street the other day and thought that unusual."

"It would be in any other Georgia town of this size, I suppose. There were just enough Catholics in the valley to warrant one."

"He looked a little the worse for wear."

McAuliffe smiled and nodded. "Well, the Irish clergy have never held with the Protestant attitude toward drink, and I suppose Father Harry held with it less than most. Still, there was a time when he wasn't *always* drunk. After the lake came, his parishioners scattered, and he was getting on a bit. The archdiocese pensioned him off. He's past eighty now."

"Remarkable that the booze hasn't finished him off."

"Ah, me lad, you underestimate the resilience of an Irish constitution."

"Where is the Catholic church, then? I don't think I've seen it in my travels."

"It's under the lake," McAuliffe said wryly, "like a great many other things hereabouts."

"You're the first person I've heard who seems less than enthusiastic about the lake," Howell said. "It seems to have done a lot for the area."

"For a very small area," McAuliffe replied. "And a very few people. I'm afraid that my lack of enthusiasm for the lake is reflected in my law practice. There are two lawyers in town, you see. There's Swenson, who's the attorney for the power company and Eric Sutherland and for the quality folk hereabouts. Then there's me."

"What sort of practice?" Howell asked, intrigued.

"Whatever's going. Drunk driving, the odd bootlegger, though that's dying out, since liquor came to Sutherland. Terrible thing, legal booze. A lawyer could do very nicely in the bootlegging line a few years back. I do a will now and then, though most of my clients don't have enough to bother with a will. And I sue Sutherland and the power company for people who get mad enough. Not many of them about," he grinned. "If you're mad at Eric Sutherland, I'm the only game in town."

"Somehow it doesn't sound very profitable to get mad at Eric Sutherland."

"A good rule of thumb," the lawyer agreed. "You'll fit right in around here."

"Well, I don't expect to be around long enough for that to matter. Say, do you know the Kelly family, out near where I'm staying?"

McAuliffe nodded, but didn't speak. He simply concentrated on the stuffed cabbage, staring at his plate.

"They've been very nice to me; Brian brought around some firewood, and Dermot came and tuned the piano. Their mother apparently sent them around. I can't imagine how she knew I needed those things."

McAuliffe stopped eating and looked at him. "Mama Kelly sent her boys to you?"

"That's what they said."

McAuliffe continued to stare blankly at him. "Jesus Christ," he said finally.

Howell hardly knew how to reply to that. "Uh, how many Kellys are there?"

"There's the twins, Brian and Mary, they're the youngest. Dermot is the oldest, and Leonie comes after him, I think. There were a couple of other kids who died in infancy. Their father, Patrick Kelly, has been dead for twenty years, I guess."

"Brian's retarded, isn't he?"

McAuliffe resumed eating and nodded. "His twin, Mary, is too, from all accounts. Dermot's all right, except he's an albino, of course. Leonie . . . Leonie's very bright. She's . . . like her mother, in some ways."

"What's her mother like?"

"She's . . . unusual, I guess you'd say. After Patrick passed on, Mama Kelly made her living for a long time—raised those children—as a sort of fortune-teller. She's been sick for a couple of years now, though. Just hanging on, I hear."

"Dermot says she wants to meet me. I guess I should go by there and thank her for the wood."

McAuliffe stopped eating again. "John, let me give you some advice; you can take it or leave it." He kept his voice low. "The Kellys make a lot of people around here . . . nervous, I guess you'd say. Eric Sutherland is prominent among them. A lot of people will have a piano tuner up here from Gainesville just to avoid using Dermot. You're not going to endear yourself hereabouts if you have much to do with them. They . . . Oh, Jesus, I'm sounding like some sort of snob. That's not what I mean to convey at all."

"Well, just say it, Mac," Howell replied. He was baffled.

"Oh, shit, I suppose you may as well know about this. It'll come up sooner or later. Mama Kelly was married to her husband . . ."

Howell laughed. "So?"

"I'm really screwing this up," the lawyer said, shaking his head. "What I meant to say was, the parents, Patrick and Lorna—that's Mama Kelly—were brother and sister."

It took a moment for this to sink in with Howell. "Jesus H. Christ! And they had how many kids? Why didn't the law . . . ?"

"The valley was a remote backwoods area for a long time, until the lake came. People just minded their own business. After the lake came, though, Eric Sutherland and some other prominent locals started making noises about doing something about it—arresting Patrick and Lorna, I guess, and putting the kids into an orphanage. Then . . ."

"So what stopped them?"

"Then Patrick died—a tree he was cutting down fell on him—and it seemed better just to let things lie, I guess. There wouldn't be any more children, and nobody would ever have adopted the others. Dermot was nearly grown, anyway, and Brian and Mary were . . . well, you've seen Brian. The whole thing just died down."

"What about the priest? You said he's been around here for a long time. He would have had a lot of influence with Irish Catholics, wouldn't he? Couldn't he have stopped it in the beginning?"

"John, what I've told you so far I know to be true. But this, I stress, is just rumor. Nobody knows for sure but Lorna Kelly." He paused, seeming undecided as to whether to go on.

"Well, come on, Mac," Howell said. "You can't just leave me hanging."

"It's said that Father Harry married them in the Church."

Now Howell was speechless. "Well," he was finally able to say, leaning back in the booth and shaking his head, "every small town has its eccentrics, I guess, and its skeletons, too."

McAuliffe shrugged and returned his attention to the stuffed cabbage.

There was a parking ticket waiting for Howell on the windshield of the station wagon. He had put money in the meter, but his conversation with Mac McAuliffe had kept him at Bubba's longer than he had anticipated. Five bucks down the drain for want of a dime. The back of the ticket said that it could be paid at the sheriff's office, opposite the courthouse.

The sheriff's office was a storefront in the square. Inside, a radio operator and two female clerks sat in an open office area separated from the public by a counter. He recognized one of the women immediately. What was her name? She had been a features writer on the *Constitution* when he was there. She recognized him, too, and beat one of her coworkers to the counter. "Can I help you, sir?" She quickly held a finger to her lips, her face miming urgency. Heather MacDonald, that was her name. He had seen her byline in the paper not more than a few weeks before. "What can I do for you?" she asked, her back to the others.

"Oh, I just want to pay a parking ticket." Scotty, they called her. She was small, with short, dark hair; pretty. He had eyed her in the city room more than once.

"May I see the ticket, please?" Her eyes were begging him to go along.

He handed her the ticket. What the hell was she doing in Bo Scully's office? He glanced over her shoulder. The sheriff was at his desk in a glassed-in office at the rear.

"That'll be five dollars," she said, reaching for a receipt book. She palmed a notepad at the same time. "Name?"

"John Howell."

"Address?"

"The Denham White cottage on the north shore."

"RFD 1, that would be." She quickly wrote something on the note-pad and turned it around, then went back to the receipt. It read: "Just shut up and leave. I'll contact you later."

"I guess so. I haven't received any mail yet." Howell looked up and saw Scully coming toward them. "Hi, Bo," he said.

She quickly crumpled the note and ripped off the receipt. "Here you are, sir."

"What brings you to see us, John?" Scully asked, stepping up to the counter.

"Came to pay a fine; forgot about a parking meter."

Scully laughed. "Pity you didn't see me instead of Miss Miller here. You might have bribed me to fix it."

Howell laughed too. Miss Miller? What the hell was going on here?

"John, meet Scotty Miller, our latest addition here. She's hell on the word processor. Scotty, this is John Howell, the famous newspaper-man."

"The former newspaperman," Howell said, shaking Scotty's hand.

"So he keeps telling me," Scully said. "I was just on my way out, John. Want to take a ride with me?"

"Where you going?"

"Just to make some rounds. I'll give you the ten-cent tour, since you already contributed five bucks to the kitty."

"Sure. I've got to do some grocery shopping, though. Will we be long?"

"An hour or two, depending on what's happening."

"Fine. Nice to meet you, Scotty."

"Same here," she replied, looking worriedly from Scully to Howell.

The two men left together and got into Scully's unmarked car. "You seen much of the area?" Scully asked.

"Only what I saw driving up here. It's been raining ever since, until today. This is the first time I've even been to town since that day we met."

The sheriff wound the car idly through the streets of the town. "Eric Sutherland hired an architect from Atlanta to design the look of the town," he said, waving a hand at some storefronts. "Got the city coun-cil to pass a bill requiring any new building to conform."

"Looks nice," Howell said. "Not too contrived. Simple, neat, lots of trees, too; bet it's pretty in the fall."

"Lots of leaves to get raked in the fall," Scully said.

The sun struck the brick of the storefronts, giving them a glowing warmth.

"Those are Harvard brick," Scully said, seeming to read Howell's mind. "Sutherland went to Harvard, and I guess he liked the brick the school was built out of. When the major building was going on, he imported them by the carload. To this day, if you want another kind of brick, even to build your own house with, you'll have to special-order it. We got two building-supply outfits here, and both of them stock nothing but Harvard brick. I reckon there's some Yankee brickmaker up in Massachusetts wondering what the hell we're doing with so much Harvard brick down here."

"Eric Sutherland seems like a man who doesn't leave detail to chance."

The sheriff grinned. "You better believe it, boy."

Scully left the town and headed for the north shore, in the direction of Howell's cabin, but he continued straight at the crossroads. "You know, there wasn't even a road around the lake in the early days," he said.

"So Denham White told me."

Scully laughed. "I wish you could have seen old Denham in that canoe, towing all that lumber. Boy, he was a sight."

"I'll bet."

"He got the nicest lot on the lake, too, for my money. Only lot Sutherland leased in that cove. His father and Sutherland got along real well."

"So I gathered from Mr. Sutherland. In fact, I got the impression Mr. Sutherland would have ordered me out of town if I hadn't been old Mr. White's son-in-law."

"Yeah, well, he has a better opinion of the old man than the boy, I guess. Denham got mixed up with a local girl up here a few years back, somebody not of his station, you might say. Sutherland didn't like it a bit, called up his daddy, and old man White snatched the boy out of here pretty quick."

"Pregnant, was she?" Howell asked, interested.

"Nah, just in love—at least Denham was. Never saw anybody so much in love."

Howell chuckled inside himself, thinking of the cool, buttoned-up Denham, now married to an icy Atlanta debutante. He wouldn't have thought his brother-in-law would ever have had so much passion. "Who was the girl?" he asked.

"Nobody you'd know. Catholic family. I think that pissed off old man White as much as their social standing."

"Yeah, well, he was a pretty hard-shelled Baptist, I guess. My wife didn't take after him."

"How's your wife feel about you coming up here for such a long time without her?" Scully seemed to want to change the subject.

Howell hesitated. "Well, we're separated, really. I think it's probably best for both of us, my being up here." Now he had said it out loud to somebody. That made it official, he supposed. He was surprised he'd let it out.

"Kids?"

"Nope. Just as well, I guess."

Howell found it very easy to talk to Bo Scully. There was something companionable about the man. "You married?"

Scully shook his head. "Nah. Never got around to it. I was engaged once, to a girl in the valley, but she . . . it didn't work out. I was just a kid, anyway."

"No more close calls?"

The sheriff grinned. "Oh, sure. I found the perfect girl once, but, like the fellow says, she was looking for the perfect man."

"I wouldn't think there would be much of a supply of single women in these parts."

"Oh, it's not too bad. Fair number of divorcées. I'd have a shot at little Scotty in my office, if she wasn't so close to home. You ought to give her a call, you know. Nice-looking girl. Smart, too; she's done a lot to shape up the office."

"You said she was new?"

"Came a little more than a month ago."

"Local girl?"

"Nah, Atlanta. Said she wanted to get away from big-city life. She had real good references from a law firm—she was a legal secretary—and I just snapped her up. You don't find many girls around here with that kind of experience."

"I guess not. Seems like a pretty good life up here, too. I can see why she might want to get away." He couldn't see at all, really. She was up here with a phony name and phony references, obviously up to something.

"You better believe it's a good life. Shoot, I can't hardly believe it sometimes."

"How long you been sheriff?"

"Since '62. I got a deputy's job when I came back from Korea. When old Sheriff Bob Mitchell hung it up, I ran. Got elected. Been getting elected ever since."

"Much crime up here?"

"Not much. Not the way you've got it in Atlanta, anyway. Oh, we get our share of cuttings, and burglary's happening a lot more often than it used to. We get a murder once or twice a year, usually a domestic situation." He grinned. "We stay busy, but we don't bust our asses."

They drove on along the smooth two-lane highway, the lake appearing from time to time through the trees on their left. "How big is the lake?" Howell asked.

"Fifteen miles from Sutherland down to Taylor's Fish Camp at the other end, but I guess it's not more than a mile and a half, two miles wide anywhere. Looks like a river in the narrower parts." He pointed at a narrow place they were passing. Light reflecting from the water flashed through the pines. "You ought to get out on the water before it starts getting too cool. Denham's got a boat out to the cabin, hasn't he?"

"Yeah, there's a runabout under the house and a fifty-horsepower outboard stored down at Ed Parker's. I'll have to get it out."

They passed Taylor's Fish Camp, a jumble of ramshackle cabins with a big main building. A sign out front said "Home Cooking."

"How's the food?" Howell asked.

"Best fried chicken in the state," Scully replied. "Real good breakfast, too; homemade sausage and country ham. Closest thing we've got to a good restaurant around here. No booze, though, not even beer or wine. The Taylors don't hold with it."

"I'll have to give it a try."

They headed back along the south shore of the lake, not talking much, enjoying the sunshine on the water after the days of rain. At the outskirts of Sutherland they passed a convenience store, and Scully slowed slightly. There was only one car out front. He nodded. "Now, just have a look at that," he said. "Fellow sitting in a car with the motor running; out-of-state plates. That say anything to you?" Before Howell could reply, Scully picked up the car radio microphone and pressed the transmit button. "Mike, this is the sheriff, who's out and where?"

A voice crackled back. "Car Two's here. Everybody else is scattered around the county. Jimmy's right here."

"Good. Jimmy, I'm out at Minnie Wilson's store, and there's a possible code eleven in progress. I'm going round the back. Get out here right quick, no siren. There's a '74 Chevy with Tennessee plates parked out front with the motor running. Approach with caution and detain the driver. Watch out for whoever else might come out the front door. Don't go too heavy; might be my imagination. Read me?"

"I read you, Sheriff."

"And radio me when you're about to Minnie's. I won't go in till you're there." Scully put down the microphone, swung left into a side street, then left again into an alley. He pulled up at the back entrance to the store, switched the engine off, and got out of the car. Howell followed as he went to the trunk and removed a short pump shotgun. "Now listen," Scully said, "you stay right here until I come get you, you hear? If there's any shooting, pick up that microphone, press the button, and tell my radio operator, okay?"

"Okay," Howell replied, glad he wasn't going into that grocery store with the sheriff.

Scully stood by the car, waiting impatiently to hear that his man was in place at the front of the store. The radio came alive.

"Sheriff, this is Jimmy."

Bo picked up the microphone. "I hear you. You out front?"

"Listen, I'm real sorry about this," Jimmy came back, "but I've got a dead battery. Can you hold off till I can get a fresh one in there? Shouldn't be more than four or five minutes."

"Shit!" Bo said. He pushed the button. "Hurry up, goddamnit. Get here as fast as you can." He put down the microphone and banged his fist against the steering wheel, then turned to Howell. "Listen, I can't wait for him to get here. Minnie will be in there by herself. I could use some backup. You know how to use a shotgun?"

"Well, yeah," Howell said.

He handed Howell the weapon. "That's got eight in the magazine. The button there's the safety. You just push that and pump, then shoot, okay?"

Howell nodded. "Okay." He didn't feel as confident as he sounded. He had been around cops when there was shooting, but he hadn't been doing the shooting. He didn't like this at all.

"Now, listen, you're gonna be there to point that thing, not to shoot it—not unless you absolutely have to, and for God's sake, don't shoot me. You're deputized as of right now. There's a manager's office through the door to the left; somebody could be in there. Follow me in; if the office is empty, we'll work our way down toward the cash register."

Bo Scully walked quietly into the back hallway of the store, staying close to the wall. He tossed his Stetson onto the floor behind him, looked carefully into the manager's office, then shook his head. He held a finger to his lips and motioned for Howell to follow him. The two men walked quietly forward into the main room of the store and found themselves facing a shelf of canned goods lying directly across their path. Scully stopped and cupped a hand to his ear. They could hear the cash register beeping softly as an order was rung up. That seemed normal enough to Howell, but he was afraid to be relieved. Scully motioned for Howell to go right, then he went left.

Howell followed the shelf to its end and peeped down the aisle toward the front of the store. The store seemed empty. He could see all the way into the parking lot but could not see the Tennessee Chevy. How the hell had he gotten into this? He took a deep breath and began tiptoeing down the aisle toward the front of the store, passing other aisles between the shelves to his left. At each aisle he could see Scully, his revolver drawn, moving forward. Fearfully, Howell kept pace with him. He stopped at a cereal display and peeped around the corner toward the cash register. A man in a leather jacket and a woman in jeans stood at the checkout counter, their backs to him, watching an elderly woman bag their groceries. Howell could see the Chevy now; its motor was still running. Nothing else seemed wrong, though. The couple were just buying groceries. He began to relax a little.

"That'll be $32.41," Howell heard the elderly storekeeper say.

"Uh-uh, Mama," the male customer replied. His right hand went to his jacket pocket. "That'll be everything you got in the cash register. Then we'll go have a look in the safe."

Howell froze. Oh, God, he thought, it's on. What am I *doing* here?

"Yessir," he heard the woman say, then a ringing and the sound of the cash register drawer opening. Howell braced himself and waited for Bo Scully to make a move. Sweat was trickling from his armpits down his sides, making him shiver. Out of the corner of his eye he saw the driver's door to the Chevy open. The second patrol car was nowhere in sight.

There was an explosion, and the man in the leather jacket seemed to leap backward onto another checkout counter. A potato chip display was knocked flat, and Howell saw bits of bloody debris spattered over the bags.

"Freeze!" Bo Scully shouted. "Everybody just freeze right where you are!" Scully stepped into the open area around the checkout counter, his pistol held in front of him with both hands. A movement outside the store caught Howell's eye. The driver of the Chevy was out of the car and leaning on the top of the car, pointing a rifle at Scully. Howell pumped the shotgun, brought it up and fired. Simultaneously a six-inch hole appeared in the store's plate glass window, and the windshield of the Chevy turned white. The man dropped the rifle and flung his hands in the air. Howell could see a patrol car racing into the parking lot toward the Chevy.

"Freeze, everybody!" Scully shouted again. "Minnie, put that gun down!"

For the first time, Howell saw that the elderly storekeeper was holding a heavy revolver. She put it down on the counter as she was told. The woman companion of the robber stood, frozen, her hands out in front of her as if to ward off bullets. In the parking lot, a uniformed sheriff's deputy had the Chevy's driver leaning up against the car being handcuffed.

"Okay, now," Scully said, "everything's all right. It's all right now, Minnie." He moved forward, spun the robber's companion around, made her lean against the counter, legs spread, and thoroughly searched her. Satisfied, Scully handcuffed her hands behind her back. Only then did he approach her male companion. Howell put the shotgun on safety and stepped forward, too. The man in the leather jacket was sprawled backward across the checkout counter, eyes and mouth open. There was a hole in the middle of his chest. Scully took hold of an arm and turned him halfway over. His back was an enormous mess. Blood dripped down the stainless steel counter onto the floor. "Jesus, Minnie," Scully said, "what you loading in that thing?"

"Dum-dums," the woman said matter-of-factly. "Jesse got 'em for me last year. They robbed me twice before, and they ain't going to do it again."

"This one sure ain't," Scully agreed. He looked at Howell, then at the car outside. "Nice going, John." Scully looked at him worriedly. "You all right?"

Howell looked at the hole in the plate glass store window and at the shattered windshield beyond. He didn't seem to have hit anybody. He wiped his face with his sleeve. "Yeah, I guess so." Suddenly, the entire window collapsed with a crash. Howell jumped a foot.

Howell opened his eyes slowly and listened. There had been a noise, he thought. He had been sitting on the sofa with a drink, about to doze off, when he thought he heard a car door slam. He couldn't make himself move until the knock came at the door. When he finally swung his legs off the sofa, it seemed that every muscle in his body cried out. He struggled to his feet and walked stiffly to the door. It was Scotty Mac-Donald—or, these days, Miller.

"Hello," she said cheerfully. "You look like shit."

"Thanks. Come on in." He switched on a lamp and threw a couple of logs on the embers of the fire. "Drink?"

"Sure. Bourbon, if you've got it."

"Oh, yeah, I've got it." He looked at the bottle. He had made a large dent in it already.

"I think you're still in shock," she said, taking the drink and peering at him.

"What?"

"Bo's been telling everybody that this guy had drawn down on him with a hunting rifle when you pumped one off at him through Minnie Wilson's store window and saved his life."

"Well, that might be going a little far."

"Not to hear Bo tell it. You know, that sort of action rattles the system if you're not used to it. It can make you stiff and sore all over, like you've been beat up."

"That's an excellent description of my condition right now," Howell agreed.

"I did a piece on it once. Interviewed some Atlanta cops about what it was like after action. I think what happens is you get this huge rush of adrenalin, then when it's over, you sort of have a hangover."

"Well, I had a pretty huge rush, I guess. I was scared out of my tiny mind."

"That'll do it. Say, have you had dinner?"

"No." He looked at his watch; it was nearly nine o'clock.

"Neither have I. Have you got any food in the house? I'll fix us something."

"Yeah, there's a bunch of groceries in there. I didn't even put them away."

She walked toward the kitchen. She looked terrific in those tight jeans, Howell thought. She looked pretty good all over, really. She was petite, but beautifully put together. The T-shirt stretched tightly over her ample breasts, and the sweater thrown over her shoulders lent a cocky air to the way she walked. The short hairdo made her look cockier still. Almost butch.

"Jesus," she called from the kitchen, "all you've got in here is chili. Is that what you live on?"

A few minutes later they were eating chili and crackers and drinking beer. "All right, what are you doing working in Bo Scully's office?" he asked. He had been waiting for her to bring it up, but she hadn't, and his curiosity had got the better of him.

"Just that," she replied, scooping up a mouthful of chili. "Best little worker he ever had, he says."

"Come on, you're using a false name and references. What's up?"

"I got a really good tip that Bo's dirty," she said.

"So what else is new? What sheriff isn't these days?"

"No, I mean *real* dirty. Drugs. And in a big way."

"I thought that was a coastal phenomenon, or south Georgia."

"Folks up here like their grass and nose candy, too, I guess."

"The paper sent you up here? You've been here what, a month?"

"About that. They didn't exactly send me. It was more like they let me come." She scratched her nose. "Actually, they fired me."

"What for?"

"I asked them to. I reckoned it would take two or three months to get a story out of this, and they wouldn't assign me to it, so I asked them if I could do it without pay, sort of a leave of absence. I asked them to fire me just to cover my tracks at the office." She took a sip of her beer and gazed thoughtfully across the dark lake. "I think Bo knows somebody at the paper."

"So?"

"Well, he knows there's a reporter up here, I think."

"He's on to you already, then?"

She grinned. "Nope. He's on to *you.*"

Howell set his beer down. *"Me?"*

"Sure. I think he thinks the paper has sent you up here to get something on him and that this book you're writing is just a flimsy cover."

"Swell. That's all I need. I'm lucky *I* wasn't the one shot this afternoon." Suddenly, his mind caught up with that notion. Maybe that was why Scully had wanted him in that store with a shotgun. Then old Minnie had done the shooting first and spoiled everything.

"No, no, I don't think he's like that, I really don't."

"Listen, getting mixed up in big drugs has a way of making a murder or two seem a reasonable thing. I'd better straighten him out pretty quick on why I'm here."

"You do that, and you'll blow me," she said gravely.

"So, you're blown. That's better than me getting blown away."

"Come on now, John. You used to do this sort of thing, you know. I've read your stuff, I've read your book. There's something going on up here, and I want it. You'd want it, too, in my place, you know you would."

"Listen, don't pull that old newspaperman's camaraderie bullshit on me," he said, banging his beer on the table. "Why should I have to spend all my time up here looking over my shoulder so you can work on something so flimsy that the paper wouldn't even assign you? I don't think you've had enough experience with these country sheriffs to know how territorial they are, how dangerous they can be. Bo Scully is a very powerful man right here on his own turf, and I don't need him on my back."

"Oh, come on, he's not going to mess with you. Your brother-in-law is Denham White; you're married to the daughter of a man who was one of Eric Sutherland's closest friends. Bo isn't going to do anything to annoy Sutherland."

"I'm not so sure Sutherland would be all that annoyed if something happened to me. I've only met him once and . . ." He thought of that meeting. "Jesus, I'll bet he must think I'm investigating *him*. He behaved that way, anyway."

"Why would Sutherland worry about being investigated?" Scotty asked.

"I wonder," Howell said. "I guess you know why I'm up here."

She grinned. "You mean that cock-and-bull story about writing a book?"

"Now listen . . ."

"Oh, we hear all the local news in the sheriff's office. Bo likes to know what's going on."

"Well, he got my story this afternoon. I thought we were just having a man-to-man chat, but he was pumping me, because he thought I was you."

"Just what is your story, anyway? Last I heard, you were quitting to write the Great American Novel."

"Well, publishers have less taste than I thought. It didn't exactly get snapped up. And what's *your* story? Last I knew, you were writing bad house and home stuff and shaking your ass around the newsroom."

"I finally got a shot at something gritty, and it worked out."

"The highway bid-rigging thing?"

"Right, and I didn't get the assignment by shaking my ass." She grinned. "If I'd done that, I'd be city editor by now."

He laughed. "Well, at least you know your strengths."

"Listen, buster, my strength is investigative reporting, and I'm going to find out what's going on up here, I promise you."

"If I take the heat from Scully for you."

"I have to believe you're gentleman enough to help me," she said, arranging her features into a semblance of vulnerability.

"Don't pull that horseshit with me. You've been coming on like Jack Anderson all evening, and now you're making like Scarlett O'Hara?"

"Oh, goddamnit, can't you see what a terrific story this could make? A country-fried drug operation that nobody knows about? You've got your Pulitzer, now give me a shot at mine."

"Even if I have to give Bo Scully a shot at me?"

"You saved his life this afternoon. It would violate his dumb macho code to hurt you now."

"What's so dumb about that?"

"Oh, you know what I mean. He's seen too many Clint Eastwood movies."

"Don't you think for a minute that Scully isn't bright. He's in the catbird seat up here, and he didn't get there by being stupid. You sniff around him too much, and you'll get a nose full of hot buckshot."

"Jesus, I know he's not stupid. Neither am I. Look, just go along with me for a while on this. Let's see what happens." She stared at him worriedly across the table.

Howell shoved a cracker into his mouth and chewed it silently.

"Besides," she said smugly, "now you're just as curious as I am. Once a reporter . . ."

He washed down the cracker with cold beer. "Now that's the first smart thing you've said. Why didn't you try that tactic first instead of all that other crap?"

She laughed. "Because I didn't know it was true. I thought you really had become the novelist, but under that cruddy sport shirt beats the heart of an old newspaperman."

"What do you mean, cruddy? It's a damn fine sport shirt. And what do you mean, old?"

"How old are you?"

"None of your business."

"I'd say forty ah . . ."

"I was thirty-nine last month, and I look thirty-five, tops. And you? You're just a snot-nosed cub reporter on your first undercover—"

"I'm twenty-four, and I've got three years on a major metropolitan daily, and who told you you look thirty-five? Jesus, you look older than my father, and he's forty-six! Oh, if we cleaned you up a bit, got you a shave, and combed your hair over the bald spot . . ."

"I'm only balding if you're taller than I am and stand behind me. You wouldn't come up to my belt buckle if you stood on tiptoe . . . you could walk under tables. What're you, four ten, four eleven?"

"I'm nearly five two, and I'm probably stronger than you are. Want to arm-wrestle?"

"Let's see who can piss farthest—that's what this is all about, isn't it?"

"Don't be so sure you'd win, buster. You going to blow my cover on this one, or you going to do the right thing?"

"Oh, hell, all right, but I hate to do this to Scully. I sort of like him."

"So do I. He's a very attractive man."

"He thinks you're cute, too, but you're too close to home for him. He suggested I give you a call."

She started for the kitchen with the dirty dishes. "Why don't you?"

"Taylor's Fish Camp tomorrow night?"

"You're on." She grabbed her jacket. "You'd better soak in a hot tub and get to bed."

"Join me?"

She laughed. "I don't think you're up to it." She skipped down the steps and headed for her car.

He watched her drive away. It had been a long time since he had made a dinner date with a girl. He felt foolishly happy about it. He thought about Elizabeth, but she seemed terribly far away. While he was married, he hadn't done a lot of fooling around, but he didn't feel married anymore, somehow.

Scotty drove slowly back to the room she had taken at the home of an elderly widow, Mrs. McMahon. She could not believe how well this was working out. When John Howell had walked into the office that afternoon, she had nearly peed in her pants, but now it was going to be okay. It was going to be *better* than okay, because now Bo had a visible reporter to worry about.

She had gone way out on a limb with the paper on this one. They had always thought she was reckless, and maybe she was, a bit, but that got results. Still, she had problems; when she wanted the police beat, she got the society page; when she wanted to do investigative work, she got the second-string job at the state capitol. It annoyed her greatly that they hadn't kept her on staff for this job, that she had to do it on her own time and money. If she pulled it off, she'd be a hero in the newsroom, but if she didn't go back with the goods on Bo Scully, she couldn't go back at all. She'd be writing about women's club meetings on some county weekly.

Quite apart from Howell's taking the heat off her, she was glad to have him in town. In Atlanta, she had avoided tying herself to one man, but she was accustomed to an active sex life, even if she had to hit the singles bars to keep it up. In Sutherland, however, the only attractive man around had been Bo Scully, and he was for her, as she was for him, too close to home. Howell had turned up just in time. Another week, she knew, and she'd have been in bed with Bo. Another day, now, and she'd be in bed with John Howell. She could always tell.

In her room, she dialed an Atlanta number.

"Hello."

"Hi, Daddy."

"Hiya, kid. How're you doing?"

"Okay. Just fine." Her father was a widowed orthopedic surgeon who practiced at Emory University Hospital. Her mother had been dead for less than a year, and she made it a point to see him often. Since she had been in Sutherland, she had telephoned him two or three times a week.

"You're really okay now? You're not doing anything dangerous?"

"Honest, Daddy, it's just like I told you. All I do is work in the office. It's less dangerous than writing society stuff for the *Constitution.*"

"Well, I know you're a tough little nut. After all, dynamite comes in small packages."

"You know it." It had been his joke for as long as she could remember. "How's the practice of medicine? Left any tools in patients this week?"

"Well, there's a crowbar missing around the office, but it'll turn up. When you coming home? I miss you."

"I know, Daddy. I miss you, too, but I've got to stick it out up here for as long as it takes."

"How long is that going to be?"

"Well, who knows, but if I can't dig up something in three months, I probably never will."

"Three months, huh? Is that a promise?"

"Well . . . almost. Listen, I'd better run. Big day in law enforcement tomorrow."

"Take care of yourself now. Let me know if you need anything."

"Okay, Daddy. I love you. Goodbye."

Scotty hung up and made one other call, to the answering machine in her Atlanta apartment. A couple of calls from guys. No point in returning them; it would just make her hornier. As she brushed her teeth before going to bed, she reminded herself to take her pill the next morning. She was glad she hadn't gone off it. She had always known something would turn up, and now, something had.

8

The hangover did not help Howell's attempts to make a start on the autobiography of Lurton Pitts. He had followed Scotty's advice and soaked in a hot tub, but he had gotten through another six ounces of the bourbon in the process and had fallen asleep quite drunk. The dream had come again, most vivid just at the point of awakening, but as soon as he was conscious, it was gone, just as always.

A beer for lunch quelled the hangover enough for him to listen to more of Lurton Pitts's tapes, but what he heard did not inspire him to write. He was getting the picture, though, getting through the tapes, figuring out what sort of book Pitts wanted. He could blast through it in a hurry when he finally got around to writing, he was sure of it.

He lasted until two o'clock on the tapes, then gave up. He needed air. He drove to town with nothing particular in mind, then, on impulse, pulled into Ed Parker's service station.

"How you doin'?" Benny Pope asked, scratching his snow-white head.

"Not bad, Benny. Listen, I want to get Denham White's outboard out of storage. Is it ready to go?"

"Give it a test run, Benny," Ed Parker said, coming out of the station's little office. "It's been sitting around all summer, John; let's see if it's running good." He sat down on a cane-bottomed chair and pulled up another. "Sit yourself down for a minute. Want a cold drink?"

Howell accepted the chair and a Coke. The two men leaned against the whitewashed station wall and soaked up the afternoon sun.

"Hear you and Bo had yourselves a shootout yesterday out to Minnie Wilson's."

"Well, sort of, I guess."

"They ain't been talking about nothing else over to Bubba's all day."

"Wasn't much to it, really."

"I hear Minnie put a hole slap through that fellow."

"She sure did that, Ed. Just about scared me to death."

Ed laughed. "Yeah, must've got pretty noisy around there. What sort of book you working on, John?" Ed hadn't missed a beat on the change of subject.

"Oh, nothing I can talk about for the moment, Ed."

"I guess it's like that if you're a writer. You get superstitious about talking about it, huh?"

"Yeah, I guess, sort of superstitious."

"A novel, is it?"

"Yeah, a novel."

"And you plan to be up here just two or three months?"

"About that."

"I always thought a novel took a long time to get written; maybe years."

"Well, if you're Flaubert, maybe. I hope to work faster than that. Anyway, all I want to do is get a start up here. I'll finish it in Atlanta, I guess."

"How you like it out at the cove?"

"Pretty good. Got everything I need out there."

"Pretty place, ain't it? Prettiest place on the lake."

"Sure is. Say, Ed, how many lots has Sutherland let out to people over the years?"

"Oh, I don't know, forty or fifty, I guess."

"How come nobody else has built out at the Cove except Denham? Like you say, it's the prettiest place on the lake."

"I don't know. I tried to get a lot out there once myself," Parker said, "but old man Sutherland wouldn't lease it to me. I got a place over on the south side of the lake, though."

"Did he tell you why he wouldn't let you have a lot in the Cove?"

Parker shook his head. "Wouldn't even talk to me about it. Just flat refused. I didn't want to get him riled, so I took the other one."

Howell heard the outboard start up in the test tank behind the station.

"Sounds pretty good," Ed Parker said. "Running real smooth."

Howell got up. "I guess it'll go in the back of the wagon all right, won't it?"

"I'll send it up there in the truck with Benny. You'll need a hand getting it on the boat; that's a pretty big hunk of iron. There's the battery, too. That's been on a trickle charger."

"Thanks, Ed. What do I owe you?"

"Oh, Denham paid when he laid it up. You can give Benny five bucks for helping you, if you want to. You headed home now? I can send him right on with it."

"Yeah, that'll be great. I'll go straight there."

He didn't go quite straight to the cabin, though. He picked up a couple of bottles of bourbon and a bottle of brandy. The booze seemed to be going pretty fast.

Benny was waiting for him, sitting in the truck, when Howell got back to the cabin. The two of them stripped the tarp off the boat and wheeled it from under the house into the water on its trolley. Benny rolled the heavy outboard down to the water on a handcart, set a gas can down next to it, then pulled off his shoes and pants. "Reckon we'll get our feet wet doing this right," he said.

Howell shucked off his trousers and shoes and waded into the cold water with Benny, wheeling the outboard. Benny stopped at the right depth, then pulled the boat toward them. In a moment the motor was fastened securely to the boat's stern, and Benny was connecting the control cables which led forward to the throttle and steering. He set the battery in its box and hooked it up.

"You like it up here?" Benny asked. He had been very quiet. Howell remembered how chatty he had been at the filling station.

"Yeah, it's real pretty. Quiet too; just what I need to work."

Benny straightened from his work and looked out over the little inlet on which the cabin was situated. "You ain't, uh, seen nothing?"

"Seen what?" Howell asked.

Benny worked his jaw for a minute, but didn't answer the question. "Get in there and see if she'll start okay. Battery's all hooked up."

Howell climbed over the stern and tried the starter. The engine roared to life. "Sounds great. Want to come for a spin?"

"No sireee, not me," Benny said, backing out of the water, his skinny white legs sticking out of his shorts. He got into his trousers and started for the truck, shoes in hand, walking tenderfootedly.

"Hey, Benny, take five bucks out of my pants for your trouble," Howell shouted, but Benny didn't seem to hear. A moment later he was driving away. Howell shrugged; he would drop the money by the station next time he was in town. He looked around him; it was a beautiful summer day, hot and sunny. The engine idled quietly, waiting his bidding. He sat in the driver's seat and shoved the throttle down. The boat shot forward and shortly he was in the middle of the lake, flying along at what he reckoned was thirty or thirty-five miles an hour. He had flown for not more than five minutes when the engine coughed, then coughed again, then sputtered and died. The boat slowed to a stop, rolling, caught by its own wake.

Howell tried the starter a few times, but nothing happened. Then he remembered the gasoline can sitting ashore. He made his way aft and checked the two fuel tanks which had been in the boat all along. Both empty. Swell. He checked the boat for a paddle, but there were only some life jackets and a couple of old beer cans. He looked around him. He was drifting about equidistant from both shores of the lake. He could see the outline of the town of Sutherland a couple of miles down, the water tower hovering over it, but no boats. He looked toward the other end of the lake. There was a boat coming fast from that direction, perhaps half a mile away. It would pass close to him if it didn't change course. He started waving.

He could see four people, two couples, in the boat as it drew closer. The driver returned his wave and turned toward him. "Having problems?" he called out as they pulled alongside.

"Yeah, I'm out of fuel, and I'm afraid I've left my gas can ashore," Howell explained.

The young woman next to the driver laughed. "That's not all you left ashore."

Howell followed her gaze and found that he was wearing only Jockey shorts. "Oh, Christ, you're right. I was wading . . ."

"No problem," the driver said. "Where can we tow you?"

Howell pointed to the cove in the distance. "Over there."

A few minutes later Howell had safely secured the boat to the little dock in front of the cabin and had his pants on. "I sure appreciate your help. I'm John Howell."

"I'm Jack Roberts," the driver said. "This is Helen Smith, and in the back are Harry and Joyce Martin. We're staying at a friend's place the other side of the lake."

"Hi," Howell said, taking them all in.

"Is your boat like ours?" the young woman in the back, Joyce, asked. She was blind. Howell reflected that he had met more blind people and dogs in the last week than he had in the last year.

"Pretty much, I guess. Can I offer you folks a drink?" he asked. "Seems the least I can do for being returned to my trousers."

"We're just on our way to pick up some things in the town," Jack explained. "And we're going home in the morning. Maybe next year."

"Well, thanks anyway," Howell said.

"Don't mention it," Jack called back, shoving his boat away from the dock. He gunned the engine. The others waved as they pulled away. Howell saw them off, then emptied the five-gallon gasoline can into one of the outboard's tanks and made a mental note to fill the other one on his next trip to town.

Scotty arrived at the cabin at seven, freshly scrubbed and squeezed into designer jeans topped with a silk blouse. "I was right," she said. "You don't look half bad with a shave and your hair combed over the bald spot."

"We're taking the boat down to Taylor's tonight," Howell replied, "and if you keep that up, you can swim back."

She threw up her hands. "Okay, okay, truce. That's a great shirt, too; you look twenty . . . well, ten years younger."

Soon they were skimming down the lake, drinks in hand, through the early evening light. The air was fresh and cool as it whipped past them, and the water had turned a deep blue with the end of day. At Taylor's they tied up next to the boat that had rescued Howell that afternoon. He told Scotty about the incident.

"Listen, John, you should always wear your pants when you go out. Your mother should have explained that to you. God, I wish I could have seen that—the Pulitzer Prize winner in his little Jockeys."

The two couples were waiting on the front porch for a table, and Howell introduced Scotty. "Jesus," he said, "I forgot this place was dry. Why don't you people come back to the cabin for a nightcap after dinner?"

They ate fried chicken and catfish at a long, oilcloth-covered table, and finished up with peach cobbler, washing everything down with iced tea. The room was crowded with couples and families from miles around, all eating with both hands. Howell and Scotty sat across from Joyce, the blind woman, who alternated bursts of talk and laughter with periods of what seemed to be puzzled silence whenever Scotty spoke more than a few words. Her husband, Harry, seemed to notice it too. "Have we met the two of you before?" he asked Howell and Scotty.

"I don't think so," Howell replied. Scotty shook her head.

"I think Joyce finds you . . . familiar," Harry said.

"It happens sometimes," Joyce chimed in. "Sometimes I think it's something to do with not being able to see. Maybe there are more similar voices than similar faces, who knows? Tell me, is either of you psychic?"

"Nope," Scotty said.

Howell did not reply immediately. "Why do you ask?" he asked finally.

"I think one or both of you probably is," Joyce replied. "I am, and I sometimes get that feeling about other people. If you are, you shouldn't be afraid of it. It's a perfectly natural thing."

"Oh, I've had little flashes at times, I think," Howell said warily. "It may have been just a fluke."

"I doubt it," Joyce said.

After dinner they raced down the windless lake, the two boats abreast, over flat, glassy water, under a rising moon. It had grown chillier with the coming of dark, and Scotty huddled close to Howell for warmth. He put his arm around her and felt the chill bumps through the silk blouse. It had been so warm when they left that neither of them had brought a sweater.

They tied up at the dock in front of the cabin and waited while the two other couples disembarked. Only the crickets broke the silent stillness of the evening. Inside, Howell got a fire going while Scotty made some coffee. "There's a bottle of brandy in there," he called to her. "It would improve the coffee."

Scotty came out of the kitchen with a tray of cups and stopped. Howell, busy at the hearth, looked at her and followed her gaze. The blind woman was standing in the middle of the living room, her chin lifted and her head cocked to one side, turning slowly in a circle. "Is something wrong, Joyce?" Scotty asked.

"Oh, no," she replied. "I was just getting a feel for the place." Her husband came and led her to the sofa before the fire.

Scotty set the cups on the coffee table. "You said you were psychic."

"Oh, yes," Joyce replied.

"She's sometimes quite remarkable," her husband said. "Do you feel something, Honey?"

"I'd like some coffee, if it's ready," she replied, ignoring his question.

Scotty left and returned with the coffeepot and the brandy and busied herself with serving everyone.

Howell put an Errol Garner roll on the player piano, then switched it on. He got a cup, poured an extra measure of brandy into it, and sank into a chair. "Where are you all from?" he asked.

"Helen and I are from Chattanooga," Jack replied. "Harry is, too. Joyce is English, though you'd never know it from her accent."

"Joyce seems to have a good ear," her husband said. "When we visit London, her accent changes the moment we get off the plane at Heathrow."

Joyce spoke up. "Would you all like to have a séance?" Everybody turned and looked at her.

Scotty giggled. "A séance? Really talking to the spirits and everything?"

"Perhaps," Joyce said. "You never know for sure, of course, but I think there might be something here."

"Joyce has a feeling for all sorts of communication, not just accents," Harry said.

"I'm game," Scotty said.

Jack looked at Helen, who nodded. "Sure, why not?" he said.

Only Howell said nothing. He had the odd feeling that things were about to get out of hand.

"John?" Joyce asked. "There's no point unless we have the cooperation of everyone."

Howell felt on the spot. He didn't want to do this, but he would be a poor host if he didn't go along. "Sure," he said, unenthusiastically. "How do we go about it?"

"We need a table," Joyce said, "preferably a round one."

"We've got that," Howell replied.

"Will you place it as near the center of the room as you can? And will someone please switch off the piano?"

"Sure." Howell stopped the piano, and the three men went to the table. "This isn't going to be all that easy," Howell said as they gathered around it. "The base of this thing is a section of a tree trunk that's almost petrified. I don't know how they managed to saw through it."

"Ooph," Harry said as he tugged at the tabletop. "Maybe we just ought to tilt the thing and roll it on its base. We might pull the top loose trying to lift it."

The three men, not without difficulty, got the table tilted and, using the tree-trunk base like a wheel, rolled it toward the center of the room. "I think that's close enough," Harry said. He seemed to have done this before.

They dragged over the chairs, and Joyce indicated where they should each sit, alternating them by sex. "Would someone turn all the lights in the house off, please?" she asked.

Scotty jumped up, and moments later came back from the kitchen. "That's everything," she said. It seemed pitch dark for a moment, then their eyes began to become accustomed to it, and they discovered that the moonlight and the fire lit the cabin quite well. The only sounds were the crackling of the fire and the noisy chatter of the crickets outside. They all sat down and pulled their chairs up to the table.

Joyce placed her hands on the tabletop, her fingers spread, her thumbs touching. "Will everyone please spread your hands like this? Be sure that your thumbs are touching and that the tips of your little fingers touch the person's next to you. What we want is an unbroken chain around the table." They did as instructed. "Please, whatever happens, do not break this chain. It joins our spirits as well as our bodies, and we need the collective help of everyone. We may be at this for some time, so I must ask you to be patient, and if anyone needs to go to the bathroom, please go now."

No one moved.

"I want all of you to relax and be as comfortable as possible. Close your eyes, if you wish. It's important that you each empty your mind of everything but what is happening here. It will be much easier to establish contact if you can do that." Joyce settled herself. "We are all joined here in God to receive the spirits of those departed. If there is any spirit here, please make your presence known." She was silent for a moment, then began to speak again, rhythmically, swaying slightly as she spoke, her blind eyes wandering aimlessly. "Come to us, spirits, speak to us, communicate with us, hear our call, touch us."

Howell felt oddly relaxed. He was unconcerned with his work or his wife or the sheriff of the county or his growing attraction to Scotty. He floated on the moment and listened to Joyce. As she continued, he thought that it seemed to grow quieter, but he reflected that there had not been much noise in the first place. Then he realized that the crickets had stopped. The only sound now was the crackling of the fire.

"Hear us, O spirits, join with us—" She stopped in midsentence.

The room was as before; he wondered why Joyce had stopped. Then the table moved.

"I feel a presence," Joyce said. There was a slight stirring among the group.

The table moved again, more distinctly this time. Howell tried to figure out what was happening. There was something peculiar in the movement of the table. It seemed to slowly undulate beneath his spread hands; it seemed nearly to breathe.

"Will you identify yourself?" Joyce asked. The table moved again, even more distinctly, seemingly in response to her question.

"Can you speak?" Joyce asked. No one spoke, but the table moved again. "Please move the table once for yes and twice for no. Can you speak?"

The table moved twice, distinctly. There was no mistaking it, Howell thought. The hair on his head nearly stood on end. He could feel his scalp crawl.

"We would like to know your name," Joyce said. "I will go through the alphabet. Please move the table once when I reach a letter in your name. A," she said. "B . . . C . . . D . . . ," she continued, with no response. Then, on R, the table moved. Joyce continued and reached Z with no further response. She began again. On A the table moved, then again on B. Joyce finished the alphabet with no further response, then started over. "B . . ." The table moved, then was still as she chanted the letters. "I . . ." Movement. And again at "T." "Rabbit," Joyce said excitedly. "Your name is Rabbit."

The table moved once, for yes.

"Do you wish to contact someone at this table?" Joyce asked.

Yes, the table said.

"Who? I'm sorry, is it me?"

The table moved twice; no.

Joyce continued around the table. "Is it Jack?"

No.

"Is it Helen?"

No.

"Is it John?"

Howell tensed, resisting the urge to take his hands from the table. The table moved. No. He slumped in relief. Then he felt angry with himself. This was some sort of parlor trick, and he was getting sucked into it like a tourist.

"Is it Scotty?"

The table moved once, then stopped. There was a little gasp from Scotty. Then there was a gasp from everyone. The table had left the floor and was moving slightly up and down at about chest level.

Howell felt near to panic. He was hallucinating, he was sure of it. He felt the same way he had on the appearance of the young girl in the cabin the night of the storm. Think reality, he kept saying to himself. It wasn't working.

"Don't move, anybody," Joyce said firmly. "It's all right, just relax. It's all right, Scotty."

Howell looked at Scotty. She was sitting rigid, wide-eyed, staring straight ahead. Then he saw something else. He was sitting facing the lake, and across the room, standing, looking out the window, stood the girl of the thunderstorm.

"Why do you wish to contact Scotty?" Joyce asked, then quickly corrected herself. "I'm sorry . . . Ah, are you happy or unhappy? Once for happy, twice for unhappy."

Howell looked down at the table, a few inches below his nose; he wanted to hear this. It moved twice. Then everything stopped. Howell thought it was like when a refrigerator turned off; you weren't aware of it until it stopped. The table was back on the floor. A moment later the crickets resumed. He looked back to where the girl had stood. She was no longer there.

"It's over," Joyce said. "I don't think we'll get it back."

Later, when everyone had gone, Howell and Scotty sat in front of the fire. "You know anybody named Rabbit?" he asked her. He had to try to figure this out.

"Nope. I didn't even know there *was* anybody named Rabbit."

"Maybe it's a nickname. You know anybody around here? Have you spent any time in the area? I mean, before you came to work for Bo."

"Nope. I grew up in Atlanta—in Decatur, really. My dad's a surgeon at Emory Hospital. I'd never even seen the lake until a month ago."

"Were you frightened when it picked you out?" he asked.

"No, oddly enough. I suppose I should have been, but I just wasn't. Funny."

"I was scared shitless there for a minute," he said, "when the table came off the floor, but I'm not scared now. I mean, I don't want to flee the cabin or anything." He didn't want to mention the girl at the window. Apparently, nobody else had seen her. "I don't feel uncomfortable here, do you?"

"Not in the least," she said, and kissed him.

"Good. Stick around."

"I'm not going anywhere." She kissed him again.

Howell forgot about séances and hallucinations and gave himself to the moment.

The sun was well up, and Scotty was gone. They had made love repeatedly for what had seemed half the night and probably, he knew from his past performances, had been more like half an hour. Maybe what they had done had carried over into the dream, but still . . . The séance seemed very far in the past. As convinced as he had been of what had happened the night before, he now regarded the incident with some skepticism. Maybe he had been drunker than he thought. He had seen the girl twice, and he hadn't been entirely sober either time.

Howell rolled over and put his feet on the floor. As he stood, a needlelike pain shot through his back. He grabbed the bedstead and straightened carefully. He was clearly out of shape for sex, he thought. His back muscles were as sore as a boil. He stood under the shower for a while, directing the hot water onto his spine, trying to let the muscles relax, and they seemed to. Then, as he was shaving, he bent slightly to dip the razor into the water and it was as if a tiny hand grenade had gone off in his lower back. The pain became worse when he tried to straighten, and he forgot his half-finished shave and struggled to the bed. When he had lain stretched out for a few minutes, panting, the pain subsided, but when he tried to get to his feet, it overwhelmed him again.

He struggled painfully into some clothes, trying to stand as little as possible. It wasn't so bad as long as he sat or lay down, but to stand up was torture. He managed to get some coffee made, and sat down on the piano stool to drink it. He looked around the room. The cups and glasses from the night before were still scattered about. Thank God they had moved the table back to its usual position. He shuddered at the thought of trying to move it in his condition. As the pain subsided again, he doodled a few bars on the piano, then flipped on the player. The old machine turned and wheezed and began to play "I'll Take You Home Again, Kathleen."

That was too sentimental for this early in the morning. He removed the roll and inserted another, the Gershwin one. Immediately the piano began again to play "I'll Take You Home Again, Kathleen." Howell stopped the mechanism and looked on the roll. "Gershwin Plays Gershwin" was clearly printed on the paper. Surely George Gershwin had not written the old Irish-American tune? Puzzled, he tried another roll—Earl Hines. Same tune. Howell shut off the piano. The goddamn thing must have some sort of mechanical memory that got stuck; now it was repeating itself, like a windup music box. He suddenly needed a drink. Forgetting his back, he started for the kitchen, then fell to the floor, shrieking, as the pain swept through him.

When he could move again, he got gingerly to his feet and, using a peculiar, Quasimodo-like gait, he made it to the station wagon and pointed it toward Sutherland. He had passed a doctor's office half a dozen times, and now he needed a doctor.

After half an hour with old *Reader's Digest*s and *Guidepost*s, he was ushered into the doctor's examination room, where he related what had happened to him.

"What the hell is the matter with me, Doctor?"

"Incipient middle age," the doctor replied, filling a syringe.

That was not what Howell had wanted to hear. "So what can you do about it?"

"Not much, to tell you the truth. I'm going to inject a muscle relaxant into the area, and I'll prescribe a painkiller. After that, hot baths a couple of times a day and plenty of bed rest."

"For how long? When is this going to clear up?"

"A few days, a few weeks, who knows?" The doctor stabbed at him with the needle.

"Jesus, what kind of prognosis is that?" Howell howled.

"Best medical science can do, I'm afraid. I'd send you over to the local chiropractor for a little wrestling match, but I just sent him down to Atlanta for a laminectomy the other day."

"For what?"

The doctor grinned. "Back surgery. Last resort, of course." He scribbled something on a pad. "Take one of these every four hours for the pain. They're a sort of artificial morphine, so don't get too enthusiastic with them. Come and see me in four or five days if you're not better, and I'll give you another injection."

Howell hobbled out of the place, got the prescription filled, then stumbled into a booth at Bubba's. The place was buzzing with locals in for midmorning coffee, and after a moment Enda McAuliffe plopped down across from him.

"How's it going, John?" he asked.

"Just terrific, Mac," Howell replied, popping one of the painkillers into his mouth and washing it down with coffee. "I've just come from the doctor's, and I think I'm crippled for life." He told the lawyer what had happened to him.

"Well, that's just awful," McAuliffe commiserated. "You know what I'd do if I were you?"

"Suicide?" Howell asked.

McAuliffe shook his head and seemed to suppress a laugh. "Not yet, anyway. Mama Kelly."

"Mama Kelly?"

The lawyer nodded. "The old lady has something of a reputation in these parts for healing. You know, warts, cross-eyed kids, the lame and the halt—that sort of thing. Of course, none of your better people would ever stoop to that."

Howell blinked at him. "You're kidding, aren't you? You're not really suggesting that I do that."

"Seems to me you come under the heading of lame and halt, and anyway, you've had an invitation, haven't you?" McAuliffe sipped his coffee and grinned a wicked little grin. "Couldn't hurt."

"I don't think I'm that bad off," Howell replied. The pill was beginning to work, and he was feeling a little light-headed with it. "Don't worry, I'll tap-dance again."

"Suit yourself. I've seen folks down for months with that sort of thing, though. Course, being a writer, you make your living on your ass, anyway."

"With my mind, buddy." Howell ordered some eggs and another cup of coffee. "Say, you'd have loved it up at my place last night. We had a regular séance up there, some people from across the lake and I."

"Oh?" McAuliffe looked both interested and wary.

Howell told him about meeting the two couples on the lake and about their experience after dinner. He didn't mention the girl at the window. As he spoke, McAuliffe's expression began to change from interest to derision.

Howell continued, "The bloody dining table, which must weigh two hundred pounds, actually spelled out a name—a word, anyway—and came right off the floor at one point. And this morning, all my player piano would play is 'I'll Take You Home Again, Kathleen.' "

McAuliffe put down his coffee cup, suddenly irritable. "Oh, come off it, John. Who've you been talking to?"

"I kid you not, Mac. That's just the way it happened."

"What was the word the table spelled?"

"Rabbit. As in bunny."

"Now look, John, you've had your fun, but this has gone far enough. I don't want to talk about this any more." He picked up his check and started to rise from the booth.

Howell put a hand on his arm. "Look, Mac, I'm not telling you all this to get you riled. It honest to God happened, at least I think it did. Could I make all this up?"

McAuliffe slumped back into the booth and mopped his brow. "No," he said cautiously. "No, you couldn't make it up."

"Mac, is there something you're not telling me? Has anybody else around here ever had this sort of thing happen?"

McAuliffe gazed over Howell's shoulder through the window and out across the mountains. "Not for some years," he said finally. "At least, not that I've heard about."

"Tell me," Howell said, not entirely sure he wanted to know.

McAuliffe looked back at him, then out the window again. His eyes seemed to go out of focus. "I'll tell you a story," he said. "True story, not a ghost story. As much of the truth as I know, anyway. As much as anybody knows, I guess." He called to Bubba for another cup of coffee, and when it came, he sat back and started to talk.

"I told you about the Irish community that used to live in the valley. My family was among them, Bo Scully's, several others hereabouts. Well, just after the war, late '46 or early '47 it was, Eric Sutherland started to put together the land for the lake, and, of course, that meant all of the valley. There was a lot of resistance at first, and for a while it looked as though Sutherland might not make it. Since it was a private, not a public project, he couldn't take the land by eminent domain, he had to buy it outright. He had a couple of Atlanta banks behind him, though—a lot of money. One or two families capitulated, then, finally, the rest of them. All but one, a family called O'Coineen. They wouldn't budge."

"I suppose Sutherland brought pressure to bear."

"Oh, he had been doing that all along. The local bank was with him, of course, and they held a lot of paper in the valley. The worst pressure on the O'Coineens came from the other families, though."

"Why was that? I mean, if they'd all held out in the beginning."

"Well, Sutherland had already paid them three or four times what their property was worth as farmland, and he was smart enough to offer them a hefty bonus beyond that—but only if they all sold. Sutherland was confident enough of the outcome to start building his dam. When the dam was nearly finished—this would have been early 1952—the O'Coineens were the only holdouts, and things started to get nasty."

"Friend against friend, neighbor against neighbor," Howell said.

"Exactly. Donal O'Coineen's barn was burned and some well-digging equipment destroyed—he had a well-digging business in addition to his farm. Things started to get rough for his child at school—there were two daughters; one of them had already graduated. Donal developed what I guess you'd call a siege mentality. He pulled the child out of school and wouldn't let his wife shop in the town. They grew most of what they needed, and he went over to Gainesville for the rest. There were rumors that Sutherland had offered them more than the others, under the table, and that made things worse. The O'Coineens just pulled their heads in, like turtles, and refused to budge. Then Eric Sutherland closed the dam, and the water started to rise."

Howell sat up straight. "Jesus, how could he do that?"

"Well, it was pretty high-handed, all right, but he had the signatures of all the landholders except O'Coineen, and they'd all been paid everything but the bonus. These people had allowed their homes and farm buildings to be pulled down and their timber cut; they'd found other farms and had money in their pockets. They'd scattered, of course; the old Irish community was gone. So Sutherland had the right to fill his lake right up to the road which was the boundary of O'Coineen's property. The law prevented him from flooding the road and cutting O'Coineen off, but suppose there was some error in calculation on the part of the engineers? The roadbed was pretty high and formed a sort of earthen dam for O'Coineen's property. After two or three weeks, the water on the one side of the road was actually higher than the level of his land, which fell away downhill from the road into a sort of hollow. That's where his house was. He knew that if the roadbed caved in, he'd be flooded. And he still had his wife and daughters there, convinced, apparently, that they were all that was keeping Sutherland from letting the water rise any farther. Things were getting pretty tense."

"So, what happened?"

McAuliffe grinned; he was enjoying the storytelling now. "What do you think happened?"

"How the hell should I know?" Howell cried. *"What happened?"*

"One of two things," the lawyer said. "Some folks believe Eric Sutherland's story, that he went out to the O'Coineen place one night and talked Donal into selling. O'Coineen signed a deed of transfer for his land and instructed Sutherland to put the money into his account at the bank. Then he took his wife and children and left the county that very night. The water continued its inexorable rise over the roadbed and flooded the farm."

"And the other thing?"

"Other folks believe that Sutherland never saw O'Coineen, that the roadbed gave way and Donal O'Coineen, his wife, and two daughters were drowned in the ensuing flood."

"So? Which of those two things happened?"

"Nobody knows."

"What do you mean, nobody knows? How could they not know?"

"Because the O'Coineen family was never seen again—not by anybody who knew them, anyway."

Howell was speechless for a moment. "What about the money? Didn't O'Coineen take that?"

"The money is still right down the street there, in the bank, drawing interest."

"You mean, then, that Eric Sutherland may be a murderer?"

"I wouldn't put it as strongly as that. Manslaughter, maybe. Around here, your view on that depends on how close are your economic ties to Eric Sutherland."

Howell slumped back into his seat. "Jesus, that's the most hair-raising thing I ever heard."

McAuliffe grinned maliciously. "You ain't heard nothing yet."

"There's more?"

The lawyer nodded. "The elder daughter was about my age, nineteen or twenty at the time. She was blind. Her name was Joyce." He waited a moment for that to sink in.

The hair on the back of Howell's neck began to move around.

"The younger girl, who was twelve or thirteen, I guess, was named Kathleen."

Howell tried to speak but swallowed hard instead.

McAuliffe took a sip of his coffee, put down the cup, and sat back. "And in the Irish language, me bucko," he said with a sigh, "the name O'Coineen means 'rabbit.' "

10

Bo Scully drove from his office south along the lakeshore. He tried breathing deeply to dissolve the knot that grew tighter in him with every mile. It was always this way, he thought; he supposed it always would be. He turned through the wrought-iron gates, which stood open to receive him.

Their relationship had always been peculiar, he thought, since the very night Eric Sutherland had first spoken to him, as he limped off the field after a particularly bruising game in his junior year of high school. He had just turned seventeen. Sutherland had invited him to lunch the next day, and the event had been awkward for both of them. Sutherland had never married, had no immediate family; Bo was fatherless, so he reckoned the man was simply extending a kindly hand to a fatherless boy. But there was nothing kindly about Sutherland, even when he was working hard to be hospitable. It had occurred to Bo that Sutherland might be queer, but there had never been any hint of that in their relationship, not since that first day when they had eaten club sandwiches on the back terrace of the big house and talked stiffly of Bo's football career.

He saw Sutherland infrequently, though they talked on the phone more often, when Sutherland needed something or wanted something done. The summonses to the house were infrequent, a few times a year, not counting the big annual party, and there was always something specific and of importance to discuss, as there had been when Sutherland had suggested—nearly ordered—that Bo run for the dead sheriff's unexpired term. Bo wondered what it would be today.

His heavy shoe struck the tiles of the front stoop with a hollow sound that somehow reminded Bo of the whole house. It was certainly well furnished, he thought, as the white-jacketed black man showed him into the house and down the hall to the study. But the house seemed unused, uninhabited by any real person. It might have been a photograph in a glossy magazine. Even the study, which he now entered, seemed to belong to some absent spirit rather than its owner, who had built it. Its order was too perfect, almost obsessive. Bo suspected that the leather-bound classics on the shelves had not been read, and he had never known Sutherland to use the expensive shotguns in the polished mahogany case. He thought that many of the things in the study might have belonged to Sutherland's father, whom Bo had never known. Sutherland nodded at a chair, and Bo sat in it. The servant noiselessly closed the door behind him.

"You all right?" Sutherland offered a box of cigars.

"I'm real good, Eric." The man had insisted on being addressed by his Christian name ever since Bo had come back from Korea. Bo was the only person he knew who called him that, and he was not comfortable with it. He accepted the cigar; he thought it must be Cuban, though he had no way of knowing, since he despised cigars.

Sutherland came to the point quickly, as he always did. "I think it's time Mr. John Howell departed us," he said.

Bo stopped himself from objecting; first he wanted to know exactly what Sutherland meant by "depart." He put the cigar in the ashtray next to him and left it there.

"I want you to see to it," Sutherland said.

Bo leaned forward and placed his elbows on his knees. "Eric, I don't think we should overreact to Howell." He still didn't have a firm grasp on Sutherland's intentions, but he was worried by what the old man might mean.

"He's up here to spy, isn't he?"

"I'm not at all sure that he is," Bo said, as calmly as he could manage. He thought that Howell probably was at the lake to spy, but not quite the sort of spying Sutherland had in mind, and he felt this was no moment to agree wholeheartedly with Sutherland. This felt very dangerous. "My best information is that he left his job some time back to write a book. He hasn't worked for the paper for a long time now."

"He knows them, though, and they know him. He's just the sort of fellow they'd put up here if they were being sneaky, don't you see that?"

"Well, since he knocked an editor of the paper halfway across the newsroom when he left, I don't know that he'd be the sort they'd send."

He was trying to sound reasonable; he'd never seen Sutherland quite so worked up. "His name seems to be mud around that newspaper."

"Well, maybe he's doing it on his own then. Maybe he thinks he can work his way back into their good graces if he comes up with something here."

"Our information is that the paper was sending one of its reporters. It just doesn't add up." Bo thought it just might add up, but he was fighting his way out of a corner now.

Sutherland slapped his palm on the leather surface of the big desk. "Well, just why in hell can't they leave it alone, for God's sake? It's been nearly twenty-five years."

"Of course it has," Bo said. "What could he possibly dig up that could be embarrassing after this long?"

"Nearly twenty-five goddamn years," Sutherland said, then sagged back into his chair.

"Now, Eric, I don't want you to worry about this," Bo said, as soothingly as he could manage. "I'm keeping an eye on Howell, and so far there's been nothing to be alarmed about." That wasn't true, but he didn't want Sutherland alarmed. Sutherland alarmed was dangerous. "You just trust me to handle him; it'll be all right, I promise you." He wanted Sutherland calm for his own reasons. Anyway, Howell had probably saved his ass during that holdup, and he liked the man. "Let's not overreact," he said again.

"I wish I'd never put that money in the bank," Sutherland said. "It eats at me to this day."

"You did the best thing in the circumstances," Bo replied. "You covered yourself. There might have been serious trouble if you hadn't done that."

Sutherland sagged even further. "All right. You keep an eye on him. If there's the slightest sign that he's after something, I want to know about it, you hear?"

"Why, sure, Eric. You just leave it to me."

Bo's shirt was sticking to him when he left the house a few minutes later. He had to keep Sutherland happy; the man didn't have an important heir, and Bo knew he was in line for something, maybe everything. The old man had brought it up often enough. John Howell might be a problem, or he might not be. Bo thought the best thing to do was wait. As a rule, he preferred waiting until he had to move. He still didn't know what Sutherland's intentions toward Howell had been. He had been afraid to ask. He didn't want to know.

Bo glanced at his watch as he left the house. Just four minutes to go. Sutherland had nearly kept him too long. He drove quickly out of the south side of town and pulled up at a telephone booth in the parking lot at Minnie Wilson's convenience store. The phone was already ringing when he got to it. He snatched the receiver off the hook.

"Yeah?"

"That you?"

"Yeah, I got your teletype."

"Don't say that on the phone, for Christ's sake."

"Sorry. What's up?"

"I've got a big one for you."

"When?"

"Soon enough. They're getting cranked up down south now. A few weeks, maybe. It takes time to put together a big one."

"A big one means big at my end, then?"

"Don't get greedy, friend. You've been very well taken care of so far, haven't you?"

"I'm not complaining."

"I think I can get you seventy-five, maybe eighty for this one. Trust me to deal for you."

"You've done okay by me so far. I'll trust you."

"Okay, I just wanted you to know what's in the works. We'll be doing it as a training operation; there'll be a bigger carrier involved than usual."

"There's not all that much room, you know."

"Our man has been there before. He says he can do it. I believe him."

"If that's good enough for you, it's good enough for me."

"Good. You'll get the schedule in the usual way. Postpone if there's serious trouble, but if you confirm, it's go all the way. I'm depending on you to see that this comes off without a hitch."

"I don't have hitches. I'll do everything but drive it in and out. That's your man's job."

"Right. I'll be in touch."

Bo hung up the telephone and leaned against the booth. Seventy-five or eighty. Funny, it didn't seem as much as it used to. Still, it wasn't bad for a few hours' work. He headed back to his car.

11

For two days Howell was an invalid. Scotty came and rubbed his back and saw that he ate, but he wasn't sure she believed it was as bad as he made it out to be. It was, in fact, worse. Every time he got to his feet he had about two minutes of mobility before his legs began to cramp horribly, then it was into a chair or back to bed. As long as he sat or reclined, the pain was manageable. Even then, it was manageable only because of the painkillers the doctor had given him, mixed with generous doses of Jack Daniel's.

He was in no mood to think about work, so he thought about the séance and the girl at the window. He could not bring himself to give any credence to the idea that the house might be haunted, but he was intrigued by the double coincidence of the medium's being blind and being named Joyce, like the elder O'Coineen daughter. It was clear that they could not be the same person, since Joyce O'Coineen would now be in her late forties, and the medium had been much younger, or at least, she *seemed* younger. Still, he was intrigued. Both the visiting couples had left the lake the morning after the séance, apparently, to go back to Chattanooga. He couldn't remember Jack's last name; Helen's name was Smith, and that was tough to trace; and Harry and Joyce Martin weren't going to be easy either, he thought, an opinion confirmed when the Chattanooga information operator was finally persuaded to give him the numbers of all the Harry, Harold, Henry, and H. Martins listed. There were some two dozen. Halfway through the list, he got lucky.

"May I speak to Joyce Martin, please?"

"Speaking."

"Is this the Joyce Martin who was at Lake Sutherland a few days ago?"

"Yes. Is this John Howell?"

"Yes," he replied, surprised.

"I thought so; I'm good at voices," she said.

"I'm sorry to trouble you, Joyce, but I've been thinking about the séance the other night and . . ."

"You're psychic yourself, aren't you, John?"

"Well, I've had a few minor episodes that were hard to explain away, but . . ."

"You shouldn't suppress it, you know."

This was making Howell uncomfortable, and he pressed on. "Joyce, may I ask your maiden name?"

"It's Wilks. Why?"

"And may I ask where you were born and grew up?"

"At Newport, on the Isle of Wight, in England."

"Of course. I had forgotten you were British. I'm asking because there was a girl who lived in this area many years ago whose name was Joyce and who was blind."

"Someone still living?"

"I'm not sure."

"Well, I'd never been to that area before last week, and I assure you I'm not a ghost revisiting an old locale."

Howell laughed. "I didn't think you were."

"Tell me," she said. "Were you frightened by what happened the other night?"

"No, just intrigued."

"Did you experience something you didn't tell the rest of us about?"

"Why do you ask?"

"Because sometimes people who are uncomfortable at séances, as you were, either don't want to admit an experience, or don't want to draw attention to themselves. Anyway, I just felt you did."

"Well, yes, I thought I saw a young girl standing at the window."

"Was that the first time you'd seen her?"

"No, there was one other time." He told her about the thunderstorm.

"Does any of this have any meaning to you? Something in your personal life, perhaps?"

"No, nothing at all. At least not until after the séance." He was beginning to trust her now, to want to confide in her. He told her Enda McAuliffe's story, and about the player piano's behavior.

"Well, now," Joyce said. "You've got something very interesting going on there, haven't you?"

"Well, maybe."

"The piano interests me a lot. The manipulation of an inanimate object by a spirit is often part of the poltergeist phenomenon, something often associated with the presence of a pubescent child in the house. I take it you have no children there."

"No."

"But you say the girl you saw was of that age."

"Yes, I think so."

"And the O'Coineens had a daughter of that age named Kathleen, and now the piano is playing a song with her name in it."

"That seems to be what's happening."

"So, what does this mean to you?"

"I'm not sure."

"Oh, come on, John. You just don't want to acknowledge what's going on. You don't need me to tell you that somebody wants to contact you."

"Then why did the . . . whatever it was, say it wanted Scotty?"

"I don't know, but Scotty is your friend; maybe it felt you were offering resistance and was trying to get to you through Scotty."

"Well, that's very interesting, Joyce. I . . ."

"And it's obvious that this event wasn't induced only by the séance, since you had seen the girl before on your own."

"What's your advice, then? What should I do about it?"

"If you're frightened by all this, you can always find a priest and try to persuade him to do an exorcism, but it would be hard to get one to do it, and, anyway, you say you aren't frightened."

"No. Not yet, anyway."

"Well, I think it would be a lot more interesting just to see what happens. Lie back and enjoy it, John."

"Should I speak to her?"

"Sure, if you like. I should tell you, though, that people who see ghosts don't usually get much conversation out of them. Their actions are more important. What did you say she was doing when you saw her?"

"She was looking out the window over the lake, both times."

"Well, if it happens again, why don't you have a look out the window?"

"Well, all right. Can I call you again for advice?"

"I'm afraid Harry and I are leaving tonight for New York, and we've got a flight to London tomorrow. My father is ill, and I expect to be in England for several weeks. Try me in a few weeks, though, if it's still going on."

He thanked her and hung up. It hadn't been a very satisfying conversation. He had called her to dispel one notion, and she had planted another, one he didn't like very much.

When Howell woke on the third day, the pills were gone, and the bourbon wasn't enough. Scotty was at work, and the thought of waiting until she could refill the prescription was more than he could bear. So was the thought of going back to the quack in Sutherland, with his drugs and injections. The man obviously knew no way to cure his problem. If quacks were all that was available, then what the hell?

When he reached the crossroads, he very nearly turned right toward the town, but a twinge from his sciatic nerve kept him on course, straight ahead. As he passed the mailbox, he reflected that this was the closest he had come to the house. He wasn't sure why he had been avoiding it; odd people had always appealed to him, and he had never had any trouble talking with the eccentrics and freaks that so repelled most people. In his early days as a reporter, he had gotten more than a few readable features out of just such people—quirky stuff that filled in the cracks between police and political reporting, stuff that caught the attention of editors and, eventually, helped convince them that he might be good for a column.

The house was like hundreds he had seen all over the South; together, he thought, they must form some backwoods school of architecture. It was frame, with a wide porch, deep eaves, and a heavy, gently pitched roof, the house of a moderately prosperous farmer or sawmill operator. It was different, though. There was no lawn, just a hard-packed, pebble-strewn yard, and only scrawny remnants of shrubbery. But if the residents had no enthusiasm for beautification, neither did they hold with neglect. There were no missing shingles, no broken panes, no rusting automotive heaps on the grounds. The place had a tidy, well-mended look to it.

He stopped in the dirt driveway at a corner of the porch. A young woman was sitting in a porch swing, rocking gently, shelling peas. Her thick, pale-red hair fell to her shoulders, and her skin was powdery and freckled. Her cheekbones were wide and high, her jaw firm, square, her shoulders broad, and, from what Howell could see from that angle, her breasts were full and high under the flowered cotton dress. He sat staring at her for a moment. He could immediately see what her younger brother, Brian, might have been had he been born with his full senses.

"Well," she said, tossing her hair over her shoulder, "whatever it is you want, you'd better come get it; we don't offer curb service."

Howell climbed carefully from the car and ambulated, crablike, up the porch steps. By the time he reached the top, the leg cramps were coming again, and he nearly dived into the swing next to her to get the weight off his feet.

She held on to the pan into which she had been shelling the peas and waited for the swing to settle down after his lunge for it. "Have a seat," she said dryly.

"Sorry, I just couldn't make it any farther. I've come—"

"I know why you've come," she interrupted.

"Yeah, yeah, I know," Howell said, nodding wearily. "Mama told you."

She looked at him sideways. "That's right, Mama told me. What took you so long?" She didn't sound particularly glad to see him.

"Well, I haven't been getting around too well these past few days. You're . . ."

"Leonie," she said. She pronounced it Lee-OH-nee.

He started to tell her his name, but then, she already knew it, didn't she?

"So you're the famous John Howell," she said, as if she doubted it. "I used to read you in the paper."

"Well, I've been surprised at how many folks around here have. I wouldn't have thought people this far up would read the Atlanta paper."

"Oh, yes," she said with mock gravity. "We have to struggle with it, but we manage to get through a newspaper if we move our lips."

"Look," he said irritably, "that's not what I meant, I . . ." He stopped, realizing that she was goading him and that it was getting to him. He didn't want an argument with her. He was, in fact, quite attracted to her. "Do you think I could see your mother?"

"She's asleep."

"Well, maybe I'd better come back another time, then." He shifted his weight in preparation for getting up again.

"Just sit tight. She knows you're here; she'll wake up soon."

He sat tight and watched her shell peas, which she did very quickly. She seemed to concentrate on the job, though he knew she didn't have to. He wondered what she was thinking and tried to think of something to say, but she didn't seem to be very receptive. He heard a footstep from inside the door and the screen door swung open. He had expected the mother, but a girl came out. He knew immediately that she was Brian's twin. There was the same beauty, marred by the vacant look.

"You finished the peas yet, Leonie?" the girl asked. She looked shyly at Howell.

"Just about, honey," her sister replied. "Mary, this is John Howell. He's come to see Mama about something."

"Hey, John," the girl said, and smiled.

"Hey, Mary," Howell said back to her. She had the same beautiful teeth her brothers had. He wondered if Leonie had them too. He hadn't been able to tell yet.

Leonie held out the pot. "Here, honey, you can take them to the kitchen. Don't cook them for more than five minutes, now. Remember to set the timer." The girl took the peas and went happily away.

"She seems like a nice kid," Howell said. "So does Brian."

"Well, they're as alike as two of those peas," Leonie said, and permitted herself an affectionate smile. "And just as sweet."

Howell thought of how they had surely come to be retarded and was suddenly stuck for something to say. He was saved by a voice from inside the house.

"Leonie!"

Howell was brought sharply back to why he was there, and he was suddenly as nervous as a cat.

"Yes, Mama," Leonie called back. "All right," she said to Howell, "let's go see her." She stood up and led the way into the house, walking slowly so that Howell could keep up with her. In the living room she stopped and said, "Wait here for just a minute, while I sit her up and brush her hair. She likes to look nice when people come."

Howell sank gratefully into an easy chair and looked around the room, trying to get some further sense of the Kelly family. The first thing he noticed was books; there were books everywhere. They seemed to be mostly book-club selections, fiction and biography, but then he saw a familiar binding stretching eight feet or so along a bottom shelf. The Harvard Classics. He had the set too; he'd bought them in a used book shop years before with the best of intentions, but he'd never cracked a one of them. He wondered if somebody in this house had. He scanned the other shelves quickly, looking for his own book, like any author. It was there; it had been a selection for a book club. The bookcases meandered around the room, banged together, it seemed, by a poor carpenter. The shelves sagged and fell off at odd angles. There were a number of family photographs, some of them quite old. He picked up one from the table next to his chair. It was a group of people sitting on the steps of a house much like the one he was in, but not quite. Must have been during World War II or just after; a man was in an army uniform. The others' clothes looked about right for the period. There was an oddly familiar face in the group, a child. Not the child in the window; he hadn't seen her face. He was trying to place it when Leonie's voice made him jump.

"All right, you can come on in now." She was standing in the door of what must be Mama Kelly's room.

Howell struggled up and shuffled across the living room, feeling more and more nervous with each step. He entered the bedroom slowly and, at first, saw only the foot of a hospital bed and some covered feet. The head of the bed was behind the door he was entering. Leonie was standing at the foot of the bed and beckoned him to join her. He was glad of that, because when he reached the end of the bed he could lean on it. He turned to face Mama Kelly.

He had built up a fantasy of some shriveled old hag who would be waiting for him, and he turned his eyes reluctantly toward the head of the bed to be met with a steady gaze from large blue eyes set in a handsome, nearly unlined face. He was sure that, before her illness, she had been a beautiful woman. She seemed large, like Leonie, though frail; she must have lost considerable weight, he thought. Her hair was very white and quite thin, and Leonie had arranged it carefully. She smiled broadly, as if welcoming a long lost friend. The teeth were perfect.

"Welcome, John Howell," she said. "I've waited an awful long time for you to come."

His unease left him immediately. "How do you do, Mrs. Kelly. I'm sorry I didn't get by sooner. I wanted to thank you for sending Dermot to me and for the firewood. I've let too much time pass before coming to see you."

"Oh, I've been waiting for longer than that, John—may I call you John?"

"Of course. I don't quite know what you mean, though."

She smiled again. "Oh, you will in time, don't you worry." She patted the bed beside her. "Will you come and sit down here next to me?"

He moved carefully to her side and sat on the edge of the bed. She took his hand in the two of hers. Her hands were warm and rough, as if they had done hard labor. He felt perfectly comfortable, as if he were visiting a favorite aunt that he hadn't seen for years.

"You're in a great deal of pain, aren't you?" she asked.

"Yes, it's . . ."

"It's in your back, I can feel it," she said, and a shadow, a wince, crossed her face.

"Mama," Leonie said, "don't you do this. You're not up to it."

Howell was alarmed that she might be somehow taking on his pain. "No, ma'am," he said, withdrawing his hand. "You mustn't do that. I can go back to the doctor."

She took his hand back and held it. "I'm perfectly all right, it's just that I'm a little tired. I know that you had trepidations about coming to see me. I know this is all a little strange to you. But we're going to help you with your back, and with the other thing too. You see, you're stronger than you think, but you need the help."

Howell frowned. There was no question that he needed all the help he could get with his back, but the rest of what she was saying baffled him.

"Don't worry," she said again. "You'll know, you'll understand in time. It will come to you one way or another." She looked up at her daughter. "Leonie, come around here." She gestured to the other side of the bed. Leonie came and took her hand. Then, one hand holding Leonie's and one holding Howell's, Mama Kelly said, "John, my powers are waning with my own sickness, but my daughter's are just beginning."

Leonie looked embarrassed. "Mama, I don't think . . ."

"Hush, girl, listen to me. God gave you these powers, and it didn't matter that you didn't want them—not until now, it didn't. But now, I can't carry on, and it's time for you to take this on. Now is a good time, because John has come here to help us, and it's only right that we help him. Do you understand?"

Leonie nodded and squeezed her mother's hand.

Mama Kelly turned back to Howell. "Now, John, I need to talk to Leonie for just a minute. You go up to her room—it's the first door at the top of the stairs—and lie down and rest for just a bit. It's better if you're relaxed, and I know you're uncomfortable standing up."

Howell looked up at Leonie questioningly. She nodded.

Mama Kelly spoke again. "You go on up now, and I want you to come and see me again if things seem to get too much for you, you hear?"

"Yes, ma'am, I'll do that," Howell said, and left the mother and daughter alone. He found the stairs and limped painfully up them, putting as much weight as he could on the bannister. At the top of the stairs he opened a door and found a neat, sunlit room filled with country arts—needlework and quilts—and a fourposter bed. The pain was gaining fast on him; he kicked off his shoes and threw himself onto the bed, panting, and waited for it to subside. It was a feather mattress, and he sank gratefully into it. The pain slowly drained away and, with it, the tension that he had brought to this house. He let it go and soon fell into a light doze. What must have been a few minutes later he heard the bedroom door open and close and a light footstep on the rug. There was the tiny rasp of a window shade, and the light in the room grew dimmer.

"Turn over," she said softly. Then he felt her hand at the small of his back, just to the right of where his spine ended, at the very epicenter of his pain.

"How did you know?" he mumbled, half into the soft mattress. "How did you know exactly where?"

There was a hint of a laugh. "I just knew," she said. "Undo your pants."

He managed to lift enough to get the buckle and zipper undone, then helped her peel away the jeans and undershorts.

She pushed upward on his polo shirt. "This too."

He pulled the shirt over his head, tossed it aside, and sank again into the feather mattress. The sunlight had warmed the room, and the air felt good on his naked skin. He felt her climb onto the bed next to him.

She placed both her hands on his back again and held them there, as if feeling for something. She took them away and put them back again in a slightly different position. Then again.

He had nearly drifted off, but now he became fully alert. Her hands were growing warm. Not simply the warmth of skin against skin, but a heat he had never felt before from another human being. It grew so intense he thought he would be burned. Then she withdrew her hands. When she replaced them, they were cooler, and she began to gently massage the place at the center of the pain. He felt a deep relaxation come over him, of muscles he had not known were there.

"Have you ever done this before?" he asked.

"No," she said.

"Did your mother tell you what to do?"

"No. She just said I'd know."

Howell moved his body gingerly in a way that would have, a few minutes before, caused him agony. Nothing happened.

"Not yet," she said. "Don't move yet. Let me do the moving." She began to move her fingers up his back, feeling her way, seeming to pull at his spine. She placed the heel of one hand at the base of his skull and the other in the small of his back and pushed in opposite directions. She began massaging his neck and shoulders, then stopped, got up for a moment and returned. She began again, this time using oil, which she warmed in her hands. She moved slowly down each side of his back, rubbing away tenseness, then to his buttocks, pressing hard with the heels of her hands into the large muscles. At one moment, her hand brushed across his anus and made his breath quicken, then she moved down to his legs and eventually his feet. She stopped and sat quietly for a moment. He lay still, breathing deeply. "That's all I can do for your back right now," she said. She seemed to be breathing rapidly. "Lie still for a few minutes and rest. Then get dressed and come downstairs. I want to check on Mama." She left.

He lay on the bed and tried to recapture what had just happened, but it flew from him. Finally, knowing that she would not come back, he got up and dressed. It was not until he was halfway down the stairs that he realized that he was moving without pain or restriction for the first time in days. There was some soreness in his back, as if he had just played some strenuous game, but no pain. He felt light and easy on his feet. As he reached the bottom of the stairs, Leonie came out of her mother's bedroom. They walked out onto the porch together.

"I'd like to thank her," he said.

"She's asleep. You can see her another time."

"I hardly know how to thank you. I've no pain at all in my back. I can tap-dance again."

She laughed. "I'm glad to hear it. Mama says I'll have to do it again, to make it permanent."

"Well, you won't get an argument from me. I could come back whenever you like, or . . ." He hesitated. "Will you come to the cabin?"

"Yes," she said.

"Tomorrow night?" He was already thinking of what to say to Scotty. Work, maybe. He would say he could only work at night.

"Not at night. Only in the daytime, when I can get away." She laughed again. "Anyhow, you're busy at night."

"I can get free."

"Only in the daytime."

"All right."

Driving back to the cabin, he thought about the Kelly family, why
they were the way they were. He pushed the thought away. That was all
over. The old man, Patrick, was dead, and there was nothing wrong
with Leonie. He wanted her. Elizabeth came into his mind for a moment, but he pushed her away.

Howell was setting the dinner table when Scotty arrived. She stepped inside the door and stopped in her tracks.

"You sonofabitch!" she cried. "You've been faking all along."

"No, no, I . . ."

She advanced toward him across the room. "You just wanted to be nursed and have your back rubbed, didn't you?"

"No, listen, I'm healed! Really, I am!" He did a mock soft-shoe.

She watched him in amazement. "You really went to Mama Kelly, right? You did it!"

"I did indeed." It didn't seem necessary to tell her that he had been ministered to by daughter, not mama.

"And it worked? It really worked?"

Howell put down the plates he had been holding, bent over, and touched his toes.

"Well, I'll be damned!"

"Probably. But before that, you'll be served my famous spaghetti."

"Famous for what? Ptomaine?"

Howell clutched his chest. "You wound me, madam. Before the evening's over, you'll apologize."

An hour and a half later, she drained her wine glass and put it down. "I apologize," she said contritely.

"Told you so."

"I didn't get ptomaine, just ordinary indigestion."

"There's nothing ordinary about the indigestion you get from my spaghetti. It matches anything you might get in those greasy spoons you have to eat in when you're a reporter. It's a Pulitzer indigestion."

"Say, now that you bring it up, what happens when you get the Pulitzer Prize?"

"They give you a thousand dollars, and you become a legend in your time."

"No, no, I mean, what happens on the day? How do they tell you you've won it?"

Howell leaned back and took a sip of his wine. "I think somebody knows something a little early," he said. "I got a call from my editor at the *Times* asking me to come to New York; he didn't say for what. The news came over the AP wire that afternoon. There were five bells on the teletype, and the thing started to print: 'The Board of Trustees of Columbia University today announced the winners of this year's Pulitzer Prizes for Journalism.' They didn't keep me in suspense. 'The Pulitzer Prize for National Reporting was awarded to John Howell of the *New York Times*.' Then all the others were announced. There was a little impromptu party in the executive editor's office, and then he took a bunch of us to '21' for the best dinner I ever had."

"Wow," Scotty said softly. "I want it to happen to me just like that."

"Hang in there, kid; you never know."

"Do you ever miss the *Times*?" she asked. "Would you go back?"

"Sometimes," he said. God, how he missed it. "I think it's highly unlikely I'll ever go back. They say you can leave the *Times* once for another love, so to speak, but not twice. I've only left once, of course, but somehow I don't think they liked it very much." That was an understatement, he thought. They had offered him the best thing going, and he had turned it down. They didn't like being turned down.

"Listen," she said, "is your back really cured?"

"You bet."

"You can screw, and everything?"

"And everything."

"Don't tell me, show me," she said, pushing her chair back from the table.

As she headed past him toward the bedroom, he grabbed her wrist and pulled her toward him. With his teeth he pulled the front of her T-shirt out of her jeans and pushed his tongue into her navel.

Scotty made a little noise and peeled the T-shirt over her head, exposing the beautifully shaped breasts which had always appealed so much to Howell. He bit the nipples, which leaped out at him.

She unzipped her jeans, pushed them down, kicked them off, and surprised him by climbing so that her knees were resting on the arms of his chair. He pushed his face into the mound of hair and opened her with his tongue. Scotty was now biting off tiny yells. She was pulling his head into her, and for a moment Howell thought he would suffocate, but he couldn't stop. Within less than a minute she was coming noisily, shouting her delight.

Howell scooped her up in his arms and swept her toward the bed. Then he was out of his own clothes and into her, moving with slow, shallow strokes. He pulled her legs up over his shoulders and, very slowly, slid more and more of himself into her until, finally, she was panting and laughing.

His arousal had started with Leonie that afternoon, and now he had an outlet for it. Both women were in his mind as he brought Scotty to orgasm again, then again. Finally, he came with her, shouting with her, rocking the bed until he thought it would collapse. He rolled over, and she lay on top of him, their sweat mingling.

"Johnny," she said, "I've done my share of fucking, but never in my whole life was it like that."

"Me, either," he said weakly. "Listen, Scotty, I want to be straight with you . . ."

"Yeah?"

"Look, I'm just coming out of a marriage that didn't work, and it was my fault, all of it. I feel as if I'm in bed with you on false pretenses."

"Listen, sport, there was nothing false about what we just did."

"Yeah, well, I feel that way too, but I just don't want you to expect too much of me."

Scotty turned on her side and put her head on his shoulder. "Johnny, I've been stuck up here with nobody, and I mean *nobody,* even to spend an evening with, let alone make love to. I like you, really I do; I think we've become friends. But that's enough for me. Is it enough for you? Are you looking for somebody to be in love with you?"

"Oh, no," Howell said, with sincerity. "I don't think I could handle that right now."

"You like me? Are we friends? Do you feel close?"

"Yes, I do. I really do."

"Well, then, as long as we seem to have slid into this wonderful patch of screwing, why don't we just ride it out, so to speak, and see how it goes?"

He kissed her on the top of the head. "I think that's a marvelous idea," he said. Then, exhausted, he fell soundly asleep.

Sometime past midnight, Howell woke with a start and sat straight up in bed. The linens were in disarray. Scotty lay sprawled beside him, face down, naked. He was immediately aroused, wanted her.

But what had wakened him? He had been dreaming the dream, he knew that, but some sound had interrupted. Had it been inside the house? He got his feet on the floor and made his way gingerly into the living room. He didn't want to turn on the lights. Anyway, the embers of the fire cast some small light. As his eyes became used to it, he saw the girl again. He froze. She was in the same position as before, standing at the window, her back not quite to him. The light wasn't good, but he had never seen her for more than a second or two, and he wanted a longer look. Afraid even to blink, he studied her dim outline carefully, and this time saw something different. Although she was small and slight, she seemed to have more shape than he had noticed before; there was something more mature about her. He took a deep breath.

"Kathleen," he said softly.

She turned slightly toward him; her face was in shadow, but she seemed to be looking directly at him. After a moment, she turned back to the window.

Howell took a step toward her, then another. She stepped back into a shadow and seemed to become part of it. She was gone. Howell moved to the window; he wanted to see what she had seen. Outside, lit only by stars, was the lake, just as it always was. He pushed open the French doors and walked onto the deck, out over the water.

There was no moon, and the silence was complete; the crickets had stopped. A chill climbed up his naked skin. Now he knew what had awakened him; not a sound, but a sudden absence of sound. Once before, he remembered, the crickets had stopped.

He looked about him in the darkness, but he could see nothing, no one. His fingers found the deck's railing, and he leaned against it, stretching to see further. Then, with a loud crack, the weathered wood suddenly gave way and he pitched forward into the darkness, down toward the black waters of the lake. He grabbed a breath, held it, and waited for the cold shock.

But there was no water, only grass at his feet. He was standing in another place, and he knew with certainty that he was not himself; he was another man. He felt ill, felt terribly hung over. He looked wildly about him, completely disoriented. It was still night, but there was no cabin in this place. And no lake.

He stood in a patch of grass and ferns on a forested mountainside and looked out over a valley. There was a house below him, something less than a mile away, with cheerfully lit windows and smoke curling up from the chimney. The floor of the valley was covered with a thick ground fog which reached the steps of the house. Suddenly the noise of a car engine caused him to turn to his left. An old car, a convertible, sped past him, perhaps twenty yards away, and headed down a road which led into the valley. A childish compulsion to identify all automobiles caused him to say aloud, "Lincoln Continental, 1940." The voice was not his.

He watched as the car moved into the ground fog of the valley and approached the house. It stopped in the front yard, and a man got out and approached the house. Someone met him at the door and admitted him. Howell heard the screen door slam and, a moment later, a yell, a scream—a man's voice. Howell was gripped with a thick dizziness, and time seemed to pass. Then he heard the slam of a car door and heard the engine start. The car turned onto the road and headed back the way it had come, toward where he stood. It was moving fast, and in a moment he would be able to see the driver. Already, he could see a glow from the instruments inside the car. There . . . there, he could nearly see . . .

A blinding white light filled his vision, obliterating house, car, everything, then the light was black, and he was upside down, cold, choking, struggling desperately for his feet and for air. He surfaced, gagging and spitting, sucking air into his starved lungs. He brushed the water from his eyes, saw the dock, and made for it. When he had climbed out of the water, he did not stop to rest until he was up the steps and back on the deck. Avoiding the broken railing, he looked out over the lake. A cloud drifted away from the moon, revealing everything as it was before. The crickets were chirping loudly.

He moved into the house, found a terrycloth robe, and poured himself a stiff drink. For half an hour he sat at the table in the living room, looking out over the lake and trying to shape what had happened to him into an acceptable form. He had nearly drowned, he decided finally, and in his panic had hallucinated. But the hallucination had been his dream, he was sure of it. He had experienced his dream while awake. He had been somewhere else, had been another person, had seen the car and the house, but not the driver. The hallucination had stopped too soon. He was sure that, in the dream, he had seen more.

He finished his drink and went back to bed. Scotty was still as he had left her. She stirred as he climbed onto the bed. He ran his hand lightly down her back. She made a small noise and snuggled up to him.

"What a night," she said softly into his shoulder.

"What a night, indeed," he said back to her, then fell asleep.

13

Scotty drove to work feeling pleasantly tired, drained, and happy. With a lover now available, she felt that some lost part of herself had been restored. She reflected that if she ever were sent to prison, she would kill herself. She had tried it with women, and there had been something, quite literally, missing. Scotty liked men, and she was delighted to have one again.

She arrived at the sheriff's office simultaneously with a furniture delivery van. Two men were struggling with a large, apparently very heavy filing cabinet. She thought that odd, since she usually ordered that sort of thing for Bo Scully, and she had not ordered this. She preceded the two men into the office and was surprised to find the sheriff there ahead of her. He ordinarily did not arrive before midmorning.

"Is that for us?" she asked him, waving toward the two men, who were now rolling the thing into the office on a dolly.

"It's for me," Scully replied hoarsely. "I ordered it a while back, before you joined us."

He looked a bit odd, and Scotty thought at first he must be hung over. Then, as she brushed past him to get to her desk, she realized that he was drinking. She was astonished. She knew Bo knocked back a few with the boys—she had seen him hung over often enough—but she had never seen him drinking in the morning.

"Where is everybody?" she asked. There was usually at least one other clerk or deputy in the office besides herself.

"Sally called in sick; I got the rest of 'em out patrolling," Bo replied, waving the furniture men into his office and pointing out a place for the file cabinet. "Eric Sutherland's been bitching about speeders. I thought we'd have a little push, hand out a few tickets." He signed for the furniture and the two deliverymen left his office and walked through the squad room, past Scotty, to the front door. One of them turned and dug into his pocket.

"Oh, nearly forgot; here's the keys." He tossed them accross the squad room to Scotty. She caught them and thought they were very heavy for file cabinet keys. She glanced again at the cabinet and saw for the first time that it was equipped with a thick steel bar that ran the length of the cabinet, through the heavy handles. This was no ordinary file cabinet; this was practically a safe. There was already a safe in Bo's office, but she and Sally both knew the combination. There were three keys on the ring; she slipped one off and palmed it.

"Here are your keys," she said, holding up the ring with the remaining two. Bo was already transferring files from his old cabinet to the new one. "You want me to keep one in my desk?"

"Nah," Scully replied. "I'll keep them both."

She tossed him the ring, and he put it in his pocket. She turned and slipped the third key into her bra. It couldn't hurt, having that key. She wanted to know what Bo wanted to lock away from his clerks and deputies.

Scully shifted files for most of the morning, occasionally discarding a few papers, putting some of the others into the new cabinet, and returning the rest to the old one. Finally, he slid the steel bar through the handles and snapped the lock into place. "I'm going out for a while. You know how to handle the radio?"

"Sure." He had taught her himself. He really was tanked.

"Hold the fort, then," he said, jamming his Stetson onto his head.

Then he was gone, and she was alone in the office.

Howell woke to a room full of sunlight. For a few seconds he was afraid to move at all; finally, he rolled carefully onto his side and looked at the alarm clock on the bedside table. Half past ten. Scotty was long gone. Still carefully, he swung his legs over the side of the bed and sat up. He stood. He was joyfully aware of the absence of pain. It had happened, it had worked, this laying on of hands. He could move without fear of agony.

He should be exhausted, he thought, but he was not. He felt rested, relaxed, and eager for the new day. What was happening to him? Was he having, in what he liked to think of as his late youth, some sort of reawakening? Was he emerging, after a couple of years of sexual numbness, from some peculiar, midlife change? He felt oddly youthful. And hungry. He pulled on a pair of jeans and headed for the kitchen.

Howell made himself a huge breakfast of scrambled eggs, sausages, grits, and toast and put on a pot of coffee. He felt like working today, and the coffee would help him along. He had not written a word of Lurton Pitts's autobiography, and it was time he got his ass in gear. He was just mopping up the last of the eggs, washing them down with orange juice, when he heard the crunch of tires on gravel and the slamming of a heavy car door. He opened the front door before Bo Scully had a chance to knock.

"Hey, Bo, come on in," he said, genuinely glad to see the sheriff.

"How you doin', John?" Scully asked, walking carefully into the cabin, looking warily about him.

Howell thought he looked a little drunk, but it was awfully early in the day for that. "I've got a pot of coffee on the stove. Want some?"

"Sure, I could use it."

Howell poured the coffee and set it on the table with the cream and sugar. To his surprise, Scully pulled a pint bottle of bourbon from his hip pocket and poured a generous slug into the coffee.

Scully grinned. "Gotta get my heart started. Join me?"

"No thanks, I've got to get some work done today. You taking the day off?" It surprised Howell that he hadn't wanted the drink. First time for a while he hadn't wanted a drink.

"Ah, well, my time's pretty much my own. I'm sort of in business for myself, you might say."

"Well, I guess a sheriff's more his own boss than most men," Howell said. "Who does a sheriff report to, anyway?"

"Not a damn soul, if he's smart. Oh, to the judge on some things, to the county council on others." He grinned wryly. "Course, we got a slightly different hierarchy in Sutherland County."

"Old man Sutherland takes an interest, does he?"

"Damn right he does." Scully knocked back a swig of the spiked coffee. "Oh, not every day and not usually on small things, but he keeps his hand in. Right now, it's speeders he's worried about. Watch your ass driving into town. Mike's sitting down there on the road with the radar on. He'll take your picture, and I'd have to fine you."

"Thanks for the advice; I'll do that." Howell felt himself automatically shifting into his reporter mode. It was too good to pass up, a chance to quiz a sheriff with a couple of drinks inside him. "I guess those fines make a nice little retirement fund, huh?"

Scully looked at him sharply. "You kidding? Shoot, I could take you down there to the station and show you a record of every traffic ticket since I been sheriff, and which account the money went into. My operation's as clean as a hound's tooth, boy, let me tell you. Some asshole wants to haul me or one of my people in front of a grand jury, I'll have him armpit deep in records of every penny that's passed through my office. I *believe* in records, boy. The fuckin' FBI don't have any better records than I do. I'm gonna buy a computer and computerize 'em when the machinery comes down a little bit. Next year, maybe. We already got a word processor. I've got the most modern operation in the state of Georgia, maybe the whole South." Scully pulled at the coffee again. "Let me tell you something, John, you better not do business in Eric Sutherland's county 'less you back yourself up every which way. He thinks he sees a crack in your dam, and whoomp! You're treadin' water 'fore you know what hit you."

Howell thought the metaphor appropriate, considering the source of Sutherland's power. Suddenly, before he had time to think why, he asked, "Bo, does anybody around here have a 1940 Lincoln Continental convertible?"

"Nah," Scully answered without hesitation, "not anymore. Eric Sutherland used to have one, but that was a long time . . ." The sheriff turned and looked at him oddly. "That's a weird question."

"Oh, I just saw one on the road yesterday. Hadn't seen one since I was a kid. I thought if somebody local owned it I'd like to have a closer look."

The sheriff looked relieved. "Oh. Well, nobody around here has one I know of. Sutherland sold his in the fifties sometime. I remember, it was still in perfect shape. I'd of bought it myself if I'd had the money." He glanced at his watch. "Hey, I gotta get going. Just thought I'd drop in and say hello."

Howell nodded, then, for reasons he couldn't fathom, leaped again. "Bo, do you ever have dreams?"

Scully emptied his coffee cup and looked out over the lake, his eyes red and cloudy. "Nah," he said, getting to his feet and shuffling toward the door. "Just nightmares."

From the cabin door, Howell watched the sheriff drive away. Last night, he remembered, he had been another man. He wondered if he had been Bo Scully. Or, perhaps, just having Bo's nightmare.

• • •

For the better part of the morning, Scotty was busy with the phone, the radio, and with visitors to the office. Finally, near lunchtime, the place was empty and quiet. She went to the door and looked up and down the street. No sign of Bo or a patrol car. She fished the key from her bra, walked quickly into Scully's office, and unlocked the new filing cabinet. She tucked the key back into her bra, then lifted out the steel bar and leaned it against the door, glancing every few moments through the glass partition for visitors.

For ten minutes she combed through the drawers, file by file. By the time she got to the third drawer, her excitement was turning to exasperation. There was nothing but old department files—old traffic tickets, old payroll forms, old everything. She opened the bottom drawer and started on that. More of the same. Why the hell would he order an elaborate, security file cabinet and then shift useless old files into it that nobody would be interested in anyway? She finished flipping through the last of the files and closed the drawer. Then she glanced across the street and saw, over the tops of parked cars, the blue lights of a patrol car gliding to a halt across the street.

Scotty quickly threaded the steel bar through the file drawer handles, mated the lock to its closure, and pressed. Nothing happened; the bolt, instead of retracting and snapping into the closure, remained rigid. The goddamned thing had to be locked with the key. She looked around in time to see Bo Scully starting across the street toward the office, looking both ways at traffic. Panicked, she dug a hand into her bra for the key, but just as her fingers reached it, it fell through the elastic to her waist, under her blouse. There was no time to pull out her shirttail and dig for the key. She dived sideways out of Bo's office toward the coffeemaker. As Bo came through the door, she was shakily pouring a cup.

"Hi," she said brightly. "Want some coffee?"

"Yeah," he said. "I think I need some." He went into his office. "I only got as far as John's place on my rounds, then I didn't feel so good."

She took her time fixing the coffee, trying to get her breathing back to normal. Then she realized that he was in there with the unlocked file cabinet and she should be in there distracting him until she could find a way to get the thing locked again. She hurried into his office with the coffee.

She set down his cup. "I think I'll join you," she said. She took her own cup across the room and leaned against the file cabinet, the lock behind her.

"Have a seat," Scully said.

"Oh, I've been sitting all morning. Do me good to stretch."

"I like that blouse," he said, grinning. "How does it come off?"

"With great difficulty." They both laughed. Scotty realized it was the first time she'd ever been alone in the office with him. She still found him attractive in a bearlike way. She wondered for a moment what it would be like to have that great weight on top of her, and her breathing grew a little quicker.

"Well," he said, "you been up here, what . . . a month now? How do you like us?"

She smiled. "I like you all right."

"You know, if I didn't have a rule about fooling around in the office, I'd of asked you out by now."

"Oh? I never paid too much attention to rules myself." She couldn't think of anything else to say. He really was quite good-looking; she thought he knew it too.

"You've been seeing a good bit of John Howell, right?"

She nodded. She'd rather he hadn't known that, but what the hell, it was a small town.

"Well, John's a friend of mine, and I'm not going to go tracking up his territory. But if that cools off, I'd like to know about it. Okay?"

She smiled. "Okay." She meant it, too. Then Bo reached for his coffee; his hand struck the edge of the desk blotter, which bumped against a paperweight, which fell onto the floor and rolled toward her. Instinctively she bent to catch it, and before she could straighten she heard him say "Shit," and knew he had seen the lock. As she straightened, the heavy paperweight in her hand, he was coming around the desk toward her. She could hit him with the paperweight and run, she thought. But run where? She'd have to talk her way out.

"Damn lock," he said, brushing past her. He fished in his pocket and brought out the keys. "I guess I haven't learned how to work the damn thing right." He inserted the key, banged on the lock with his fist a couple of times, and jangled it to make sure it was closed.

At that moment a deputy walked into the station waving a fistful of traffic summonses. Scully went out to talk with him, and Scotty was left standing in his office, breathing deep breaths.

14

Howell sat at the desk and let the droning voice of Lurton Pitts wash over him. He searched through the self-serving mush for a way to begin, and just as he thought he might have an idea, there was a soft rap on the door. He quickly switched off the tape recorder. Pitts's voice was familiar to millions from his television commercials for the fried chicken chain, and he wanted no one to hear it. He walked to the door, wondering who it might be. He had not heard a car. He opened the door and found Leonie Kelly standing on his doorstep.

She looked quite different today, more contemporary. She was wearing jeans instead of the rather dowdy dress of the day before, and a man's blue workshirt was tied in a knot above her waist, showing three or four inches of powdery, freckled skin. She wore sneakers without socks, and her hair was pulled back into a ponytail.

She gave a little laugh. "Well, you did invite me to drop by, didn't you?"

"Oh, sure," he replied, suddenly aware that he had been staring at her. "Come on in."

"Here's your mail," she said, handing him some letters.

He winced. The top one was from Elizabeth. "Thanks," he said, tossing them on his desk.

She wandered about the room, looking carefully at things. "I've never been inside here," she said, poking her head into the kitchen, then lingering for a longer look at the bedroom.

"Don't you know Denham White? He's been coming up here for years."

"I've seen him in town a couple of times, I guess." She strolled out onto the deck, and he followed. The midday sun was hot. She motioned toward the broken railing. "That looks kind of dangerous. You better fix it."

Howell stared at the railing. "Yes, I'd better take a hammer and a nail to that, I guess," he said.

"I remember this place from a long time ago," she said. "When I was a little girl." She seemed about to say something else, but then suddenly blurted out, "It's a gorgeous day, how about a swim?"

"Sure," he said.

She was already untying the knot of her shirt. She ran down the stairs to the dock, leaving her shirt, jeans, and shoes in a trail behind her. There was no underwear. Struggling with his own clothes, he saw only a flash of the tall, full body before she was into the water. A moment later, he dove in and surfaced, shouting, gasping. He had forgotten how cold the water was. She still had not come up, and he looked around for her. Ten seconds passed, then another ten. She must have been under for nearly a minute, he thought. He forgot the cold and started to worry.

Something brushed his thigh, then she was on his back, ducking him under the water. He'd had no chance to draw a deep breath, and he struggled to free himself from her and get to the surface. She pushed away, and he thrashed upward, gasping at air. "Jesus!" he shouted. "You want to drown me?"

"No, I don't want to drown you," she said, swimming over and putting her arms around his neck. She kissed him. He put his arms around her and held onto her buttocks. They sank together from a lack of swimming. He was the first to break free and return to the surface. She came up a moment later. "You've got to learn to hold your breath longer if you're going to have any fun in the water," she shouted, then made for the dock.

She pulled herself up and sat trembling, rubbing at the chill bumps on her body. He climbed out beside her. "I'll get some towels," he said. When he came back, she was on the deck, still naked, piling their clothes on a chair. There was a touch of sun on her lightly freckled skin, and her hair, darkened by the water, contrasted more than ever with her paleness. She took the large towel, dried herself thoroughly, did the best she could with her hair, then wrapped the towel about her and flopped down into a reclining deck chair. He dragged up another.

"How's the back today?" she asked.

"Terrific," he replied. "That was some sort of miracle, you know. How did you do it?"

"I don't know. I'd never done it before. I think Mama did it through me, somehow. She says her powers will come to me when she's gone—that it's already started to happen. I guess it has. It's more than the healing, too. I get flashes of thoughts, sometimes, from lots of people. I can nearly always tell what the other kids in the family are thinking. Never with Mama, though. She can be as much a mystery to me as to everybody else. Only Dermot seems to read her easily."

"It's hard to believe that you . . . well, that you're all brothers and sisters," Howell said.

Her face clouded briefly. "I don't want to talk about that, please." Then her expression changed, became laughing, mischievous. "You know, I think I enjoyed your backrub yesterday as much as you did."

"You couldn't possibly have liked it as much as I did," he said.

She laughed. "Well, nearly as much." She reached over and kissed him gently. "I wanted to do that yesterday, but I might have forgotten myself."

He kissed her back. Oh, God, he thought to himself, what is going on here? There were a couple of times in his life when he had been seduced by a girl, but never as directly as this. He felt himself drifting into a soft haze. Whatever it was, they were both experiencing it. He slipped a hand under her towel, parted her, and stroked gently for a moment. She sighed and opened her legs slightly. He kissed her again, then moved slowly down her body with his lips and tongue, pulling away her towel. She was fresh from the lake water, and he was amazed at the sweetness of her.

In what seemed to be one long motion, she took his head in her hands, pressed him back in the reclining chair, threw a leg over his body, and drew him inside her. She had moved so gracefully, aimed so perfectly that she had not even needed her hands. She began to move slowly up and down him in long, smooth movements.

Howell lay back and looked up at her, her head thrown back to receive the sunlight, her pale-red hair stroking her shoulders as she rolled her head, an expression on her face that seemed as much acute thought and concern as passion. She opened her eyes and looked at him with surprise, moving faster, silently opening and closing her mouth, her eyes going in and out of focus. "It's happening," she said huskily. "Come with me! You must, you must!"

He sat up and hugged her to him, pouring himself into her in floods until, at last, he had only the strength to lay his head on her shoulder and hold on. She ran her fingers through his hair and rested with him, both of them twitching involuntarily. Then she pushed him gently back into the recliner and stood up. She passed a hand over his eyes and said, "No, just rest. Don't get up." A moment later he opened his eyes, and she was standing over him, her jeans on, tying a knot in her shirttail.

"Don't go," he said, attempting to rise.

She pushed him back in the deck chair and kissed him. "I must. Mama will wake up soon. I need to be there." She kissed him again, then started for the steps.

"Leonie," he called, and she stopped and turned. "Why me?"

She paused, and for a moment he thought she would tell him. Then her expression changed, and she shrugged. "Why not?" She ran down the steps and away.

Howell gathered up their towels and started toward the bedroom, feeling just a bit pleased with himself. It was a nice thing, having a sex life again; it did wonders for the ego. It was the best of all worlds, he thought. The relationship with Scotty was such that he felt no guilt about sleeping with Leonie; they had both made their declarations on that subject. Scotty was available only in the evenings, and Leonie had said she could see him only in the afternoons. He felt a little guilty about feeling so good about that, but pushed the thought aside. He didn't need guilt right now. Then his eye fell on Elizabeth's letter.

He picked it up and weighed it in his hand. At least two pages of her heavy, cream-colored writing paper. He dreaded reading it; she would probably beg him to come back, making him feel even more guilty. He tore it open and sat down to her bold, precise handwriting.

Dear Johnny,

If I were a braver person I would have come up to see you, or at least called you, but I'm not, so I'm taking the coward's way out.

I've been doing a lot of thinking since you left. I felt when you went that you probably would not come back, but then I thought you might come back out of a sense of obligation and not because you wanted to. I don't want that, and, after a lot of agonizing, I think it would be better if you didn't come back in any case.

I may as well tell you, too, before you hear it from somebody else, that I've met a man that I'm strongly attracted to. You don't know him; his name is Winston Behn. He's not one of the people we ran around with, he's a fashion designer, and a good one. (*Definitely* not gay.) We seem to have a lot in common, and I've grown very fond of him very quickly. I don't know if it will work, but I have to try.

I know you feel badly that it was you who drew away, but I don't think you should. I honestly think you did the best you could. We never fought or tried to hurt each other, and I have a lot of good memories. A part of me will always love you, and I'll always think of you as my friend. I hope you'll think of me that way.

I'm in no hurry for a divorce, but I think when you've finished your work up there we should sit down and discuss it. Denham will handle it for me, and, since I can't see us squabbling over things, you might ask him to do for you, as well.

Again, I'm sorry to have to tell you all this in a letter instead of face to face, but I don't think I could have done it any other way.

I hope you're taking care of yourself and that your work is going well. We'll talk when you come back.

Affectionately,
Liz

On the second page there was a postscript.

P.S. Although Winston and I aren't living together exactly, he is spending a lot of time here, so I've packed all your things from the dressing room and the library and moved them out to your study over the garage. I've had the gardener put the Porsche under cover and attach a trickle charger to the battery. Please feel free to leave these things here until you've found your own place, or as long as you like. Unless you particularly want it, I would like to have the station wagon back for the cook to use when you come back from the mountains.

L.

Stunned, Howell read the letter again. *Winston.* What kind of name was that? Bulldogs were named *Winston.* *"Definitely* not gay." Oh, swell, that meant they were screwing the socks off each other twice every night of the week and four times on Sunday. And his things were in the fucking garage now; that was considerate of her. We wouldn't want *Winston* to have to look at Johnny's toothbrush in the bathroom, would we? Howell wadded the letter and threw it at the fireplace as hard as he could.

He stood there, breathing hard, livid. He kicked a chair across the room and walked out onto the deck. Then he began to get some control of himself. It was his fault, all of it, he knew. She couldn't have been better, not at any time. Maximum wife. He hadn't deserved her. And, after all, he was screwing the socks off *two* women; what did he have to be jealous about? He had wanted out of the marriage, hadn't he? He sat down on a deck chair and looked, sightlessly, at the lake. He felt something solid, something permanent breaking inside him. He put his face in his hands and wept like a child.

15

Scotty attacked the large steak with both hands. "Now I know he's dirty, I just don't know how."

"What's changed?" Howell tried to get interested; he needed to think about something else besides Elizabeth and *Winston.*

"He's bought this great huge filing cabinet with a steel bar and transferred a lot of his files to it. Sally or I have a key to everything else, but not to this. I mean, I do, but I'm not supposed to." She told him, with some relish, how she had palmed the third key.

Howell laughed aloud at her audacity; with that sort of brass, she might well make a good investigative reporter. "Pretty swift, Scotty. So what's the problem? Pillage his fucking filing cabinet, and get the goods on him."

"I've already pillaged it, and there's nothing in it but regular stuff— ordinary office records. I went through all four drawers, file by file."

Howell chewed his steak thoughtfully. "Is there anything else in the office—another filing cabinet, a safe—that only Bo has access to?"

Scotty dumped sour cream onto a baked potato. "Nope. Just that one filing cabinet."

"Then that's where it is."

"What is?"

"The goods, if there are any."

"It ain't. Trust me."

"It is. Let me tell you a story. A few years back, I got a tip from a secretary at the capitol that her boss, the guy who handled the physical plant, all the repairs and maintenance, was on the take from contractors. She and I went into his office late of an evening, you might say, and we went through every filing cabinet in the place. Nothing. So, over breakfast, after a night of fruitless endeavor, I asked her to tell me all about the guy, what he was like. He was a maniac for records, a regular pedant about office procedures. That told me that he had to have some records somewhere; he couldn't have lived with himself unless he had records. We went back to the office the next night, and this time we really took the place apart. Nothing. Three nights later, we found it. It was a tiny notebook, and it was hidden in a cut-out book, just sitting there on a bookshelf in plain view."

"Bo's that way about keeping records."

"Damn right. He told me so himself only yesterday. Stopped by for a cup of coffee that turned into a drink."

"I noticed he was drinking at the office."

"So, I'm telling you that if Bo is as hipped on record keeping as he says he is, and if he's dirty, he's got a record of it. And I'll give you odds it's in that filing cabinet."

"But I've already been through the goddamned thing, I told you."

"Yeah, but you're forgetting something. A guy, a public servant, an accountant who's an embezzler, anybody with a game on the side who keeps a record, doesn't do it in one of those big old ledgers out of Dickens. He does it small, compact. A notebook, like my guy at the capitol, maybe a few sheets of paper. He doesn't bury it in the backyard —he's got to make entries in it from time to time. He doesn't stick it in the safe—that's the first place a prosecutor would look if things went sour. And anyway, you and Sally know the combination to Bo's safe."

"So?"

"So he gets himself this lockup filing cabinet, very conspicuous, and he puts a lot of old crap in it and . . . ?"

"Oh, come on, Johnny, I've already told you . . ."

"And he hides his records in plain sight; he picks himself out a nice, dull file—say, unpaid parking tickets or something, and he sticks his notebook in there. Did you think you'd find a file labeled 'Dirty Money'?"

Scotty had stopped chewing. "Jesus, why didn't I think of that?"

"Grand jury wants to go after him, they're going to do what you did. Who wants to waste his time going through old parking tickets? Now the FBI, they'd lock themselves in and read everything, if it took 'em a year. But all Bo needs is two minutes' notice, and he whips out the incriminating stuff and *then* he buries it in the backyard, or burns it. Except a true-blue keeper of records would never burn it. Never happen."

"So I've gotta go back in there and go through every file. And Christ knows when I'll be able to do it. There's always somebody else in the office."

"Middle of the night?"

"A radio operator, minimum. Always."

"Then you're going to have to get clever, aren't you?"

"Yeah, I'm going to have to get clever." Scotty chewed her steak and narrowed her eyes.

"But not cute. You get cute and slip up, and Bo will hang you out to dry, kiddo, I mean it. I've tried to tell you before how territorial these country sheriffs are. The Mafia couldn't make you go away any faster or better. Bo's in control up here, and don't you ever forget it."

There was a rap on the door that made them both jump. "Jesus, he's come to get you," Howell laughed. He got up and went to answer it. A small, gray-haired black man in a white jacket stood on the porch. He looked like a butler.

"Good evening, sir. My name is Alfred," the man said. "Mr. Eric Sutherland asked me to bring you this." He held out a white envelope.

Howell took it. "Thank you, Alfred."

"Mr. Sutherland asked me to wait for a reply, sir."

Howell opened the envelope and pulled out a heavy, engraved card. Eric Sutherland was requesting the pleasure of his company for cocktails on Saturday afternoon. "Thank Mr. Sutherland for me, Alfred, and tell him I'd be pleased to come. And I'd like to bring a young lady, if that would be all right."

Alfred bowed slightly. "I'm sure that will be just fine, Mr. Howell. I'll convey your acceptance to Mr. Sutherland." And he was gone.

Howell closed the door and tossed the card to Scotty. "Alfred is conveying my acceptance to Mr. Sutherland. Want to come?"

"Well," she said, "it would be nice to see what the crumbs of the upper crust are like around here. All I've seen so far are the drunks and speeders."

"You own a dress?"

"You betcha. How much of a shock shall I give old Mr. Sutherland?"

"None at all, please. I've still got a few weeks to go around here. This must be Sutherland's annual bash. I've heard something about it."

"It is. Bo got his invitation this afternoon."

"By hand?"

"Yep. Apparently old man Sutherland doesn't trust the post office."

"Sort of courtly, that—hand-delivered invitations."

"From what I hear, once a year is the most Eric Sutherland can manage courtly. He probably didn't want to spend the money on the stamps."

"Well, we'd better take advantage, hadn't we?"

Very late that night, he wasn't sure quite how late, Howell came gently, fully awake. Scotty slept beside him, quietly, almost like a child. He had a curious sensation of unease; something seemed out of kilter. Then the silence came to him. There were no crickets.

He stopped himself from getting up immediately. He asked himself questions: Was he really awake? Yes. Was he sober? Yes. He looked around the room, which seemed perfectly normal; he felt the sheet over him, rubbed it through his fingers; all senses working, performing normally. Finally, sure that he was in complete charge of himself, he got up and walked through the silence to the living room windows. Once again, the lake was not there, but another place; the house, tranquil in the moonlight, lay below him, and he heard the tune drifting toward him.

"Scotty!" he called out, afraid to take his eyes from the scene. "Scotty, come here quickly!"

"What?" her sleepy voice answered from the bedroom.

"Get out of bed and come here right now, goddamnit!" He heard the bed creak and her bare feet on the living room floor. She came onto the deck beside him.

"What? What is it?" She sounded fully awake and alarmed.

He reached out behind him for her hand, then stood her in front of him. "Look," he said, taking her head in his hands and pointing her at what he could see. "Tell me exactly what you see before you."

He felt her go rigid.

"What's happening?" she asked, her voice trembling. "What's going on, Johnny?"

"What do you see?" he asked urgently. "Tell me exactly what you see."

"A road, a house. It's misty."

"How many windows in the house?"

"Uh, two . . . three . . . four that I can see."

"How many chimneys?"

"Two."

"Do you hear anything?"

"Your hands are over my ears."

He moved them. "Now?"

"A piano."

"What's it playing?"

"I don't know. It sounds familiar, but . . ." She turned and buried her face in his chest. "I'm scared, Johnny."

"It's all right. Nothing's going to happen to us." He lowered his head and kissed her hair, and, as he did, he heard the crickets. He looked up, and the lake looked back at him.

He showed her the lake, then put his arm around her and walked her into the living room. He sat her down on the piano bench and inserted a roll into the piano.

"What are you doing?"

"Listen." He switched on the instrument; it began to play.

"That's the song, the song I heard out there on the deck," she said after a moment. Her voice was small and frightened. "Johnny, do you know what is happening here? Please tell me if you do."

"No," he said, "I don't. But I know now that I'm not crazy."

"Why?" she demanded. "What makes you so damned confident about that? You may be crazy, and I may be too."

"No, we're not crazy, either of us."

"Why not?"

"Because two people, even two crazy people, can't have the same hallucination. What we saw was real."

16

The morning after Scotty, too, had seen the vision, which is how Howell had come to think of it, he woke with an oddly pleasant feeling. It was mysterious, but faintly familiar, and it took him a couple of hours to bring it into focus. For the past year, and perhaps for the better part of two, he now realized, he had been, more than anything else, bored. For all of his life, boredom had been foreign to him, and his work as a newspaperman had been boredom's antithesis. Now, on this bright, cool August morning, in this most beautiful of places, in the throes of what could only be a classic male-menopausal crisis, he was experiencing anew the intellectual and emotional condition which had always driven him: curiosity. He was once again, at long last, *interested* in something.

The fact of Scotty's seeing the vision convinced him that he was not mad, not hallucinating. He was by no means convinced that what he had been experiencing had a supernatural basis. The experience was, in some sense, real; it had a rational, if unfamiliar basis, and he was a rational man. He would proceed rationally.

Scotty did not entirely share his view of the situation. "Listen, John, this place is screwy—haunted or something."

"Or something. Does it scare you?"

"Well, yeah, a little." She cocked her head to one side and looked thoughtful. "I mean, I'm not terrified, no more than after the séance, but that didn't seem quite as real."

Howell had been about to tell her about the girl; but now he felt that the introduction into the situation of what Scotty might interpret as a ghost could disturb her too much, and he didn't want her to panic on him. "Well, I think it all means something, and I want to find out what."

"How do you figure on doing that?" she asked.

"I'm not sure exactly, but before I can proceed, there's something I need."

"What's that?"

"I'll tell you when I've got it."

Howell knew where to get it too, he thought, as he drove into Sutherland. He read the directory at the courthouse and bounded up the stairs two at a time. A young woman asked if she could help him.

"What a lovely dress," he said enthusiastically. She blushed. "Lovely. Uh, I'm interested in the local geography, and I wonder if I might see a survey map of the area?"

"Why, sure." She was putty in his hands now. "The whole county?"

"Oh, no, not the whole thing, just the town of Sutherland and the surrounding area."

She reached under the counter and pulled out a sheet of typewriter paper with a map printed on it. "Here's the official Chamber of Commerce map of the town, and it shows a little bit beyond the city limits."

"Well, I really had something on a little larger scale in mind, something with a lot of detail."

"How about a mile to the inch?"

"Perfect."

She went to a wide-drawered cabinet, fished in a drawer, and pulled out a large sheet. "There you are," she said, spreading it on the counter before him.

And there he was. It took only a moment to find the crossroads and follow the road down to the cabin. True to life, the line of the road stopped at the lake's edge. "Oh, that's terrific," he said, grinning at her and making her blush again. "Now, do you think you might have a map of the same area, on the same scale, before the lake?"

She wrinkled her brow and looked doubtfully around the room. "Gee, I don't have the slightest idea where that would be. Just a minute, I'll ask Mrs. O'Neal. She's been here forever, and she'll know just where to put her hand on it."

The girl walked across the room to a door and knocked. Howell could see, through a glass partition, an older woman working at a desk. She looked up and heard the girl's question, then looked out for a long moment at Howell. Then she got up from her desk, still looking at him, brushed the wrinkles from her skirt, walked out of the office and across the room to the counter where Howell stood waiting. "May I help you?" she asked, in a manner which immediately told Howell she had no intention of doing so.

"Gosh, I hope so," Howell replied, in the manner of a high school junior doing research for a term paper. "I was just wondering if I could have a look at a map just like this one, except before the lake."

"This is a map of the town of Sutherland," she said evenly. "The town was much smaller before the lake, so, of course, there can be no such map."

"Oh, sure, I see," Howell said, as cheerful as ever. "Well, then, do you reckon I could see a map of the area without the town? Just the valley, and all?"

"Sir," she said, not quite so evenly now, "you are missing the point. The courthouse was not built until the town was built, so we would not have such a map."

"Oh, yes, sure, that was dumb of me. Uh, where was the county seat before it was at Sutherland?"

"It was over in Pinewood, but when it was moved here, the old courthouse was torn down to make way for a school."

"And the records were moved here?"

"Yes."

"Well, is there, maybe, somebody here now who worked in the old courthouse who might be familiar with the old maps?"

"I worked in the old courthouse," she said icily. "I have been in charge of these records for thirty-eight years."

"Well, someone with all your knowledge is just the person I'm looking for," Howell said, exuding charm again, and watching it ricochet right off the old bat.

"When we moved the records, we naturally discarded a lot of outdated material, including old maps. I did it myself. I tell you again, no such map exists."

A glance at the astonished face of the girl standing behind her told Howell that the woman was lying. "Oh, shucks. Well, I guess I'll just have to go to the Army Corps of Engineers in Atlanta," he said, anxious to let her know she had not won.

"I'm afraid that would be useless," the woman replied with a triumphant smirk. "Lake Sutherland was privately built. The Corps of Engineers was not involved."

Howell glanced at the girl, who looked embarrassed and shrugged.

"Oh, well, I guess I'll just have to forget about it," he said ruefully, and slunk out of the room, hoping the woman believed him.

He thought about approaching the girl after hours, but she seemed thoroughly intimidated by her superior. He would have to think of something else.

The party had been under way for an hour when Howell and Scotty arrived, and it was clear that everybody who was anybody in Sutherland was there. The lord of the manor had summoned, and all had responded. Eric Sutherland spotted them almost immediately and came over with the butler, Alfred, in tow, bearing a tray of champagne glasses.

"Why, Mr. Howell, I'm so glad you could come."

"Thank you, sir. Have you met Scotty Miller?"

"Of course, but only briefly. I understand you've made Sheriff Scully's life easier down at his office, young lady."

"Well, that's nice to hear," Scotty replied, turning on her best smile. "I'd better ask for more money."

Sutherland chuckled appreciatively. Howell marveled at the difference between the man now and the first time they had met. Sutherland the host was an improvement on Sutherland the town father. "Please wander as you like," he said. "There's food here and there, and Alfred will keep you in drinks." As if on cue, Alfred materialized again and topped off their glasses. Sutherland moved off to greet another arrival.

They wandered among local merchants and businessmen and their wives, dressed in their Sunday best. A couple approached them.

"I'm Dr. Joe McGinn," the man said, extending his hand, "and this is my wife, Maeve." They were both short and plump, and the woman was wearing a bit too much jewelry. "We're both old fans of your column."

"Thank you, Doctor," Howell replied, and introduced Scotty. "Beautiful place Mr. Sutherland has here, isn't it?"

"Ah, yes," the doctor replied, "and made all the more beautiful by his crowning achievement." He waved a hand toward the lake.

"Have you lived in Sutherland long, Dr. McGinn?"

"Oh, yes, ever since the lake. Maeve and I both grew up in the valley, and we married right after I got out of the army. That was just after the lake was built, and we knew Sutherland would need a doctor."

"You must have known the O'Coineen family, then," Howell said.

The two people froze for a moment, then the wife, expressionless, said, "Yes."

"Tell me," Howell said, taking care to sound only pleasantly curious, "in what part of the lake . . . or rather, the valley, was their farm?"

They both seemed frozen again, then the doctor managed to shape his face into a regretful frown. "That was a very unfortunate thing, and it's not something I'd care to discuss, especially in Mr. Sutherland's house." He took his wife's arm. "Would you excuse us, please?" The couple did not wait for a reply, but fled.

"I don't think you'd better bring up that subject again at Eric Sutherland's party," Scotty said.

"Tactical error," Howell agreed.

They wandered through the house for half an hour, rubbing elbows with the prosperous-looking group, exchanging a few banalities here and there, peeking into the dining room and into Sutherland's study, with its leather-bound volumes and rack of custom-made English shotguns. Howell received an admirer here and there. He waved at Bo Scully across the living room. The sheriff waved back, but his ear was being held by Dr. McGinn and his wife, who looked grim. Alfred materialized whenever a glass was half empty, and they got a little drunk.

Scotty excused herself to look for the powder room, and Howell wandered onto the broad rear terrace, which overlooked a long, gently inclined lawn, rolling down to the lake. There Howell encountered Enda McAuliffe, looking oddly well groomed in a new suit.

"The Fourth Estate," McAuliffe cried, raising his glass.

Howell thought the lawyer must have been drinking awhile, too. "Justice," he replied, raising his own glass.

"You seem remarkably ambulatory, my lad, considering your posture the last time we met," McAuliffe said.

"Indeed I am," Howell replied. "I could run the high hurdles on short notice. Well, the low ones, anyway."

"Medical Science," McAuliffe intoned, raising his glass again.

"Not a bit of it," Howell said, clinking glasses. "Faith Healing."

"Y'didn't," McAuliffe said, looking astonished.

"I did, and I owe you a large drink for your guidance in these matters," Howell said, thinking he owed the lawyer a case of the stuff at least.

"Jesus, John, I never thought you'd go up there. I was just having you on. It really worked?"

"Believe your eyes," Howell replied, affecting a golf swing. "I am whole."

"Mother of God. What was it like up there?"

"Pleasant enough place, I guess. No goblins. Mama Kelly looks like going soon, though."

"So I hear. You met the lovely Leonie, then?"

"I did."

"Ah, the lads used to howl after her, when their folks weren't looking. Some of them got in her pants, but none of them got close to her. A pity, but what with her family history and all, nobody would go calling, proper-like."

Howell was immediately uncomfortable. "You're looking very prosperous, I must say, Counselor."

"Oh, I've a new client," McAuliffe replied, nodding toward Eric Sutherland across the terrace.

Howell was astonished. "I thought you were the only game in town if somebody had a beef with him. What's happened to your principles?" He had meant it as a joke, but McAuliffe took him seriously.

"They got tired of eating Bubba's chicken-fried steak," he shot back. "The old boy popped up with a plum of work, and I took it." He knocked back the rest of his drink, and Alfred zoomed in to refill it. "I've decided instead of fighting him, I'll break him with my fees. Altogether a more satisfactory method, don't you think?"

"I can't argue with that." Howell searched for a way of changing the subject. "Say, do you know where I can lay my hands on a map of the area before the lake was built?"

McAuliffe looked at him sharply. "I doubt if one exists, and if I were you, I wouldn't go around asking about one."

"Why not?" Howell asked innocently. "Why would anybody be touchy about that? This neck of the woods interests me; I'd just like to know more about it."

McAuliffe lowered his voice and spoke earnestly, nearly soberly. "Now, listen, John, you're getting into things that shouldn't concern you, and I suppose it's my fault, telling you stories and sending you up to the Kellys', so I want to give you the best advice I can muster. Go up to that cabin and write your book, and then go back to Atlanta. Stay away from the Kellys and don't tell anyone else about that séance nonsense of yours, and for Christ's sake, don't go blundering around asking a lot of stupid questions about maps and before the lake and all that. It doesn't concern you—it doesn't concern anybody anymore. Just leave it alone, all right?"

Howell was stunned for a moment. "It seems to me you had a different attitude about all this before Eric Sutherland became your client," he was finally able to say.

A flash of anger crossed McAuliffe's face, then passed. He put his hand on Howell's arm and squeezed. "John, you're a good fellow and a bright one, and I've enjoyed your company. But I've no more to say to you." He turned and walked into the house, upending his glass on the way.

Howell looked after him, puzzled. He thought himself good at reading people, and he had read McAuliffe as tough, stubborn, and unlikely to yield to pressure, let alone money. If the lawyer had suddenly got into bed with Eric Sutherland, there must be a better reason than Howell knew about. Mac, he thought, if you wanted me to forget this, you couldn't have gone about it in a worse way. He walked down the steps to the lawn and strolled down the hill toward the lake.

He had gone only about halfway to the water, fifty yards or so, when he noticed a small building to his right, in the trees. It looked like a guest house, and Howell wandered in its direction. He stopped outside a pair of French doors and put his hands up to shield his eyes from the reflection in the glass. There was one large room, and it was furnished as an office, with a steel desk and furniture and, in a corner, a drawing table. He tried the door; it was locked.

"You're wandering very far afield, Mr. Howell," a voice said, from a few yards behind him.

Howell started, then turned. Eric Sutherland was standing on the grass, holding a bottle of champagne.

"Come, let me fill your glass, and join me in a stroll down to the lake."

Howell joined him, and began the stroll down the hill, but his mind was on what else he had seen in the office. The wall behind the desk had been covered with maps.

17

Howell told Scotty about his conversation with Enda McAuliffe. They had finished dinner and were on coffee and brandy, having never entirely sobered up since their afternoon of drinking at Eric Sutherland's.

"I'm damned if I know what's going on around here, but I'm going to find out," Howell said.

She grinned. "The investigative reporter rears his ugly head."

"Yeah, I guess so. I think the whole thing that drove me when I was reporting was I couldn't stand it when somebody knew something I didn't. Now I get the impression that *everybody* knows something I don't. And I don't like it." He took a healthy swig of the brandy. "The funny thing is, I think I know *something,* and yet I can't seem to figure out what it is."

"You wanna run that by me again?"

"You got any department-store charge cards?"

"Huh?"

"Not Master Charge or any of those; department-store cards."

"Sure. A walletful of them. You need some Jockey shorts or something?"

Howell got up and started toward the kitchen. "Dig 'em out, let's have a look at them." He found a large flashlight, switched it on to see if the batteries were fresh, and dug a roll of black electrical tape from a drawer.

Scotty found her purse and plucked her credit cards from her wallet. Howell rummaged through them and chose one. "Neiman-Marcus, huh? They must be paying green newsies better these days."

"Daddy helps out with clothes. And who's green? What do you want with that, anyway?"

Howell picked up her American Express card and thumbed it. "Stiff as a board, right?" He did the same to the store card. "Nice and flexible."

Scotty watched as Howell began winding black tape over the lens of the flashlight. She placed a hand on his forehead. "You running a fever?"

He pulled off his necktie and began to unbutton his shirt. "Get changed. Put on some jeans and a dark sweater."

"This is beginning to sound like some sort of commando raid."

"It is."

Howell throttled the engine back to an idle and let the boat glide toward the trees. There was a breeze from the shore. That was good; some of the noise would go with it. A few yards out, he cut the engine and let the boat drift until it touched bottom. He threw a leg over the side and eased into the water, which was knee deep, then pulled at the boat until it was held firmly on the bottom.

He turned to Scotty. "Now, listen. I shouldn't be more than fifteen or twenty minutes. If I'm not back in twenty, start the engine and head slowly back to the cabin at the same speed as we came. If you hear any sort of commotion, go like hell, but not toward the cabin. Head down the lake toward Taylor's Fish Camp, and when you're halfway or so down there, cut toward shore and work your way back to the cabin at low speed. Okay?"

"I want to go with you."

"Goddamnit, do as I tell you. There's no need of both of us taking the risk, and anyway, you've got to take care of the boat. We can't get close enough to shore to tie up here, and we're sure as hell not going to drive up to Sutherland's dock."

Howell turned away without another word and waded ashore. Well into the trees, he cut toward Sutherland's place and emerged a couple of minutes later at the edge of the long lawn. He walked up the slight hill, keeping just into the fringe of trees, until he came to the small building. No lights were on. Up at the house only an upstairs light, apparently Sutherland's bedroom, and a ground-floor light, probably the kitchen, still burned. Howell looked at his watch; just past two. He'd reckoned Sutherland and the servants would be asleep by now. There must have been a lot of cleaning up to do after the party.

Howell switched on his masked flashlight. He stepped onto the little raised porch, approached the French doors, and slipped on a pair of driving gloves. In the dim beam he had a closer look at the doors. He had been right; the lock was in the knob. The bolt would be spring-loaded. He fished Scotty's charge card from his pocket, inserted it into the crack between the French doors, and felt for the bolt. He pressed the strong, flexible plastic card hard against it. Nothing. He pressed harder. The bolt slipped back. The door opened an inch.

Then, behind him, there was the soft scrape of a footstep on the concrete steps. Howell froze, clenched his teeth. He didn't want to jerk around and invite nervous gunfire. He slowly opened his hands, held them away from his body, and turned around.

"Hi," she whispered.

He resisted a heartfelt urge to strangle her. "What did you do with the goddamned boat?" he asked her through teeth still clenched.

"It's okay, don't worry. It's stuck on the mud; it won't move."

"If it's not there when we get back, I'll drown you, I swear."

"Let's get on with it, okay?"

"Wipe your feet," he said, pointing at the doormat. He wiped his own feet, then entered the office. He went immediately to the wall covered with maps, and played his light over them.

"This is a larger-scale version of the map I saw at the courthouse," he said. There was a date in the corner: 1969. He turned the flashlight to the other maps. There was one of the state, one of the county, both recent—nothing else on the walls.

He shone the thin beam around the room: leather sofa, some steel chairs, the drawing table he had seen that afternoon. Next to the table, a tall, wide drawing cabinet. The drawers were unlocked and unlabeled. He began at the top: aerial photographs of the lake and dam. He worked his way down, drawer by drawer: engineering drawings of turbines; architect's drawings of Sutherland's house; more photographs of the lake and the town; a smaller-scale version of the 1969 map which hung on the wall. There were several copies; Howell slipped one out of the drawer. One more drawer; Howell prayed.

He saw the corner of the map before he had the drawer fully open. It was dated 1936. The topography was wholly unfamiliar to him; he could find no landmark. Finally, he looked back at the box containing the date. There was a set of coordinates. He quickly compared them to the 1969 map. Identical. He could have shouted with joy.

The door behind him slammed, hard. Scotty emitted an involuntary cry.

"What? What?" he said aloud, throwing the dim beam on the doors.

"The wind," Scotty gasped. "There was a gust; sucked it shut, I guess. Oh, God, I think I wet my pants."

Up the hill toward the house, a dog began to bark, a small dog, a yapper. Howell quickly folded the two maps and stuck them in the waist of his jeans, under his sweater. He played the light around briefly to see that everything was as he had found it. The dog sounded closer. "Let's get out of here," he said.

Scotty opened the door and peered out. Howell jerked her hand from the knob and wiped it with his glove. "Sorry," she said.

Now Howell could hear a man's voice, calling the dog. It sounded like the butler, Alfred. They eased out the door and stepped around the corner of the building, then looked back. A flashlight was bobbing toward them from the direction of the house.

"Duchess? Duchess?" Alfred was closer now. Howell couldn't see the dog.

"Head for the boat through the woods," he said to Scotty. "I'm right behind you."

She started to run. Howell glanced back at the bobbing flashlight for a moment, then turned to follow. At that moment, there was a high-pitched snarl and a small ball of fur hit him just below the knee and bounced off. Howell ran, but this time his route was more directly toward where the boat lay, and there was brush to slow him down. It didn't slow down Duchess.

The little dog was all over him as he moved, going for his throat. Fortunately, being a short dog, it couldn't reach much above his ankles. Still, it was a damned nuisance. It boiled around his feet, tripping him, hanging on to his trousers when it could, slowing him all the way. Once, he stopped and threatened it with the flashlight, hoping to scare it away. It wouldn't scare, and he couldn't bring himself to hit it. It was a Yorkshire terrier. It was too cute.

Finally, he broke out of the trees at a point where he had estimated the boat would be. Neither the boat nor Scotty was there. It must be farther up toward the town, he thought, and anyway, he didn't want to go back toward Sutherland's. He could hear Alfred calling the dog again.

Then he saw the boat, and he saw Scotty. The boat had been another hundred yards along the shore toward the town, but now it was a good thirty yards offshore, and drifting, and Scotty was in the water, half that distance from the shore, making for the boat. He began to run down the shore, the dog still, amazingly, with him every step of the way. At the closest point to the boat, he turned and hit the water running.

Scotty was three-quarters of the way to the boat now, and up to her chest in the cold water. But then, she was short. Howell yanked the maps out of his waistband and held them above his head as he plowed through the deepening water. Duchess stood at the water's edge, still yapping.

When Howell made the boat, Scotty was clinging to it, apparently too exhausted to climb aboard. Howell, who was swimming now, as best he could with the handful of maps held out of the water, tossed them into the front seat, held on to the side of the boat with one hand, and with the other, grabbed Scotty by the seat of her pants and heaved. That got all but her legs into the boat, and Howell, with his last strength, gave a kick and hoisted himself in with her.

They lay in the bottom of the boat, gasping for air, too exhausted to move. Perhaps a minute later, Alfred's voice, borne on the breeze, drifted out to them.

"Duchess, what's the matter with you? Don't you know how to mind anymore? You been after another rabbit? I keep telling you them rabbits bigger than you, they going to eat you up one of these days. Come here to me! What you barking at?" There was a silence. "Oh, somebody's boat done gone adrift, huh? Well, it ain't none of your business and ain't none of mine, either. Come here to me." Then, still talking to the Yorkie, his voice faded into the distance.

"You incredible jerk," Howell wheezed, when he got a little of his breath back. He still could not move, and they lay tangled together in a heap. "When I get my health back, I'm gonna strangle you, if you aren't already dead." There was no response. "Scotty? You hear that? I'm going to strangle you with my bare hands." Nothing. She was lying awfully still, he thought. He struggled up onto an elbow. "Scotty?" He wrestled himself into a sitting position. Over the gunwales of the boat, he could see Alfred's flashlight moving jerkily toward the house, nearly there.

He got Scotty by the shoulders and shifted her limp form until her head was in his lap. He brushed the wet hair away from her face and felt for a pulse at her throat. "Say something, for Christ's sake!"

"I can't," she said suddenly. "You'll strangle me." Then she began to laugh. "Jesus, you should have seen yourself," she managed to say. "Some cat burglar you are—not even a Doberman, either, a Yorkshire terrier! I couldn't believe it!"

"Well, I'll tell you this, sweetheart, it was the biggest fucking York-shire terrier I ever saw. Must've been a four-pounder!"

It was another ten minutes before they could stop laughing enough to get the boat started.

They huddled in front of a roaring fire, naked, swathed in blankets, sipping hot coffee heavily laced with brandy.

"We did it," Scotty said elatedly.

"Your first illegal entry?"

"Yep. It was terrific."

"You're crazy. We damn near got caught, we damn near drowned, and it was terrific?"

"Well, we got it, didn't we?"

"Yep, we got it."

"What did we get?"

"The maps, dummy."

"I know that, but what's in the maps?"

"Confirmation of a theory of mine, maybe."

"Look, you're acting as though you've taken me into your confidence, but I don't have a clue to what's going on here."

"Well, something is wrong around here, and somebody's trying to put it right. Whoever it is, is using me to do it. I think."

"Okay. What's wrong?"

"I told you about the O'Coineen family, the story that Enda McAuliffe told me. Rabbit, remember?"

"Yes, I remember. They were the holdouts when Eric Sutherland was buying the land to build the dam."

"Then they disappeared, after Eric Sutherland *says* they agreed to sell. His story was that he went out to their place, got the deal signed, then put the money in their bank account."

"And McAuliffe says it's still there."

"Right. Uncollected. Building up interest for twenty-odd years. Then

I turn up, we meet these people at dinner, we have this little séance, and somebody named Rabbit, which is English for the Irish name O'Coineen, turns up and says howdy."

"To me."

"Yes, but mostly, I think, to me."

"Whaddaya mean, you? It was *me* the table liked, remember?"

"Well, I don't exactly understand this myself, but Mama Kelly thinks it was me."

Scotty shifted her weight, tugged on the blanket, and looked thoughtful. "Now let me see if I've got this," she said. "You think Eric Sutherland knocked off the O'Coineens for their land to build the lake, and now somebody from the spirit world has tapped you on the shoulder and whispered in your shell-like ear that you're supposed to bring him to justice."

Howell was quiet for a moment. "Maybe."

"You think the house we saw is real, then?"

"I don't know, but it might be best if it were, because that would put us firmly back on this earth."

"And if it's not real?"

"That would be nearly as good, because I'd know I was making the whole thing up in my mind and somehow communicating it to you, and I could spend some time in a rubber room and, maybe, be all right again."

Scotty was shaking her head. "You're losing me. If it's real, everything's okay; if it's not real, everything's okay."

Howell held up a restraining hand. "What if it used to be real, but isn't anymore?"

"Huh?"

"That's what I hope the maps are going to tell us. We know the O'Coineen place is under the lake, but we don't know *where* under the lake." He went to the maps on the desk and unfolded them. "Come over here."

Scotty went to the desk.

Howell spread out a map. "This was made in 1969. Now look here, this is where we are now, at this moment. Crossroads, road to the lake, cabin." He pointed to a lakeside lot and a house marked "Denham White Property."

"Right."

Howell unfolded the other map. "Now this is the 1936 map, covering, according to the coordinates, exactly the same area in the same scale." He switched on the word processor and turned the brightness control on the monitor all the way up, then placed the newer map on top of the older one and spread them across the screen, using it as a light box. "Now, what we have is the new map superimposed on the old one . . ."

"And?"

"And, presto, we can see under the lake."

Scotty peered at the map. "So?"

"Well, let's see." He pointed to the crossroads. "Let's start from here and follow the road toward the lake." He moved his finger along the backlit map. "Here's the point where it enters the lake, right by the cabin. Now we continue along the road; we're going downhill sharply now—see the elevation markings? And we come to— What do we come to? Your eyes are better than mine."

Scotty stared at the map. "We come to a farm. It says . . . oh, Christ, it says 'O'Coineen Farm.' "

Howell peered closely at the writing. "You're right, it does. Come with me." He put down the map, took her wrist, and led her onto the deck. The moon illuminated the cove brightly, sparkling on the water. He pointed out over the water. "There," he said. "Down there, about a hundred and fifty feet under the lake, lies the O'Coineen farm. You and I saw it together the other night."

Scotty stared, transfixed, at the shimmering surface of the lake. "It *was* real, but it isn't real anymore."

"But sometimes I can see it. Something wants me to see it."

"Me, too. Why me?"

"I think something is using you to convince me that I'm not crazy."

19

Bo Scully was later than usual getting to the office. He came in, glanced at the mail, then went into his office and closed the door. Then he opened it again.

"Scotty, will you get me the number of the Neiman-Marcus department store in Atlanta, please, ma'am? I think it's at the Lenox Square mall."

He turned away and closed the door, missing the stunned expression on Scotty's face. Quickly, she opened her handbag and checked her wallet. It wasn't there. Oh, God, this couldn't be happening. She recovered enough to dial information, get the number, and take it to him. "Want me to call them for you?" she asked hopefully. "Those stores will keep you hanging for hours. You ordering something?"

"No, it's okay, I'll call 'em myself. Close the door, will you?"

She closed the door and returned to her desk but watched him through the glass partition. He dialed the number, said something, waited a while, said something else, something longer, waited another while, then spoke for about a minute to someone. God, she wished she could hear him. He wrote down something, then hung up and dialed another number. Eleven digits, she counted, watching his hand move— long distance. He talked for another few minutes, then hung up, and came out of his office.

"Scotty, write me a letter, will you? Neiman-Marcus in Dallas— here's the address—attention of a Mr. Murray in the credit department. Say that, confirming our phone conversation of today, I request a copy of the charge account application of"—he glanced at the paper in his hand—"an H. M. MacDonald, account number 071107. Say it's in conjunction with an investigation being conducted by this department, and the information on the application will be kept confidential." He handed her the paper. "Sonofabitch wouldn't tell me nothing on the phone," he said, and walked back into his office.

Scotty quietly thanked God that she had used her initials on the card. If Bo ever got his hands on that application he'd see that the card belonged to a Heather Miller MacDonald, who was employed by the *Atlanta Constitution* as a reporter; he would figure out in milliseconds who that was, and she'd be dead in the water, or maybe just dead.

Well, she'd take a couple of days to write that letter—that would give her time to think.

Bo opened his office door again. "Do that letter now, will you, please? I want to get it right off."

She typed the letter on the word processor, ripped it from the printer, and took it in for Bo's signature. She addressed the envelope, sealed it, ran it through the postage meter, and tossed it on top of a pile of letters waiting to go to the post office. She'd take them herself at lunch and ditch that particular one.

Bo came out of the office. "I'm going to make a round or two, and I'll go straight on to lunch. Be back about two, I guess." He reached into Scotty's out basket and scooped up the pile of letters. "I'll drop these by the post office for you," he said, starting for the door.

"Hey," she called. He stopped and turned. "No need to go to the trouble. I've got to go down there anyway."

Bo grinned. "Oh, no trouble." He left.

Scotty buried her face in her hands and tried not to cry. She'd kill John Howell, the clumsy bastard. She was blown, or would be before the week was out. And what could she do in that short a time?

"Hey, Scotty," Mike, the radio operator, called, "will you keep an eye on the radio for me? I gotta get a haircut."

"Sure, Mike," she said brightly. "Be glad to. Take your time."

Mike left, and she was alone. Alone with Bo Scully's Great Iron Filing Cabinet. It was now or never. She took a big breath and dug for her key.

20

Howell spread out the maps again and peered at them, hoping for some new inspiration, but none came. What did come was an overwhelming sense of guilt. His earlier contention that he could whip Lurton Pitts's autobiography off in a hurry had turned out not to be true. He had made no sort of real beginning on the book, and that was supposed to be his reason for being here, what was paying for his being here.

He folded the maps and stuck them in a desk drawer, then got out his old Uher voice-activated tape recorder, which he had once used so often for interviews. Maybe when he had some sort of outline, it would be easier to do the actual writing. He began to organize and speak his thoughts into the machine. He liked the recorder; it paused when he did.

An hour or so later, with a rough outline nearly completed, he stopped, hearing a car pull up to the cabin. He went to the door and opened it before Bo Scully could knock.

"Hey, Bo. You're getting to be a regular visitor. Come on in."

The sheriff settled himself in a chair next to the desk. "Well, I was in the neighborhood, and a little bit more sober than the last time I was. Sorry about that. I'd had a bad night."

"I know the feeling. Coffee?"

"No thanks, I just had some. Tell you the truth, this isn't entirely a social call."

"Oh? Something official I can help you with?"

"Well, not exactly official either, I guess. I hear you've taken an interest in cartography."

"Boy, word sure moves fast, doesn't it."

"Small town. Word doesn't have far to go."

"Yeah, I was trying to locate a map of the area before the lake was built."

"And one after it was built."

"Oh, I located that. A Mrs. O'Neal down at the courthouse had one squirreled away. I must say, she wasn't too eager to help me find an earlier map."

"Well, Nellie O'Neal's been in the courthouse for so long, she sort of takes a proprietary interest in her records, I guess."

"I mentioned my interest to Enda McAuliffe," Howell said, beating the sheriff to the punch, "and he wasn't too anxious to help, either."

"Oh, there's nothing real significant about that. Most folks hereabouts would have the same attitude. Y'see, this area around here was just an unproductive backwater before the lake came. Folks' memories of that time are pretty hard, I guess. It wasn't easy to scratch out a buck around here. Now it's different, of course. We've got the lake and everybody's real proud of it. I guess we like to think of our county the way it is instead of the way it was."

Howell wanted to yell "Bullshit!" at Scully and demand to know what was going on. "I see," he said.

"I hear you took an interest in Eric Sutherland's office too," the sheriff said, still friendly.

"The little place down from his house? I had a brief peek in there from the outside; just wondered what the place was."

Scully's demeanor changed ever so slightly. "Looks like somebody might've had a little peek on the inside."

"Oh? How do you mean?"

"I mean a little breaking and entering."

"Was a lot of stuff taken?"

"What do you think might get taken from Eric Sutherland's office?"

"Beats me. What's he got in there?"

"Maps."

Howell let the word sit right there.

"Tell me, John, you acquainted with an H. M. MacDonald?"

"H. M.? Don't think so. Went to school with a Bob MacDonald. Don't remember a MacDonald since. Local fellow?"

Scully shook his head. "Nope. Nobody around here by that name. Not a MacDonald in the county."

"Why do you ask?"

"Well, Mr. Sutherland found a credit card from a store with that name on it, right at the door to his office. Card was bent, sort of.

Looked like it might have been used to jimmy the lock. Tell me, what did you do after the Sutherland party the other night?"

"Came back here, cooked a steak, ate it, passed out pretty early. We had a lot to drink at Sutherland's."

"Scotty with you, then?"

"Yep, for dinner."

"What about after dinner?"

"Is that an official question, Bo?"

"Not really."

"None of your business, then."

"Did you go out at all after you came back from the party?"

"Nope."

"Take your boat out?"

"I just said I didn't go out again."

"Sorry, John, I don't mean to make this sound like a third degree."

Howell grinned slightly. "That's just what it sounds like."

Scully chuckled. "Yeah, I guess it does. Why did you want the maps?"

"Oh, I just got to looking out the window a lot, and I wondered what was under the lake, that's all. I'd about forgotten it until you brought it up." Howell leaned forward. "What *is* under the lake, Bo?"

Scully threw back his head and laughed. "So that's it. Well, you're not the first. People seem to think that when a big lake like this gets built, there's all sorts of stuff under it. There are still stories among the schoolkids around here about houses and farms and trees being down there. They used to say that when the lake got down low in the winter, when they were using a lot of water for power, then an old bridge and a church steeple would surface again. That the sort of thing you had in mind?"

"Sort of."

"Well, let me tell you what they do when they build a lake, buddy. They tear down all the houses and sell what scrap they can; they cut all the trees for timber and pulp, and to keep 'em from being hazards to navigation later, and they painstakingly demolish every standing thing in the whole area that's going to be underwater. So if you want to know what's under the lake, the answer is a plain, old-fashioned *nothing.*"

"What about the O'Coineen place?" Howell asked, and watched Scully closely for his response.

The sheriff didn't bat an eye. He shrugged. "Well, I guess that was a little different. By the time Mr. Sutherland and Donal O'Coineen had made their deal, the water had already risen against a roadbed that cut across O'Coineen's place. Right after that, before the crew could get in there to break the place up, the roadbed gave way and the place was flooded."

"That's Sutherland's story, is it?"

Scully blinked. "I never had any reason to doubt it. Do you?"

Howell leaned back in his chair and locked his fingers behind his head. "Well, let's see now," he said. "O'Coineen, who's held out bitterly against Sutherland for years, suddenly gives in and sells; his house vanishes under the lake, then he and his whole family disappear and are never heard from again. Come on, Bo, you're a lawman; doesn't that sound just a little too convenient?"

Scully looked at him in surprise. "But they were heard from again," he said.

Howell sat up straight. "By whom?"

"By me, for one. Listen, I don't know whether you know this, but I was engaged to marry Donal O'Coineen's oldest daughter."

Howell sat back in his chair. "Joyce? The blind one?"

"That's right. We went together since high school, then started making plans to marry after I got out of the service. I was working for the county by then—I was a deputy—and that meant Eric Sutherland to Donal O'Coineen. He was pretty much of a hard case. Anyway, the whole business about the lake started to get in our way. Old Donal looked at me as being on the other side, which I guess I was, technically, but I never went against him; I stayed out of it. Still, things got tenser and tenser, and finally, Joyce backed out of the engagement. I guess it got to the point where she figured she had to choose between her family and me, and she made her choice."

"How long was this before O'Coineen finally sold out?"

"Two or three weeks, I guess. Less than a month anyway."

"And you heard from them afterwards? Personally?"

"That's right. A couple of weeks after they left the county I got a letter from Joyce—her little sister wrote it for her."

"Kathleen?"

"That's right. She was Joyce's eyes in a lot of ways. Anyway, I got this letter from Joyce saying goodbye. It was postmarked Nashville, and she said Donal was taking them farther north, maybe Virginia or Kentucky, to look for some land, and we wouldn't be seeing each other again. Donal had money in the bank here, of course. What Sutherland had paid him for the land. But Joyce said he was bitter and wouldn't touch it. He'd drawn out just about everything else he had—and believe me, he was pretty well off—several months before he left. They'd stopped doing business in town, they took Kathleen out of school, and they just wouldn't have anything to do with anybody local anymore."

"And the money's still in the bank, I hear."

"So it is, and with a lot of interest on top of it. Course the bank don't give a shit if Donal never turns up and asks for it. They got a nice fat deposit, just sitting there."

"Bo, is there any possibility that somebody else could have written the letter? I mean, since it wasn't in Joyce's handwriting, couldn't somebody have forged it to make you think the family was still alive?"

"No, no. It was in Kathleen's handwriting. She'd written all of Joyce's letters to me when I was in Korea. There must have been a hundred of them. I'd know that handwriting anywhere."

"Then there's no chance at all that the O'Coineen family could have been drowned when the roadbed gave way and let the lake in?"

"Absolutely none. Look, John, now I see what all this interest in the maps was about. People like to think the worst, and that story has been making the rounds periodically for years, but I'm in a position to know the truth of things. First of all, I know the money's in the bank; I'm a director of the bank. Second, Joyce communicated with me after the family left, and I know for a fact the communication was genuine. I was in a position to know; there was some personal stuff in that letter, stuff that only Joyce and me—and Kathleen—could have known."

Howell felt badly deflated, and he must have looked it.

Scully leaned forward. "John, I can see how this tale of the O'Coineens must've looked pretty sexy—especially with somebody like Eric Sutherland being the villain. But there's just nothing to it. Oh, Sutherland was the bad guy, all right, putting pressure on people to sell land they'd owned for generations, but he did it legally all the way, and at the end of it all, it meant a whole new world for the people who live here. And let me tell you something else. If I thought for a minute that Sutherland had been involved in something like a murder, I'd of had him long ago. I respect the man, but I don't like him much, and I loved Joyce. I wouldn't be a party to covering up her murder. I hope you believe me."

Howell did believe him and said so. "I'm sorry, Bo, if I've ruffled feathers around here with all this, especially Sutherland's. I know that can't make life any easier for you."

"Well, you're right about that, John. I don't think I've ever seen

Sutherland quite so riled. Look, I'm going to run down this credit card —like as not, there'll be some perfectly logical reason why it was there, somebody from out of town at the party, I expect—then I'll do what I can to quiet him down. I don't know if you were in there the other night, but even if you were, I think I understand why, and the hell with it as far as I'm concerned. So just forget this visit, okay? But listen, if you get the old man flustered again, he's going to start making life difficult for me, and I can't have that, and I'll have to do something about it. Do you understand me?"

"Sure, Bo. Believe me, I don't want to make life difficult for you."

The sheriff left, and Howell went to the phone.

Scotty moved through the files with almost reckless speed. She knew she might miss what she was looking for at the rate she was going, but she also knew that, with events closing in on her, she might never have another chance. Still, after three-quarters of an hour, she was only finished with one drawer and half finished with another. She was aided, though, by the neatness of the files. Nothing seemed mixed up or out of place. Finally, it was color that led her to what she wanted.

In a file marked "Miscellaneous," full of a standard form used for domestic disturbances, peeping toms, and other minor offenses, she saw something green. Everything else in the file was white. She fished half a dozen sheets of loose ledger paper from the file and looked at her watch. Ten past two. She had been luckier with time than she could have dared wish for. The telephone rang.

"Sutherland County Sheriff's office."

"It's John. Sutherland found your credit card outside his office."

"I know, you sonofabitch. Bo has already written to Neiman's to find out all about it."

"He was just here, asking questions. Just so our stories match, I told him we cooked a steak and got to bed early."

"You told him I slept there? Thanks a lot."

"He asked, but I told him it was none of his business. We had what you might call a very frank discussion about what's under the lake, and I think maybe I've been on the wrong track."

"Well, judging from what I've got in my hand, here, I'm not on the wrong track. There were some ledger pages stuck in a file where they shouldn't be. That's not like Bo." She glanced quickly through them. "There are a lot of figures on them."

"Well, you'd better get a copy of them quick. Bo's already been gone from here a couple of minutes, and if he's headed for the office, that means you've got very little time."

"See ya." She hung up the telephone and ran for the copying machine. It hadn't been used yet that day, and it took a couple of minutes to warm up. She drummed her fingers restlessly on the machine, waiting for the green light to go on. She had copied only two of the pages when the front door opened. She froze. The filing cabinet was still unlocked, the file was on Bo's desk, and papers were in her hand that shouldn't be.

"Thanks for covering for me, sugar. How do I look?" Mike sauntered by, stroking his hair.

"Slick, Mike," Scotty managed to croak. She kept making copies. "You're gonna knock 'em dead."

"You know it, sugar," Mike said, arranging himself in his chair and opening a copy of *Playboy*.

Scotty grabbed the last copy and, as quickly as she could without seeming to hurry, walked back toward her desk. When she was around the corner and out of Mike's sight, she ducked into Bo's office, stuck the sheets back into the file, got it into the drawer, and locked the cabinet. She had been back at her desk, the copies safely in her purse, for five seconds when Bo walked in.

"How'd you like Sutherland's party?" he asked casually as he strolled past her desk.

"Not bad. He was really pretty nice."

"Stay late?"

"No, I went back to John's for a steak."

"Stay long?"

She looked at him sideways. "None of your business."

He laughed and went into his office.

In her mind, Scotty ran through what she had just done, just to be sure. She'd replaced the ledger sheets at exactly the place in the file where'd they'd come from; she'd put the file in exactly the same place in the drawer; and, this time, she'd made sure the lock was firmly engaged. Then she stopped in the middle of a sigh of relief. There was something wrong, something out of order, something she hadn't done properly. The copying machine. In order to make copies, she had to place the originals, one at a time, under a flap on top of the machine. The machine drew a sheet of blank paper from a stack on one side and spat out a copy on the other. She had, she now realized, made the first five copies in the ordinary way, placing an original under the flap, pushing the button, then replacing the original with the next page. She had her own copies, now of all six pages. But, she knew in her bones, she had left the last original under the flap. It was still there.

Bo came out of his office, a letter in his hand, and headed for the copying machine.

"No!" Scotty practically shouted.

Bo stopped and turned. "Huh?"

It was hard to talk with her heart in her throat. "Uh, don't use that just yet. The paper isn't feeding properly, and I haven't had a chance to get at it."

"Well, I'll take a look at it. I need this right away."

Bo never liked to wait for anything, she knew that. She walked over and muscled between him and the machine. "Get out of the way, Bo," she said playfully. "You'll just screw it up. You know you can't fix anything." She popped open the side of the machine and removed the stack of blank paper.

"It looks all right to me," Bo said impatiently.

"It would look all right to you if it were upside down." She rapped the stack sharply against the side of the machine, squaring the corners. "Give me that," she said, snatching the letter from his hands. "I'll do it."

"Jesus Christ, Scotty, you're beginning to act like nobody else around here can work any of this stuff but you."

"That's exactly right," she said. Scotty lifted the flap on the machine slightly and slid Bo's copy underneath, at the same time flicking the green ledger sheet already under the flap with her fingernail. It slid across the glass surface, under the back edge of the flap and down between the machine and the wall. She pressed the button, gave Bo his copy and original, and went back to her desk, hoping against hope he had not seen what she had done.

"You know, Mike," Bo said as he strolled back to his office, "I don't know why we have all these service contracts with the office machine people when we've got our own mechanical genius right here."

Scotty put her hands on her desk and pressed, so that no one could see them shaking. She had pulled that off all right, but now Bo's files were missing a sheet, and it was stuck behind a machine that weighed a ton.

21

Howell huddled over the ledger sheets and studied them for some minutes. "Look at this," he said to Scotty.

"You bastard. How could you leave my credit card there for Eric Sutherland to find?"

"Listen, Scotty, if you'd stayed with the boat like I told you to, it never would have happened. But no, you had to sneak up behind me and scare the shit out of me and make me drop the card. I might also add that if you'd done what I told you to, we'd have saved ourselves a cold swim in the wee hours."

Scotty pouted. "You know, I think it's extremely rude of you to point out a person's little mistakes and make a big thing of them. That's all in the past."

"Good. Now look at this." He rattled the pages.

"Except my credit card isn't in the past, it's in Bo Scully's pocket, and my charge account application is on its way to him!"

"Well, just intercept the goddamned letter, all right? Don't you handle the mail around there?"

"Usually."

"Well, just make sure you handle it every day until the letter comes. Now for Christ's sake come here and look at these pages, and help me figure this thing out."

Scotty heaved herself off the sofa and came to the desk. "What, then?"

"Okay, look. The letters LSCA and a number are written here alongside a date in the margin. There's a long list of them. The dates go back just over three years, and they're numbered one through twenty-eight.

Then, out here in the margin, there is another number opposite each LSCA. I don't think this is any sort of a code. I think it's a schedule."

"And the numbers in the right margin?" Scotty asked, pointing to a matching column.

"Well, they're two-digit numbers, varying from fifteen to sixty, but always increasing or decreasing in increments of five."

"Could be money. Add some zeros, and it would be a lot of money."

"Good thought. So what have we got here? A schedule of deliveries and payments, maybe?"

"Sounds good to me. Deliveries of drugs."

"We've nothing to indicate that, unless the right margin numbers are money. If he's either paying or receiving sums from fifteen to sixty thousand dollars per shipment, it's drugs."

"That doesn't seem so much. I thought drug deals went into millions."

"Sure, but what if these numbers represent commissions?"

Scotty ran a finger down the pages, pointing out another series of letters and numbers. "What about these? They're interspersed after every four or five of the LSCA dates."

"I don't know," Howell said. "We've got an A and a number, an F and a number, Z, number, F, number, A, number. The numbers are all seven digits, group of three, group of four. There's a date next to each letter, too. Probably some other sort of schedule, but not as frequent as the other one."

"Could be. But a schedule for what?"

"Who knows? But it's important enough for him to hide it very carefully. Tell me about your original tip, the one that put you on to Bo."

"Not much to tell. Let's just say that it was somebody in state law enforcement, who would be in a position to pick up some scuttlebutt."

"Is somebody running an investigation on Bo, then?"

"Nope. That was his point. Somebody *should* be running an investigation, but nobody is." She smiled. "Except me."

"Somebody's protecting him, then? Heading off any investigation?"

"My source didn't say exactly that, but that was my impression. You think there's some sort of organization?"

Howell shrugged. "We don't know for sure whether there's even a crime, let alone a conspiracy. But if you're right, and there are drugs involved, then there would have to be. It's a long way from South

America to north Georgia, and to move anything in quantity would take all sorts of help."

Long after Scotty had gone to bed and left him trying to work, Howell woke with his head on the desk. He had an awful headache. It was pitch dark, and only the glow from the word processor's monitor screen lit the room. There was a half-empty bottle of Jack Daniel's next to the machine, and an empty glass. Howell poured himself a stiff drink. Maybe it would dull the headache. He could not bear to look at the blank screen any more, so he walked out onto the deck, taking his drink with him.

Scotty had gone to bed early, and he had determined to make a start on the actual writing of Lurton Pitts's book. He had it outlined on tape and in his head. He knew where to begin. But he had not been able to.

The moon was low, making a long streak of silver across the water. It was very beautiful, he thought, and he should know. He had spent enough time looking at it instead of working. He wondered why he could not clear the hurdle of Chapter One. Perhaps it was because once he actually started to write, he'd know he was a hack, finally and confirmed; a man who would ghost-write something he loathed, just for the money. He cherished the irrational thought that, until he actually wrote Chapter One, he could give Pitts back his expense money and save his self-respect. But the more he thought about it, the more he understood that his point of no return had been reached when he had packed the car, left his wife, and come to this place.

He looked out over the lake. No hallucinations, no spirits, crickets chirping loudly, all normal.

It began to be chilly, and he went back into the living room to retrieve a sweater from the back of his desk chair. As he reached for it, his eye traveled to the empty monitor screen. It was not empty. It was filled with words.

Puzzled, he sat down and read the heading. "Chapter One," it read. "How I Found God." He pressed the scroll button, and more lines worked their way up the screen, lines that were somehow familiar but that he simply couldn't remember having written. It was all there, eight or nine pages of it, the fruit of his outline, in a prose style close to the manner of speaking of Lurton Pitts. He read it to the end, then pressed another button, sending the text to be stored on a disk.

Could he have been so drunk that he had written that without remembering it? Was that possible? Maybe, but that drunk, he wouldn't have been able to write. Or would he? The last thing he remembered before resting his head on the desk was a totally blank screen, glowing eerily in the dark room.

He tossed back the rest of his drink and lumbered toward the bed, baffled and exhausted.

Scotty sweated out the mail for a week. Each morning, the postman arrived about nine thirty, dumped the usual load of circulars and letters on the station counter, tipped his hat, and went on his way. Each morning, Scotty contrived to be at the counter instead of her desk when the postman arrived, beating Sally and Mike to the mail. Bo never arrived before ten.

On the eighth morning, the postman was a little late, and Bo, inexplicably, was a little early. Scotty looked up from the counter and, to her horror, saw them practically bump into each other just outside the front door. The postman went on his way, and Bo walked in with the mail under his arm.

Scotty's first impulse was to vault over the counter and wrest it from him. Stifling the urge, she walked back to her desk, to be in his path as he went into his office. She could see the letter as he came toward her; the envelope was the same watermarked gold as her monthly Neiman's bill. She tried not to stare at it, but she knew she was a minute or so from an extremely, perhaps fatally embarrassing moment. Bo stopped at the radio to talk to Mike.

Scotty sat down, then stood up and pretended to go through some papers on her desk. Bo started to walk toward his office. It was time to panic, Scotty thought. All she could think of was to faint.

Scotty had never fainted before, not even in the very worst moments of her life, but she was so frightened that very little acting was required. She simply placed a hand on her forehead, then crumpled in sections at Bo's feet, falling across his path like an elongated sack of oranges.

Bo's inexperience with fainting apparently matched Scotty's, because he reacted as if she had taken an arrow in the chest. He shouted for help from Mike and Sally, swept her onto the sofa in his office, loosened a lot of her clothing, demanded a wet towel for her face, and generally dithered about like a white, male Butterfly McQueen. Scotty half expected him to call for boiling water.

She had time to reflect that she enjoyed the loosening of her clothing; then she stirred, moaned, and went into her routine. "What happened?" she asked weakly.

"You passed out, sugar," Bo replied, sponging at her face and ruining her eye makeup. He looked whiter than she did, she was sure.

"Oh, I'm sorry, Bo. I've been fasting for a couple of days to lose some weight. I guess I overdid it." She cast an eye about for the mail. Somebody had put it on Bo's desk.

"Well, Jesus Christ, Scotty, you've gotta eat something, you know. No wonder you're so weak. Mike, run over to Bubba's and get a cheeseburger with everything on it and a glass of milk."

Scotty sat up. "What I really need is to go to the bathroom," she said. There was a toilet at the back of Bo's office. She aimed so as to pass as closely as possible to his desk.

"Are you sure you can make it?" Bo was still terribly concerned.

"Oh, yeah. I think that was just temporary." She turned her back to him to squeeze between him and the desk, pinched the letter, and held it in front of her as she walked toward the toilet. She closed the door, sat down on the john lid, and tore it open. There it was, a clear photocopy of enough to get her killed. She tore it into the smallest possible pieces and flushed it down the john, doing it twice and checking for pieces that didn't make it.

When she came out of the toilet, Mike was waiting with the food, and Bo forced her to eat half of it on the spot.

"Come on," he said, when he reckoned she had eaten all she would. "I'm going to take you home. You need some rest."

Scotty went meekly with him. Her landlady was at work. The room looked odd to her, she had spent so little time there since meeting John Howell. Bo walked her up the stairs as if she were in the last stages of a difficult pregnancy.

"Really, Bo, I'm feeling great now," she said, showing him into her room. "The food is working. That's all it was, just too much fasting."

"You ought to take better care of yourself," Bo said softly. He raised a hand and brushed at her hair. The hand stayed, resting on her cheek. He suddenly bent and kissed her, and Scotty met him halfway. They kissed again, then again. In moments, the action had escalated.

It was wild. There was much heavy breathing and tearing at clothes, then they were on the bed, locked together, moving, moaning, coming together. The whole thing couldn't have lasted more than three minutes, Scotty reflected, but she liked it, and so, apparently, did he. They had had this carnal curiosity about each other, and they had both enjoyed satisfying it.

"Christ, I want a cigarette," Bo said, swinging his legs over the side of the bed and sitting up.

"I didn't know you smoked."

"I don't. I mean, I haven't for damn near ten years, but suddenly I want a cigarette."

Scotty laughed. "Some old reflex, I expect."

Bo laughed too. "Yeah, maybe." He fingered the framed photograph on the bedside table. "Your folks?"

"Yes. My mother's dead."

"You don't look like either one of them. Who do you look like? Grandparents?"

"Who knows? I was adopted."

"Yeah? How old?"

"Brand new, I gather. A regular foundling."

Bo was quiet for a moment. His face seemed filled with pity. "You mean you were left on their doorstep?"

"On the doorstep of the Georgia Baptist Children's Home in Hapeville, in a wooden box. My folks were already on the waiting list. I was theirs in a day or two."

Bo started to get dressed. "Well, I gotta get back," he said. "Lot to do."

"Sure. Thanks for the day off."

Bo stopped at the door but did not turn. "Scotty . . ." He seemed to be having trouble speaking.

"Yeah?"

"You think we could just . . . forget about this? Try and believe it never happened?"

"You're worried about John."

He waited a moment, then nodded. "Yeah."

"Sure. It never happened."

"Promise me you won't ever tell anybody. Not John, not anybody. Not ever."

Jesus, Scotty thought, he sounds like the girl. "Okay," she said, "I promise." And I sound like the guy.

"Thanks," he said, and left.

Scotty got up and went to the window. She watched as he went down the walk. Before he got into the car, he put his elbows on top and rested his face in his hands. When he lifted his head again, he looked crushed, shattered.

Bo and she were different generations, in more ways than one. She had never placed a whole lot of importance on sex; apparently he did. It was rather sweet, she thought, as he drove away.

She stretched out on the bed. Well, it had finally happened—though, from Bo's reaction, it wouldn't happen again. It had been nice, if a little rushed. She certainly felt no guilt about it; it was simply not in her nature to take sex that seriously. Then she remembered that Bo was not just a passing man but the subject of her investigation, that she hoped to put him in jail. Now she felt not a moral guilt, but a professional one. She had always thought of herself as a pro, and now she had crossed a line that was supposed to separate her professional judgment from her personal feelings. She wondered if cops ever liked or pitied the criminals they tried to convict.

She would just damn well have to steel herself and do her job. She was tough enough to do that, she knew it. Some secret part of her, though, began to hope that her information about Bo was wrong.

22

Enda McAuliffe stood over Eric Sutherland and pointed. "Sign here, Mr. Sutherland, and then initial every page, please." Sutherland signed, then McAuliffe and the two men from the bank witnessed the document.

"Stay a minute, Enda," Sutherland said, waving the two other men out.

McAuliffe took a chair next to the desk. He felt odd being called Enda; everyone had called him Mac since he was a kid in the valley. Only Sutherland used his Christian name, and that was a recent event, since he had become McAuliffe's client.

Sutherland looked a bit uncomfortable. "I just wanted to tell you how pleased I am with the way things have been going since you signed on," he said.

"Well, thank you very much, Mr. Sutherland," the lawyer said.

"Why don't you call me Eric," Sutherland said. "All my friends do."

McAuliffe was taken aback. "I . . . well, you have to understand, you've always been Mr. Sutherland to me, all my life, and I don't think I'd feel comfortable this late in the game . . ."

"All right, all right," Sutherland said resignedly. "I understand. In fact, the only person in town who calls me Eric is Bo Scully, and I think he does it only because I insist."

McAuliffe felt sorry for the man, something he had never thought would be possible. He had spent so much of his life feeling nothing but contempt for Sutherland that, even now, when he knew more about the man's life and felt some real sympathy for him, he still had trouble pushing his old feelings aside.

"Enda," said Sutherland, "tell me what you think of this John Howell fellow."

"Well," McAuliffe replied, "I like him. We've had a few lunches down at Bubba Brown's. I think he's bright; he certainly was a solid newspaper reporter in his day, although I thought his column wasn't all that good the last few months he was doing it. To tell you the truth, he strikes me as being sort of unhappy in his personal life."

"Do you think he bears me any ill will?"

"Why, no, sir, I don't. I think . . . Well, he's just the sort of person who's . . . curious, I guess. He's spent most of his working life asking a lot of questions, and now it just comes naturally to him."

"Enda, you understand that I can't have him asking questions around here."

McAuliffe nodded. "I certainly see why that would make you uncomfortable, sir, especially after what you've told me, and after this." He held up the document Sutherland had just signed. "But I don't think it's anything to worry about. Howell is not here to write about us. He's just curious, that's all."

Sutherland shook his head. "I just don't want the whole thing opened up again. It's been twenty-five years."

McAuliffe decided that since Sutherland was now his valued client, he should tell him everything he knew. "Mr. Sutherland, I don't think you should assign too much weight to this, but not long after John Howell arrived here he had some out-of-town people out to the cabin and they . . . well, they had a séance."

Sutherland winced. "Oh, my God," he said quietly. He took a deep breath and let it out. "Tell me about it."

Bo Scully was admitted to the house by Alfred and was taken straight to the study; Eric Sutherland was waiting for him.

"Morning, Eric," Bo said, taking care that he sounded relaxed and confident. He was never either relaxed or confident in Sutherland's presence.

Sutherland offered no greeting. "Tell me about the credit card," he said.

He looked angry, Bo thought. He had probably been working up to it for days. "I called Neiman-Marcus in Atlanta immediately. They referred me to the credit manager in Dallas—that's the main store—and he refused to tell me anything without a written request."

"So?"

"So I wrote to him, asking for a copy of the credit application."

"And?"

"And I'm expecting a reply any day now." Bo leaned forward in his chair. "Eric, I think this whole business with the credit card is easily explained. Somebody at the party—"

"Dammit, I've told you there was nobody named MacDonald at the party!"

"Look, this guy MacDonald could be a friend or relative of somebody who was there. There are all sorts of possible explanations. Have you had any workmen around the place lately?"

"No, not a one, except the gardener, and believe me, he doesn't have a charge account at Neiman-Marcus. I don't pay him enough for that."

"Eric, when we hear from Neiman's, I promise you it's going to be the most logical, ordinary thing. Besides, you're not missing anything from the office, are you?"

"What may be missing from the office is not an object that somebody has walked away with. What may be missing is information that somebody has now that he didn't have before. Knowledge is a dangerous thing in the wrong hands, and I think you know I mean Howell. I *saw* him looking in there, and the dog just went berserk that night."

"I talked with Alfred about that, Eric. He says the dog gets after rabbits down there in the woods. It's happened before."

"What about the boat?"

"Alfred says it was just adrift. That's happened before, too."

"We're going to have to get rid of Mr. John Howell, Bo. That's all there is to it."

Bo leaned back in his chair. "Well, now, I had a little talk with Howell a couple of days ago, and I think he's off your back."

Sutherland looked at him in surprise. "What did you say to him?"

"Well, he'd heard the O'Coineen rumors, all right, and I gave him the whole story."

"Did he believe you?"

"I told him about the letter from Joyce. I think that clinched it. You see, Eric, even if he did get into your office, all he wanted was a look at the maps. What he knows now makes the maps unnecessary, irrelevant. He understands that." Bo hoped to hell Howell did understand that. "He didn't come up here about that, Eric. He came to write his book, just like he said. He heard the O'Coineen story after he was already up here, and I guess he was a little bored, and it got him all excited."

"Damn right he got excited," Sutherland said. "Did you know he and some people had a goddamned séance up there? Enda McAuliffe told me."

Bo's blood ran cold. He didn't show it. "So what? You don't believe all that crap that half-wit Benny Pope spreads around, do you? His brain has been pickled for years."

"Howell's been to see Lorna Kelly, too."

Bo felt as if he'd swallowed a block of ice. "For what?"

"McAuliffe says Howell slipped a disc or something."

"Did she fix it?"

"Apparently. He certainly seemed agile enough at the party."

"Well, then . . ."

Sutherland wiped a hand across his brow. "I wish she'd die, damn her. I'd like to spend my last years in peace, without her around."

Bo stood and placed a hand on the old man's shoulder. "Eric, it's my job to see that you have the peace you deserve. You're making much more out of all this than is called for, really you are. I'm going to take care of everything. Just trust me."

Sutherland stood and took Bo's hand in both of his. "Bo, I've always trusted you, and you've never let me down. Help me enjoy my last years, and I promise you, when I'm gone, you'll be remembered."

"Thank you, Eric," Bo said, and took his leave.

He drove back into town, afraid to the very bottom of him. Too much new was happening—the business with Scotty, the séance, Howell's acquaintance with Mama Kelly. Bo felt as though control of things was slipping through his fingers, that there were more holes in the dike than he could plug. He didn't trust Sutherland, either. He'd heard that promise before, and he'd believe it when the old man was in the ground and the will was being read. In the meantime, he was making his own provisions, just in case.

As soon as Bo had left the office, Scotty began to fidget. She had thought she'd be nervous with him, after the events of yesterday, but he'd been much the same as usual, though she thought she'd caught a trace of sadness about him. But now, she wanted Sally out, and Sally was taking her time about going to lunch.

"Listen, Scotty, why don't you go first?" Sally said. "I'm not real hungry yet."

"Oh, I don't think I'm going to have lunch today, Sally. I've still got a couple of pounds to go."

"Listen, you keep up that fasting stuff, and we'll be scraping you off the floor again. I think you scared Bo half to death."

"No, no, I had a big breakfast this morning. You go ahead and eat."

Sally took what seemed like half an hour to check her makeup and brush off her dress, then finally left the office. Scotty waited until Mike was on the radio, then picked up some papers and went to the copying machine. She placed them on top of the machine and pressed the On button. When Mike was finishing his radio call, she turned her back to him and flipped the papers behind the machine.

"Oh, dammit," she shouted.

Mike turned. "What's the matter, Scotty?"

"Oh, I've dropped some papers behind the copying machine, and you know what the thing weighs. Give me a hand, will you, Mike?"

"Sure I will." He came over and helped her wrestle it away from the wall.

"Just a couple of more inches, and I'll be able to get behind it," Scotty said. The gap opened; she wedged herself around the machine and recovered both the papers she had deliberately dropped and the lost ledger sheet of Bo's. She shuffled them together to conceal the green paper among the others. "Got 'em. Thanks, Mike." Together, they moved the heavy machine back into place.

"You shouldn't be doing that sort of shoving, Scotty," Mike said. "You might not be recovered yet."

"Oh, I'm fine, thanks. I am a little hungry, though. And I was going to skip lunch."

"Well, I don't think you should do that."

"Tell you what," she said brightly. "I'll split a pizza with you."

"Hey, you really are hungry."

"I'll keep an eye on the radio, if you'll go get it."

"Sure." Mike put on his hat and left.

"Anything but anchovies," she called after him. Scotty ran for her purse, got the filing cabinet key, threw herself at the thing, and got it open. She pulled out the Miscellaneous file, removed the five other green ledger sheets, made sure they were in the proper order, added the sixth sheet, and started to replace them in the file. They stuck halfway in. She ran her fingers between the pages to push aside the obstruction, and they met something small and thick. A notebook, she thought. John said there'd be a notebook. The front door to the office slammed. She spun around, the forbidden file in her hand. A man she did not know was standing at the counter.

"I'd like to pay a parking ticket," he said.

"Oh, sure," she said, relieved. She hesitated for a moment, then put the file on top of the cabinet, and went to help the man. This would take only a second, and she'd be rid of him.

She took the ticket. "That's five dollars."

He opened his wallet and thumbed through some bills. "You got change for a twenty?"

"Haven't you got anything smaller?" she asked, looking toward the door nervously. Mike might be back at any moment; or worse, Bo.

"Sorry, that's all I've got."

Swearing under her breath, Scotty took the twenty, went to her desk, opened a drawer, took out the cash box, unlocked it, put the twenty in and took out a five and a ten, conscious all the time of the unlocked cabinet and the deadly file, lying there, waiting to be discovered.

"There you are," she said, stamping the ticket and tearing off the stub. "And here's your receipt."

The man left, and Scotty raced for the file. She reached in for the notebook and came out with a small green booklet with a gold American eagle stamped on it. A passport. Quickly, she thumbed through the pages. Bo's face stared at her from the photograph, but he was wearing glasses. Bo didn't wear glasses. The passport was issued to a Peter Patrick O'Hara. The address was Bo's.

Scotty wanted a copy of this, badly, but she looked up and saw Mike standing across the street with a pizza box in his hand, talking to somebody. She went quickly through the passport; there were a lot of stamps, but only for two countries—Switzerland and the United States. She repeated the passport number to herself three times, returned it to the file, and the file to the cabinet. She was sitting at her desk again, making a note of the passport number, when Mike came in with the pizza.

At ten minutes to twelve, Howell parked the station wagon where he could see the front door of the courthouse and waited. Bo's story had been gnawing at him for days. It was plausible enough, but the reporter in him wanted it confirmed. At the stroke of noon, the girl who worked in the records office left the courthouse and turned a corner, out of sight. Howell went and did some grocery shopping and returned just before one o'clock, in time to see the girl go back in. Shortly, Mrs. O'Neal, the battle-ax of County Records, left the courthouse. He had an hour.

The girl looked surprised to see him. "I thought we'd run you off," she said, laughing.

"I lost the battle, but not the war, I hope."

"You want me to look for the map for you?"

"Actually, there's something else I'd rather see. Can you find me an old deed of transfer? Maybe from twenty-four, twenty-five years ago?"

"Sure. We've got all those. I don't need to ask Mrs. O'Neal."

"Good." Howell read her the lot numbers he'd copied from the maps.

"Right this way."

He followed her across the room and down a long row of filing cabinets. She consulted the lot numbers and the labels on the drawers. "Here we are," she said. She opened the drawer, flipped through some files, and extracted a deed.

Howell skimmed through it, and it seemed straightforward enough. The property had been transferred from Donal O'Coineen to Eric Sutherland, and O'Coineen had signed it. Or had he? Howell thought for a moment. "Would you have a record of old business licenses?" he asked. In addition to being a farmer, O'Coineen had been a well digger, Enda McAuliffe had said.

"Sure. In what name?"

"Donal O'Coineen. Try 1951." He followed her to another row of filing cabinets.

"Here you are," she said, extracting a sheet of paper. "Here's the renewal application for 1951."

Howell walked over to a window for better light and compared Donal O'Coineen's signature on the application with the one on the deed. They were identical, or near enough. O'Coineen had signed over his land to Eric Sutherland, and almost immediately after that had taken his family and left the farm. Shortly afterward, the roadbed had given way and the farm had been obliterated. It all added up. Howell felt disappointed. The story had excited him, and now it was over. At least he could get back to work on Lurton Pitts's book now, with this O'Coineen thing settled in his mind.

He took the deed and the application back to the girl. "Thanks," he said. "I really appreciate it." As he was handing her the papers, his eye caught something, and he took them back. Under O'Coineen's signature on the deed was another signature.

The document had been witnessed by one Christopher F. Scully.

Scotty burst into the cabin, startling Howell, who was banging away on the word processor.

"I've got him, John!" she cried. "He's dirty and I've got him!"

Howell clutched his chest. "Well, do you have to give me a coronary in the process? I'm at that age, you know."

"You'll be younger than springtime when I've told you what I found," Scotty said, throwing herself on the sofa and kicking her feet in the air, her shoes flying off.

"All right, all right, what is it? What have you found?"

"Bo has got a passport," Scotty crowed triumphantly.

Howell looked at her incredulously. "So what? So have several million other Americans."

"Not in the name of Peter Patrick O'Hara, they haven't."

"Come again?"

"It's got Bo's picture in it, but O'Hara's name. It's a phony!"

"Is that it?"

"Huh?"

"Is that all you've got? You're going to ring up the FBI and turn him in for a phony passport? This is going to get you a Pulitzer? I can see the headlines in the *Times* now: 'INTREPID REPORTER CATCHES SHERIFF WITH INCORRECT TRAVEL DOCUMENT.' Swell."

"Well, listen, that's not all," Scotty replied, undaunted. "The only place he's been is Switzerland. Lots of times."

"Oh, that's different. Make that headline, 'REPORTER UNCOVERS SHERIFF'S SKIING HABIT.' "

"Come on, John, don't you know what's in Switzerland?"

"Alps."

"Banks, dummy. Secret banks. Banks you can walk into wearing a bad wig and a false nose, carrying a suitcase full of thousand-dollar bills, and they don't ask any questions."

Howell looked thoughtful. "What did you do with the copies of Bo's ledger sheets?"

"In your desk drawer."

Howell got them and spread them on the dining table. "Look at this," he said.

Scotty ran over. "What?"

"These lumps of numbers that were interspersed throughout the ledger pages. Look at this first group." He pointed.

```
D121 A 1845
F 0720
L002 F 1005
Z 1110
S241 Z 1611
F 1716
D122 F 1200
A 1645
```

"Okay, I'm looking."

Howell read through it and did some mental calculations. "Right. Yeah. It's just shorthand for an airline schedule. See? The times are on the twenty-four-hour clock. Depart Atlanta on Delta flight 121 at 6:45 PM, that would be, arrive in Frankfurt at 7:20 the next morning. Get Lufthansa 002 at 10:05, arrive Zurich at 11:10. Then back to Frankfurt on Swissair in the afternoon, and a noon flight back to Atlanta the next day."

"Great! Check the other groups."

Howell moved along the pages. "Some variations. Look, this time he came back through New York; another time he went out through New York; and here, he went through London instead of Frankfurt. Mixing it up. Doesn't want some bright immigration officer to remember his face."

"Don't they do any sort of checking on the passport in immigration or customs?"

"Yeah, they run your passport number through the computer to see if it's real and if you're some sort of problem—history of smuggling, that sort of thing."

"But his passport isn't real. Wouldn't they catch that?"

"It probably is real, just false. Bo wouldn't have much trouble running over to the courthouse, finding an old birth certificate of somebody
who's died, probably as an infant, and using that to apply. I don't know
if the State Department checks with the courthouse, but even if they
did, Bo would find that easy to handle."

"How does he get the money out, then?"

"Carries it. U.S. Customs doesn't look in your baggage on the way
out of the country, only on the way in. He wouldn't go through customs
in London or Frankfurt, because he's just changing planes inside a
restricted area. And Swiss customs, if they looked in his luggage,
wouldn't bat an eye. Can you imagine how much cash must get carried
into that little country every year?"

"How much money has he moved, then? Add it up."

Howell got a calculator and added the column of two-digit figures in
the right margin. "Well, if these figures represent money, he's got
$940,000 in a Swiss bank."

"Jesus Christ."

"Amazing how much savings a hard-working fellow can accumulate
in just over three years, isn't it?"

"But we've got him now. We've got the goods."

"Got him for what?"

"Well, to begin with, the passport. I've got the number, it could be
traced."

"Obtaining a false passport. Okay, my guess is that's a one-to-five
sentence in a country-club federal prison. With good behavior, out in,
say, eight months."

"Well, there's the drug dealing."

"What drug dealing? I don't know about any drug dealing. Neither
do you."

"But his ledger sheets."

"We don't know what the ledger sheets mean. A schedule, maybe,
but we don't know of what. Besides, all we've got is photocopies of
some numbers and letters. You could have forged those. You're familiar
enough with Bo's handwriting, aren't you?"

"Well, yes, but . . ."

"They were illegally obtained, too. Never stand up in court."

Scotty frowned. "Isn't it illegal to take large amounts of money out of
the country?"

"Nope. If you take out more than five thousand in cash or negotiable instruments at one time, there's a federal form you have to fill out, but he wouldn't bother. Now the money's gone. How're you going to prove he took it out?"

"His travel schedule. He's never spent much more than a day out of the country on these trips. It's obvious he's ferrying money, isn't it?"

"Obvious, maybe, but not provable. He likes skiing but gets tired the first day."

"How about the IRS? They could get him for tax evasion, couldn't they? I mean, that's how they got Al Capone."

"Evasion of taxes on what? I repeat, the money's gone. Nobody saw him take it, that we know of. Swiss banks don't talk to the IRS. Al Capone was a visible figure in lots of visible businesses."

"Well, Bo's dealing in drugs."

"I doubt it. Bo's too smart to push junk. I think he's being paid off by somebody to look the other way. That's what's going on. Maybe."

"Shit."

"Exactly."

"What now, then? How're we going to nail him?"

"How're *you* going to nail him, you mean. My interest lies elsewhere."

"Okay, how'm I going to nail him?"

"Well, he's been to Switzerland since his last payment, so there's no money in his mattress to find. But you've got this schedule. Whatever he's doing he does every few weeks. Let's see, it's five weeks since the last one, so, if he's still in business, he's due for another whatever-it-is pretty soon. If we can figure out what it is, and if you can catch him at it—I mean flat red-handed, squinting into a flashbulb—well, that's your best shot."

Scotty flopped down on the sofa, looking determined. "You're right," she said. "I'm going to have to catch him at it, whatever it is."

"And something else, Scotty. Something maybe a lot harder."

"What's that?"

"You're going to have to live to tell the tale."

"You're a real optimist, aren't you?"

"I'm a realist; you'd better be, too."

Howell got up and walked out onto the deck. Scotty followed him. It was dusk.

"Days are getting shorter," Howell said.

"Yeah, the leaves will be turning soon. Happens earlier up here than in Atlanta. They say it's gorgeous."

"Scotty, what is Bo's full name? Do you know?"

"Sure. He's touchy about it, though; prefers Bo. Sally told me. It's Christopher Francis Scully."

"I thought it would be."

"Why? Where'd you hear Bo's full name?"

"Pay attention for a minute. Eric Sutherland's story is that he went to see Donal O'Coineen alone and finally talked him into selling. Sutherland put the money in the bank, and O'Coineen and his family picked up and left. That's Sutherland's story, and Bo backs him up on it. Bo heard from the older girl, Joyce, later."

"That's what you've told me."

"The vision, or whatever it is, seems to back up Sutherland's story, too. A man in a 1940 Lincoln Continental convertible, top up, drives down the mountain to the farm, gets out, goes in, stays awhile—I don't know how long—leaves the house, drives away. Sutherland owned a Continental convertible, didn't sell it until the mid-fifties."

"I thought you were all through with the O'Coineen thing. What's got you back on to that?"

"I just thought it needed some more checking out. I went to the courthouse this afternoon and dug out the transfer deed that Sutherland filed and, just to check out O'Coineen's signature, his license for his well-digging business."

"Signature genuine?"

"Yep."

"So?"

"The transfer deed was witnessed by Bo Scully."

"Yeah? So?"

"That means Bo must have been at the meeting between Sutherland and O'Coineen."

"Okay, good."

"Yeah, except Sutherland says he went alone, and Bo says he wasn't out at the place for nearly a month before the O'Coineens left."

"Well, if he was at their meeting, why would Bo deny it?"

"That's what's got me stumped. The whole reason for any suspicion of Sutherland all these years—all the rumors that have sprung up—is that Sutherland's story of meeting with O'Coineen was unsubstantiated. If Bo was at the meeting and witnessed the document, then why hasn't he said so? Why hasn't he backed up Sutherland's story and taken the heat off him?"

Scotty gave a low chuckle. "You're hooked on this one, aren't you?"

"Yeah," Howell replied. "I guess I am."

"Hallooo."

Howell put down his razor and listened.

"Halloooo. Anybody home in there? *Halloooo."*

He got into some jeans and grabbed a towel.

"Hallooooo!"

It was nearly a howl now, echoing around the lake. He came out onto the deck to find a priest standing down by the water. The same priest he had seen in town early in his stay at the lake, a tiny man, very old.

"Good morning, Father," he said, wiping soap from his face. "I'm sorry I didn't hear you sooner."

"Ah, now," the priest called back. "I've come at a bad time, have I? Would another time be more convenient?"

"No, indeed. Please come on up and have some coffee."

The priest climbed the steps and at the top offered Howell his hand. "I'm Father Riordan," he said, "called by most, Father Harry. I'm very pleased to meet you, Mr. Howell."

"Call me John, please, Father Harry. Can I get you some coffee?" he asked, leading the way into the cabin.

"Would you have a bit of tea, now?"

"I think so, if you don't mind a teabag."

"Ah, that's fine, lad. Fine."

Howell made tea for both of them and took the pot out onto the deck. The sun was high; it was nearly noon. Howell poured the tea and made to sit down.

Father Harry cleared his throat. Howell stopped. "Was there something else I could get you, Father? Some toast?"

"Ah, do you think you might have a drop . . ."

"Of course, Father, but I don't have any Irish."

"Whatever will be fine," the priest said.

Jesus, he was starting early, Howell thought. He broke the seal on a bottle of brandy, walked back onto the deck, and poured a generous slug into the priest's tea.

"Ah, that's lovely," the man said, sipping it noisily. "Will you join me, now?"

What the hell, Howell thought, and poured some into his own cup.

"It's a grand place you've got here," the priest said, waving a hand at the view.

"I'm afraid it's only borrowed, Father. Belongs to my brother-in-law."

"Ah, yes, young White. I used to see him about. I've not met him." There seemed to be a note of disapproval in his voice.

"Well, now, Father, what brings you up this way? Just out for a stroll?" The priest seemed to have something on his mind. Howell wanted to make it as easy as possible for him.

Father Harry looked sympathetically at Howell. "I understood I might be of some service to you, lad."

Howell was nonplussed. He started to speak but didn't know what to say.

"Oh, I understand now. Forgive me, my boy. I was up to see Lorna Kelly, and she said you might need a word with me. I can see you weren't expecting me, but Lorna has a way with her . . . she sometimes knows these things just a bit before the rest of us."

"How is Mama Kelly?" Howell asked, to give himself time to think.

"Not well at all," the priest replied. "In fact, I don't know how she holds on. She seems to be waiting for something; I don't know what."

Howell wanted to ask about the O'Coineens but stopped himself. "Well, I don't feel any special need for spiritual help just at the moment, but I am interested in the history of this area. Have you been here for some time?"

"Oh, fifty-two years it is now, since I'm back. I'm eighty-one, you see." He looked at Howell as if he wanted to be told he didn't look it.

Howell thought he looked ninety if he looked a day. "Well, you certainly don't look it, Father," he said.

The priest accepted the compliment as his due. "Yes, it was nineteen hundred and twenty-three I was ordained at Maynooth, and I left Dublin on a steamer, eventually winding up at Savannah, as my fathers did."

"Your fathers?" Howell was puzzled. "I'm sorry . . ."

"Oh, I was born right here in the valley." He pointed out over the lake. "A fine view this spot has, then and now."

"So you went back to Ireland to enter the seminary, then?"

"I did. I was chosen to do that." The priest nodded toward the bottle. "May I?"

"Of course, Father," Howell replied, reaching for the brandy, but the priest was already pouring for both of them.

"You were chosen?"

"I'm getting a bit ahead of myself, I can see," Father Harry chuckled. "I should begin at the beginning." He resettled himself in the deck chair. "You see, our people first came up here from Savannah in the 1840s to work on the railroads."

"I'd heard that, but not much more."

"Well, not all at once and all together, but the Irish among the workers had a way of gathering, and some of them took their earnings and bought land here. Others joined them from the old country, and by about 1850 there was a thriving farm community in the valley—maybe forty families. And they needed a priest. There were not then, as now, a great many Roman Catholics in this corner of the earth."

"So I understand. The Church sent them a priest, then?"

"No, the community was too small to be sent a priest, so a lad from among the families went back to Ireland to the seminary. It was a long wait, but after a time the valley had a priest from among its own. The tradition continued, and I was the fourth in the line."

"Did the community grow a lot over the years, then?" Howell reckoned that forty Irish families could grow practically into a nation in a century and a quarter.

"No, I'm afraid it didn't," the priest said sadly. "It seemed that every time things were moving well in that direction, something happened. Nearly all the men in the community fought in the Civil War, and most of them didn't survive it. It took a great many years before the valley began to recover from that blow. Then, in '89, I believe it was, there was a smallpox epidemic that hit us particularly hard."

"I see."

"Oh, they were a hardy lot and couldn't be kept down. But there was the Great War, you know, and then a good many of the lads fought in Ireland after 1916. We recovered again, though, and after my return to the valley, things . . . well, things started to look up."

"Then came World War Two?"

The priest nodded and took a large gulp of his tea, now mostly brandy. "Exactly. Most disheartening, it was."

"And then what?"

Father Harry looked at John, then waved his hand. "Then there were . . . other problems."

"Other problems?"

"Then came the lake. Eric Sutherland's lake." The old man's voice was bitter and sad as he spoke the words. He poured himself another drink without asking.

"Tell me about Donal O'Coineen and his family," Howell said softly.

"Ah, Donal," the priest said, smiling a little. "Donal was the best of us. If we'd all hung on like Donal . . ." He let the phrase drop.

"What was he like?" Howell asked.

"A handsome lad; strong, industrious. He was always the hardest worker, the most successful. Married the prettiest girl, made the most money, had the most beautiful daughters."

"Joyce and Kathleen?"

"Yes, yes." The priest smiled. "And there'd have been more if there'd been the time." The brandy seemed to be getting to him now. God knows, it was getting to Howell. "Joyce lost her sight when only a young thing. She was the artist of the family, the musician. Sweet, kind, virginal girl."

Howell leaned forward. This was very important, somehow. "And Kathleen?"

A streak of pain flashed across the old man's face. Howell thought for a moment he was ill, but he continued. "She was the most beautiful creature I ever saw," Father Harry said softly. "A tiny thing, but strong, tough even. There was something in her I could never . . ." His voice trailed off.

Howell searched for something to say to keep the old man's train of thought going. "I understand Donal pulled her out of school when the pressure about the land got bad."

The priest shot him a scornful glance. "Nothing to do with the land, sir. You see . . ." He was fading again.

"Why did he take her out of school, then, if it wasn't because of the fight over the land?"

"She was only twelve. It was awful. Her father loved her so." He seemed on the verge of tears. "I thought it would kill him."

"What happened to Kathleen? Did she die?"

"It might have been more merciful if she had," Father Harry said. He was nodding now, with the brandy.

Howell struggled with his own load of brandy to keep the conversation going. The priest's eyes were closing now, his chin dropping to his chest. "Do you ever hear from them anymore? Donal O'Coineen and his family?"

Father Harry's eyes half opened for a moment. He looked confused. "Hear from them? Faith, lad, they're under the lake these many years." Then his chin dropped onto his chest again and he began to snore.

Howell stood up unsteadily and went into the living room. He could make no sense of all this. He dropped onto the sofa and laid his head back, just for a moment.

When he awoke, the sun was low in the sky and the old priest was gone.

Bo Scully picked up the phone on his desk, consulted his notes, and dialed the eleven digits. The switchboard answered on the first ring.

"May I speak with Mr. Murray in Credit, please?"

It had been nearly two weeks since Bo had written to Murray, and he had heard nothing. Sutherland was giving him a very hard time.

"Hello?"

"Mr. Murray, this is Sheriff Bo Scully of Sutherland County, Georgia. I talked with you a couple of weeks ago."

"Yes, Sheriff. Did you get my letter?"

"No, sir, I didn't. That's why I'm calling."

"Well, I sent you a copy of the credit application you asked for; it went out the day I got your letter, I believe."

"Well, sir, I haven't received it yet."

"That's the mails for you."

"Yessir. I wonder if I could trouble you to just give me the information on the phone? You do have my written request."

There was a deep sigh on the other end of the line. "Oh, all right. What was the name and account number again?"

"H. M. MacDonald." Bo read him the number.

There was a shuffling of papers and some muttering, then, "Here we are, Sheriff. H. M. MacDonald, 291 Cantey Place, NW, Atlanta 30327, phone (404) 999-7106. Employed by the *Atlanta Constitution*, Marietta Street, Atlanta . . ."

Bo missed the rest. He felt as if he had received an electric shock. He thanked the man and hung up. What the hell was going on here? He'd been told a reporter was being sent to Sutherland, but he had seen no one except Howell, and he knew Howell was who he said he was, because his picture had been in the paper so often. There had been no strangers at Sutherland's party; he'd known every soul there. What the hell was going on?

It made no sense to him whatever that a reporter would come to town and break into Eric Sutherland's office without asking at least a few questions around town. He dialed information and got the number.

"Good morning, *Atlanta Journal and Constitution.*"

"Mr. H. M. MacDonald, please." He would hang up as soon as the man answered.

There was a pause and the noise of pages being turned. "I'm sorry, we have no one by that name. Are you calling the *Constitution?*"

"Yes. Are you sure there's no H. M. MacDonald?"

"I'm afraid not."

"Any other MacDonald?"

"No, none at all."

He thanked her, hung up, and dialed another Atlanta number.

"You know who this is?"

"Yes."

"Is there a guy on the paper named H. M. MacDonald?"

There was a moment's silence. "No."

"You sure? I have reason to think this may be the man you warned me about."

"Positive. What makes you think so?"

"Just some recent information. I know he works there."

"Could be in classified or some other department of the paper. But there's no H. M. MacDonald on the editorial staff."

"Thanks." Bo hung up. He should have been relieved, but he wasn't. A credit card turning up at Sutherland's belonging to somebody who worked at the newspaper was just too much of a coincidence. He looked at the card. What could the initials stand for. Harold? Henry? What other names began with *H?*

He started to dial the Neiman's number again but felt embarrassed. Murray was already impatient with him. He felt a wave of annoyance with himself, and on an impulse dialed MacDonald's home number in Atlanta. The phone rang four times, and Bo was about to hang up, when there was a click on the line, followed by static. A voice distorted by bad sound quality, but somehow familiar, spoke to him.

"Hello, this is Heather MacDonald. I'm not around right now, and it might be a while before I get my messages, but if you'll leave your name and number at the tone, I'll get back to you sooner or later, I promise."

There was an electronic beep, then silence. Bo sat, disbelieving, with the phone in his hand.

There was a shriek from outside his office, followed by Mike's laughter and Scotty's shout. "Jesus Christ, Mike, will you stop that! You scared the shit out of me! C'mon, grow up, will you."

"Aw, come on, Scotty, a little goose is good for you now and then," Mike called back.

Bo hung up the phone. Heather MacDonald. Scottish. Heather M. MacDonald. Heather Miller MacDonald. Scotty. Scotty Miller. The voice was hers, static or no static.

Bo felt ill. He went into the bathroom, closed the door, and leaned on it. He ran some cold water and splashed it on his face. He sat down on the john seat and tried to think. He still felt sick. And angry, and stupid, and afraid. They weren't after Sutherland. *They were after Sheriff Bo Scully.*

Bo rested his hot face in his cool hands and tried to piece it together. How long had she been in the office? What had she seen? What could she know? Nothing, he tried to tell himself. Impossible for her to know anything. He had been too careful.

But he was still afraid. It had been a very long time since he had been so afraid.

Howell was pounding away on the word processor. He had, somehow, gotten inside the skin of Lurton Pitts, understood the man—or, at least, understood what he would want to read about himself. He had been cranking out a good twenty pages of autobiography a day since the first chapter had magically appeared on the monitor screen, and he was in full cry when the telephone rang.

"Hello?"

"It's Leonie."

"Well, hi. I'd been wondering what happened to you. I wanted to call, but you asked me not to."

"Yes, well, that would be awkward. It's better if I call you."

Howell glanced at his watch. "Why don't you come over this afternoon? We could . . . have a swim."

"No, I can't. That's not why I called."

"Oh?"

"Mama wants to see you."

"Oh. Is she better?"

"No, but she's conscious, which she hasn't been much, lately, and she's been asking for you. Can you come over?"

"When?"

"Right now. I think this is important."

"Of course. I'll be there in ten minutes."

"Make it five. I don't know how long she'll be awake."

"Okay." Howell hung up and reached for his car keys.

He covered the short distance in less than five minutes. He drove into the Kellys' yard and got out of the car. Dermot was sitting in the porch swing, picking tentatively at a mandolin.

"Hey, John."

"Hey, Dermot, how are you?"

"Real good." Riley, the blind dog, bounded down the front porch steps and pranced around Howell, apparently happy to see him. "See" seemed to fit. Howell had a hard time thinking of the dog as blind.

Howell scratched the dog behind the ears. "Hello, Riley. How you doin'?"

Leonie came out onto the porch. "Please come straight in, John. I don't think we should waste any time."

Howell followed her into the house, across the living room to Mama Kelly's bedroom. It was much as before. The room was neatly kept, and the old woman waited, a beautiful quilt thrown over her bed. Her white hair was freshly combed, and she was wearing a finely made bed jacket over her nightgown. She held out her hand for Howell's. She seemed terribly tired.

"Oh, John, I'm so glad you could come. I need to talk to you." Her voice was weak.

Howell took her hand. "I'm glad to come, Mrs. Kelly. I want to thank you for helping me with my back. Ever since Leonie worked on it, it's been really perfect."

"I'm glad we could help you, John. Now I want to say some things to you."

He strained to hear her. "Yes, ma'am?"

She took as deep a breath as she could manage. "You were brought here for a reason," she said. "I've been expecting you for a long time."

She had said this before. Howell nodded.

"You've come here to right a great wrong. I can't help you much, but I'll do what I can. You must be careful to keep your wits about you."

Howell looked at Leonie. She put a finger to her lips.

"Events are coming to a head now, and you must be ready. Please don't drink so much."

Howell said nothing.

Mama Kelly had to take several deep breaths before she could speak again. "You have seen some strange things, and they have a meaning. But all is not what it seems to be. You must be very careful."

"Do you mean the dream about the valley?"

"It may seem to be a dream, but it's not—not exactly a dream. Little Kathleen is in danger, and you must help her. If you don't help her, she may die. Do you understand?"

"No, ma'am, I'm sorry, I don't. Kathleen is either dead or gone away, isn't she?"

"All is not what it seems," the old woman said again. "I wish I could help you more." She closed her eyes and sighed.

Leonie beckoned to Howell to leave her, but when he tried, Mama Kelly clung to his hand.

Her eyes fluttered open. "Please remember that there is much here that will be hard for you to understand. You must try and understand. Your presence here has already done more good than you know. Believe me when I tell you that. But you must save little Kathleen. She is the future."

She sighed again, and her grip on his hand relaxed. Howell moved away from her and followed Leonie into the living room.

"Do you know what she's talking about?" he asked Leonie.

Leonie shrugged. "All I know is that *she* knows what she's talking about."

"She seems to think that Kathleen is still alive. Do you believe that? Or do you believe she's under the lake?"

Leonie bit her lip and did not reply.

"Kathleen would be how old now?"

Leonie sighed. "She was four years older than I was. That would make her thirty-six."

Howell thought for a moment. He knew no woman of any description in Sutherland who was that age. "Leonie, do you think Kathleen could still be alive? Please tell me."

Leonie shook her head. "I don't know, John. But if Mama believes she is, that's good enough for me."

Howell took her hand. "Listen, it's been a long time since I saw you. I miss you. Why don't you come over this afternoon?"

She put a finger to her lips, and nodded toward the front porch. The creaking of the swing could be heard. "I'll come when I can," she said.

As he drove home, Howell thought about what Mama Kelly had said. She didn't make sense. Kathleen O'Coineen was dead, and her whole family with her. Howell wasn't sure how he knew that, but he did.

When Scotty arrived at the office, Bo was there ahead of her, shut in his office working like a beaver. It was very unusual for Bo to arrive so early in the morning. She rapped on the glass and stuck her head in his office.

"Morning. Coffee?"

Bo was hunched over his typewriter. There were papers scattered all over his desk. Among them, Scotty saw the green ledger sheets. "No thanks, I've already had some. Take my calls, will you? I don't want to be disturbed."

"Sure." She closed the door and went to her desk. Bo rose, walked around his desk, and pulled down the shades between his office and the station room. She had never seen him do that before.

Scotty worked her way through the morning on routine matters. She did the mail and answered the phone, taking messages for Bo. Just before noon, the bell on the teletype rang once. Scotty went to the machine and tore off the printed message. It read:

PRSNL SHF B. SCULLY, STHRLND CO.
LSCA 0910 0330 80. CNFRM. MSG ENDS.

She ripped the message off the machine and went back to her desk, her heart pumping away. Quickly, she copied down every word and number, then put the original with Bo's phone messages. A few minutes later the shades went up in his office, and he came out with a large, thick brown envelope under his arm. The green ledger sheets were no longer on his desk, and the filing cabinet was locked. She handed him the messages; the white teletype paper was easily visible among the pink telephone message slips. Bo ignored the phone calls and went straight for the teletype message.

His face showed no emotion as he read it. He went back into his office, tossed the fat envelope onto his desk, and sat down. For the better part of ten minutes he sat there, obviously thinking hard. Then he got up, walked into the station room, went to the teletype machine and sat down.

Scotty grabbed some papers and made for the copying machine, just next to the teletype. Bo was already typing but suddenly stopped. As his hand went to the paper, she shot a quick glance at it, but he ripped the transmission copy away before she could read it. It had been a very short message; she had seen only the last word.

Bo stuffed the paper and the original message into his pocket, retrieved the large envelope from his office, and headed for the door. "I'll be at Mac McAuliffe's for a while, then at Eric Sutherland's, but don't call unless it's an emergency, okay?"

Half an hour later Bo left the lawyer's office, his business done—signed, witnessed, and relegated to McAuliffe's safe. It would be a long time before anyone read it, he reckoned. McAuliffe had not read what he had written, just witnessed his signature. Bo drove to Eric Sutherland's. He had made his decision.

Sutherland didn't waste time with pleasantries. "What have you learned?"

"I called Neiman's and talked with the credit manager. He hadn't had time to write to me yet, but he gave me all the information I wanted." Bo took a sheet of paper from his inside pocket and consulted it. "Harold Martin MacDonald is a seventy-one-year-old retired insurance salesman from Atlanta. His house was burglarized four weeks ago and his Neiman-Marcus credit card stolen. The store has already canceled the card and sent him a new one."

"What does this mean, Bo?"

"This is what's happened. Whoever burglarized MacDonald's house took the credit card. For some reason, he didn't throw it away. He's apparently an itinerant burglar. He showed up in Sutherland and was attracted to your office because it's set apart from the house. You can see it from a quarter of a mile down the road. He used the card to jimmy the lock, but your dog frightened him away before he had a chance to get into the office, and in his hurry to get away from Duchess and Alfred's flashlight, he dropped the card. Mystery solved."

"Were there any other burglaries in town?"

"No. I figure he was just passing through, and it looked tempting." Bo grinned. "I reckon that Yorkie of yours that thinks he's a Doberman scared him right out of town."

"Well." Sutherland sat back and sighed. "All that certainly makes sense. I suppose I should be relieved, but I still think Howell's up to something."

So did Bo, now that he knew who Scotty was. She and Howell were clearly working together, but they weren't after Sutherland. "Eric, I honestly don't think you have a thing to worry about. I think you've been so worked up about this that it's hard to let go of the idea, but please just try and relax, will you? Everything is okay."

Sutherland stood up. "You're probably right, Bo. Forgive me for hanging on to this idea for so long. I expect I'll get over it."

Bo left the house and drove slowly back toward town. He probably would never see the old man again, he knew. He was surprised to find that he felt some regret about that. After all, Sutherland had taken care of him. He'd demanded a lot, but he'd made Bo the second most powerful man in the county. God knows, he'd had a pretty good run.

But now, it was coming to an end. Scotty and John Howell had seen to that, even if they didn't know it. They couldn't know much, he reckoned. He'd been too careful for that. He didn't feel immediately threatened. Just one more would put him over the top. Then he wouldn't need Eric Sutherland anymore. He would be gone.

Howell looked at what Scotty had written down and compared it with the ledger.

LSCA 0910 0330 80

"Well, it fits, to a digit. I don't know about LSCA; we still have to figure that out. But if these columns are dates and times and amounts, what we've got here is September 10 at 3:30 AM and $80,000."

Scotty whistled. "That's the biggest payment so far. That'll put him over the million mark."

Howell nodded. "Must be pretty big, this one, whatever it is. And soon, too. The tenth is a week from tomorrow."

"Yeah, and the one word of his teletype I could see was 'CNFRMD.' Whatever it is, is on." Scotty wandered out onto the deck, and Howell followed. "You know," she said, "I have the feeling Bo is wrapping something up. He's been real busy the last few days, almost as if he were setting everything in order. That's the sort of person he is; no loose ends for Bo."

"Well," Howell said, "when you think about it, a million bucks is a pretty good cutoff. That's what everybody wants, isn't it? A million bucks? Maybe that was always his goal. Invested wisely, he ought to get an annual income of, say, a hundred and fifty grand out of that."

"Tax free? I could scrape by on that."

"Well, Scotty, maybe your pigeon is about to fly the coop. This could be your last shot at him."

Scotty nodded. Howell was right. It was more than just all the tidying up Bo was doing. His whole attitude seemed to have changed. Not just toward her. He still seemed embarrassed about their little roll in the hay, but there was something more. He had seemed sad, lately, as if he had lost something important.

"Well, we've got to figure out what LSCA is, that's all. We've got to catch him with his hand in the cookie jar."

"*You've* got to catch him. I don't much care about the cookie jar; I don't care how much he's got stashed in Switzerland. I want to know what happened to the O'Coineens, and Bo's got to know something about it. I still think he's shielding Sutherland."

"Well, look at it this way, old sport," Scotty said, digging him in the ribs, "if he pulls off whatever it is on the tenth and then splits, how's that going to help you? Maybe if we—I stress *we*—can catch him in the act, he'll be more in the mood to talk about what's under the lake." She went back into the house, got her purse, and sat down next to the phone.

Howell flopped down next to her. "I guess you're right," he said ruefully. "He's not going to be much help to me if he's in Switzerland."

Scotty took a small black object from her purse, dialed a number, waited, then held the black thing to the phone and pushed a button. "That's right," she said, "and don't you forget it." There was a silence on the phone, just a crackle of static, and then, from a distance, she heard her own voice shouting, "Jesus Christ, Mike, will you stop that! You scared the shit out of me! C'mon, grow up, will you." Then Mike's voice answered, "Aw, come on, Scotty, a little goose is good for you now and then." Then there was a click on the line.

Scotty hung up the phone. She felt as if she'd been struck in the chest with a heavy object.

"Scotty? Scotty? What's wrong?" Howell was looking into her face, worried. "What's the matter?"

"Oh, shit," she replied. "Bo knows."

Bo drove slowly out of town, north, then west along the lakeshore. All the car's windows were down, and the scent of pines blew faintly through. He remembered when he was in Korea; in the worst of times, when he wanted to summon some feeling of home, he would conjure up that scent, cool and evergreen.

The valley had smelled like that, too, before the lake, except when hay was being cut; then the two scents had mixed in a perfume that was headier than anything he had experienced since. He still loved the pine. The smell of new-mown hay made him claustrophobic and ill.

He circumnavigated the shining water in an unhurried fashion, taking in the trees, with their first hint of autumn color, and the light bouncing and playing on the lake's surface. Switzerland was beautiful, too, he remembered, but the thought didn't make him feel any better.

Everything was in place. The corporation had been formed—Central Europe Security—there was an accommodation address in Zurich, with an answering service on the telephone. The managing director was a Swiss lawyer who held the same position with God-knew-how-many other such paper corporations. An ad had been placed in a law enforcement journal, seeking applicants for a job with the company. The two dozen applicants had received letters saying that the job had been filled. Bo's application had, of course, been accepted. He had a stock of letterheads on which to outline the terms of his new contract, when the time came. The time was growing near.

He passed Taylor's Fish Camp and turned east along the south shore of the lake. The grocery store where John Howell had kept him from being blown away passed on his left. On the outskirts of the town, Bo stopped the car and got out. A freshly painted wrought-iron fence separated him from the cemetery. He found the gate and walked in. He had not been here for years.

It had been an oddly sympathetic thing for Eric Sutherland to do. After years of fighting the valley people for their land and finally getting it, he had, quite unexpectedly, exhumed the bodies from the valley churchyard and reinterred them here, at his own expense. Nobody had really thought about the cemetery, except, apparently, Sutherland.

Bo walked slowly among the headstones. Family names he had grown up among—all Irish—were etched on them. Most of the plots were ill-kept and overgrown. So many of the families had left when they sold their land, and others who still lived in Sutherland apparently didn't care. Bo himself had not been out here since the reinterment and consecration of the ground. He passed Patrick Kelly's grave. The plot had space for Lorna and her children when their time came. The Kellys still thought of themselves as valley, not town.

On a little rise at the center of the burial ground, under a large oak tree, he came to his own family plot. He stopped in astonishment. The grass was thick and freshly cut, and there were flowers no more than a day old on his mother's grave. He wondered who could possibly care about this when he himself had never bothered.

They were all distant figures to him. There was the small stone of his older brother, who had been retarded, and who had died at ten of polio the year a number of children had been killed or crippled by the disease. Then there were the stones of his mother, Deirdre, and her brother, Martin. Their deaths still bewildered him. When Bo was in Korea, Martin had shot Deirdre in the head, then turned the pistol on himself. Martin's mind had been going for years, people said, and had finally snapped. Bo could only remember how much they loved each other and him, and the pain of their deaths came back to him again. This was why he never visited the graves. He turned and walked quickly back to the car.

Bo sat in the car and rubbed at his eyes. He thought about Switzerland, and the thought made him homesick for where he was. Would it be this way when he was there, being paid a handsome yearly income by a fictitious firm, living high on the hog? He didn't want to go.

Maybe he could still save it here. Scotty and John Howell couldn't know anything. How could they? He had been too careful. But even if they did, why should he allow them to drive him away? He began to feel an increasingly strong resolve to stay and survive. God knows, he was a survivor if he was anything. And anyway, Eric Sutherland might really come through one of these days. McAuliffe had let slip that Sutherland had made a new will. Bo wondered what was in it. There might be a lot to stay for, after all. The money he had stashed in Switzerland was nothing compared to what Sutherland would leave.

It had been a long time since Bo had killed anybody, but to preserve what he had here, to keep from being uprooted from a place he loved, that might be a price worth paying again. Anyway, if he had to, he could find a way to do it and get away with it. The thought of doing it to Scotty stabbed at him, but, he was beginning to see, it might not be possible to avoid it.

"I thought you intercepted the letter."

"I did, but when he didn't hear from Neiman's, he must have called them."

"Well, you're fucked now, Scotty."

"So give me some advice. You're the ace reporter, what do I do now?"

"Do? Why, you get your ass out of here in a hurry, that's what you do."

"Why?"

"Why? Jesus, because Bo can't let you go on doing what you're doing. He's got to take you out of the picture, and, probably, me with you. Listen, Scotty, take the ledger sheets to the Georgia Bureau of Investigation. If you can find a sympathetic ear there, you might get somebody to issue a search warrant, then swoop down on Bo and find not just the ledger sheets, but other stuff too. There's the passport charge. You might get a decent story out of it yet. All this time undercover, working in his office—you should be able to get some good stuff in print."

"What stuff? How I collected parking tickets and ran the radio on Mike's lunch hour? Boy, that's really sexy, isn't it? No, I want more than that."

"But you can't get it now. Don't you see that? He's not going to make a wrong move while you're around—that is, if he allows you to go on living."

"He's going to make a move on the tenth of this month. Look at it from his angle, John. He's pretty cocky, you know. He'll think he can pull off this next thing right under my nose."

"Well, he wouldn't be too far off the mark, would he? All you've got is this schedule, and even though you know when it's going to happen, you don't know what or where, do you?"

"Well, no, but I've still got a week to find out, haven't I?"

"No, you haven't. You won't live a week. Listen, Scotty, if you don't pack up and get back to Atlanta *today*, I mean right *now*, I'm going to go to Bo and tell him who you are and blow your whole ballgame." Howell knew, even as he said this, that it didn't carry much conviction, but he felt he had to try to get her to protect herself.

"He already knows who I am, smart-ass, or thinks he does. If you do that, I'll come up with a good story. I'll tell him I was dipping into my expense money at the paper and got fired and changed my name out of shame and came up here to lose myself. Anyway, if I go, you've got to go too. He'll know you know everything I do. How can you find out about the O'Coineens then?"

That stopped Howell in his tracks for a moment. "No, no," he said, but with even less conviction, "if he brings it up, I'll just tell him that you came up here to find out if he was dirty, then couldn't find out anything and left."

"Oh, yeah? You think he'd buy that? Bo's a lot more careful than that."

"Scotty, please, know when you're licked. Go."

Scotty stood up. "I'm going to work," she said emphatically.

"You're going to get blown away, Scotty."

She rummaged in her handbag. "Oh, no, I'm not," she replied, pulling out a small revolver and waving it above her head. "I'll defend myself if I have to."

"Oh, no, no, no," Howell howled.

"And I know how to use it, too," she said triumphantly. "I took a course."

"Yeah? What gun did you shoot with?"

"A police thirty-eight."

"Well, what you've got there is a twenty-five caliber Saturday Night Special with a two-inch barrel. Just remember that you won't be able to hit anything more than a few feet away, and that it probably won't stop what you hit. All that will do is just help you get killed faster." He reached for it. "Give me that."

She snatched it away and dropped it into her purse again. "No, sir. I'm hanging on to it, and I'll use it if I have to." She started for the door.

Howell felt totally helpless. "Scotty."

She turned. "Yeah?"

"Bo knows. You know Bo knows, but Bo doesn't know you know he knows." Howell shook his head to clear it. "I think that's right. Anyway, that's all you've got going for you, that he doesn't know you know he knows."

"This is starting to sound like an Abbot and Costello routine."

"You know what I mean."

"Yeah, I know."

"Don't back him into a corner, Scotty. Let him think he's in control. And for God's sake, don't let yourself end up alone with him, okay?"

Scotty nodded. "Okay. That's good advice. That's what I need from you now, John, good advice. See you later."

Howell watched her walk down the steps to her car, then he closed the door and leaned on it. They were in a whole new ballgame, now, and he didn't like it at all.

28

Howell paid for the groceries at the supermarket and waited while a teenager bagged them. His eye wandered about the store and stopped. A glass partition separated the modern grocery store from its equally modern drug department a few steps away. On the other side of the glass, he saw Leonie Kelly paying for something at the prescription counter. He turned to the boy bagging the groceries and handed him half a dollar. "Just put them in the green station wagon over there," he said, pointing toward the parking lot.

He started toward the door, glancing through the glass again to see if Leonie had left, then he saw something he had not bargained for. She was walking toward the front of the drugstore, her back to the clerk at the prescription counter; as she passed near a shelf, she reached out, took a packet of something, and dropped it into her handbag.

Howell watched her leave the store without paying for it, then hurried to catch up with her. "Leonie!" he called out.

When she turned, she did not look glad to see him. "Sorry, I can't stop to talk right now. I've got to get back to the house. Mama needs some medicine. I've just had her prescription filled."

"I'll walk you to your car, then," he said, falling into step with her. She said nothing. "Listen, I could grow old waiting for you to call me. Why don't we get together the next day or two?"

"I can't. Mama needs me all the time now. I just can't get away."

She seemed very cool and distant. They had reached the Kelly truck, and she climbed into the driver's seat. Her sister, Mary, waited patiently for her. "Hey, John," the girl said.

"Hey, Mary." He turned to Leonie. "Listen, things must be pretty rough for you right now. Can I lend you a few hundred bucks to help get you through this?"

She looked at him, surprised. "Why on earth do you think I would take any money from you?" She seemed insulted by the idea.

"Well, look," he said, lowering his voice so that Mary wouldn't hear him, "taking a few bucks from a friend beats shoplifting, any day." She looked taken aback. "I saw you in the drugstore," he said, feeling immediately guilty, as if he had been deliberately spying on her.

She flushed angrily and turned to start the truck. "I think it would be better if you just minded your own business," she said, and drove quickly away, nearly knocking him down.

Howell watched the truck disappear, then walked to his own car. The grocery boy was putting the last bags into the rear of the wagon. He started the car and drove toward the Kellys' house. Leonie and her family, he was now beginning to realize, were people he had become fond of, indeed the best people he had met in this town. He felt for her, an attractive and intelligent woman, trapped in circumstances that were not of her making, who had paid him the compliment of wanting to make love to him. He had given precious little back, and he felt badly about it. He wanted to help. He didn't want Leonie stealing in order to make ends meet for her family while her mother was dying a slow and painful death.

But by the time he was nearing the Kelly house, he was reconsidering. A direct approach when she was embarrassed and angry might not be the best way. Perhaps he should wait and talk with her later, instead. When he came to the Kelly driveway he drove on past, idly following the road.

He had driven only a couple of hundred yards when an enormous roar from above made him duck reflexively. He leaned forward and looked up to see a light airplane passing over very low, gaining altitude slowly. Where the hell had that come from? A moment later, he knew. He stopped the car and stared at the sign in front of him:

SUTHERLAND COUNTY AIRPORT

Howell knew where to find Bo at this hour of the day. He tapped the sheriff lightly on the shoulder as he slid into the booth with him. "Join you, Bo?"

"Sure thing, John. Make yourself at home." Bo seemed just a bit cooler than his usual self.

"Cheeseburger and a beer, Bubba," Howell called across the room. Bubba nodded.

They traded idle chat until the food arrived. Then Howell took a deep breath. "Bo, there's something we have to talk about."

Bo looked wary. "What's on your mind?"

"It's been bothering me ever since we had the conversation about the credit card."

"Yeah?" Bo sipped his coffee and waited.

"The card is Scotty's, Bo."

Bo lifted an eyebrow, set down his coffee cup, and looked at Howell for a moment. "Tell me about it," he said finally.

He was good, Howell thought, Academy Award good. "Scotty's name is MacDonald, not Miller. Heather MacDonald. She's a reporter at the *Constitution*, or at least, she was until recently."

Bo sat back and looked at Howell, all amazement. "You kidding me, John?"

"Nope, afraid not. She heard some rumor or other about your being dirty and—"

"Where did she hear that?" Bo interrupted. His curiosity was not feigned.

"I'm not sure, from somebody at the capitol, I think. Anyway, there was nothing to back it up. Scotty just got a wild hair up her ass about it. There can't have been much to it, because the paper wouldn't send her up here to work on it. In fact, they fired her for being a pain in the ass."

"Then what's she doing here?"

"Oh, she had grand visions of breaking a big story all on her own, so she quit her job, got together some tame job references, and just came on up here. She reckoned if it panned out, they'd welcome her back with open arms."

"Well, that's the damnedest thing I ever heard," Bo laughed, slapping the table. "She sure had me for supper."

"Oh, you'd have figured it out already, but she swiped the reply to your letter to Neiman's."

"Funny you should mention that; I was getting ready to call that guy in Dallas."

"I figured you would, eventually. That's why I wanted to tell you this now."

Bo wrinkled his brow. "Why is that? Why are you telling me about it?"

"Well, I didn't want you to fly off the handle when you heard about it. She hasn't really done any harm, and she's on the point of giving up the whole thing and going back to Atlanta. She'll be coming in any day now, telling you her mother's sick or something, and that she has to leave."

"You been working on this with her? Is that why you're up here?"

"Oh, hell, no. I'm up here to work on a book, just like I told you. Well, not exactly like I told you." Howell looked around and lowered his voice. "I'm not working on a novel. I'm ghost-writing an autobiography for Lurton Pitts."

"Fried chicken Lurton Pitts?" Bo looked skeptical.

"The same, and if you ever tell anybody about it, I'll kill you, Bo. It's hack work for some fast money, and I don't want anybody ever to know I did it. Neither does Pitts, for that matter."

Bo still was unconvinced. "Listen, John, it's time you were straight with me all the way."

"Denham White is Pitts's lawyer. He got me the job. I kid you not, Bo. Come on out to the cabin and I'll play you the tapes and show you the manuscript. Wouldn't you like to hear from the horse's mouth how ol' Lurton found God?"

Bo laughed and shook his head. "No thanks, I'll take your word for it." His laughter faded. "How long you known Scotty?"

"I recognized her the first time I walked into your office—she started on the paper a few months before I left, and I'd seen her around the newsroom—so I went along with her." Howell chuckled. "I can tell you she's been going nuts and getting nowhere."

"Well, of course not. I told you I'm as clean as a hound's tooth, didn't I? What was she hoping to find out?"

"I don't know—fixing speeding tickets, taking bribes. Half the sheriffs in Georgia are into that sort of stuff, I guess."

Bo looked vastly relieved. "Well, she could grow old trying to pin any of that shit on me."

"Look, Bo, I don't want you mad at her. I mean, she's harmless. She's gotten to like you a lot, and I think she's pretty much ashamed of herself."

"Well, I ought to kick her little ass, I guess, but I'm not mad."

"Well, look, can you just let it ride? She's already given up. Really. She's just hanging on because of her pride—you know how she is."

"Yeah, she's pretty cocky, all right."

"She really thinks she's pulled the wool over your eyes. Leave her that, anyway. She'll go back to Atlanta and beg her job back thinking she's the ace undercover reporter; that there just wasn't anything to find. And if your name ever comes up again at the capitol or at the paper, she'll defend you to the death on the grounds that if she couldn't pin anything on you, nobody could. Anyway, if she ever knew I told you, she'd kill me in my sleep."

Bo roared. "Oh, Jesus, she sure would, wouldn't she?" He laughed until the tears ran down his face.

He was biting, Howell thought. Hoped. "We got a deal, then? Not a word to her? Not ever?"

"All right, buddy. She'll never know I knew. But you realize I've got something on you now. You ever cross me, and I'll tell her you told me. You wouldn't live another twenty-four hours!" He dissolved in laughter again.

Howell left Bubba's a few minutes later thinking he'd done the right thing. After all, he hadn't told Bo much of anything he didn't already know. If things worked the way he hoped they would, most of the heat would be off Scotty, and Bo might think he was home free.

He'd be damned if Bo would be home free. With what he knew now, he and Scotty had a chance of taking him. Just a chance. He didn't feel as good about that as he should have, Howell thought. He genuinely liked Bo; he wished the man were as clean as he said he was.

Howell was in gear now on Lurton Pitts's autobiography. He had outlined a book which was close to the order in which Pitts had placed things in his tape recordings, and he could sit for three or four hours at a time, marshaling all the skills that his newspaper career had earned him, typing words into the word processor as fast as he could think them. It would be a short book, he reckoned; no more than a hundred and fifty or sixty pages when set in type, an ideal length, Howell thought. It was bad enough being a hack; he would have felt like a criminal if he had needlessly prolonged the agony of a reader who, for whatever reason, felt he had to get through the book.

He stopped for a moment and searched his mind for a reference. Unable to come up with it, he flipped through the boxes of tape for the reel onto which he had dictated his original notes. He threaded the tape and fast-forwarded halfway through it, then listened. To his surprise, not his own voice but that of Bo Scully came out, talking about the O'Coineens, of having received a letter from Joyce, written for her by Kathleen. He remembered that he had been using the recorder in its voice-activated mode on the day of that visit from Bo. He listened to Bo's story again, then stopped the tape and rewound it. He wasn't sure why, but he thought it might be a good idea to hang on to that recording.

He heard Scotty's car outside, and a moment later, she bustled in. "What's for dinner? Anything left to eat around here?"

"I went to the grocery store this morning," Howell said, filing the tape away. "We've got everything."

"Terrific. I'm starved."

"The down side is, you have to cook. I'm bushed. Been working like a dog all afternoon."

"Drink?"

"Sure. Bourbon. I deserve it."

"Come on," she said, handing him his drink, "I can't believe you've been working *that* hard."

"Oh, not just the book. I've been at the deduction game today, too. I've figured some things out, I think." He opened a desk drawer and got out the sheets copied from Bo's schedule.

"What you got?"

"Before I tell you, I think you ought to know I had lunch with Bo today and blew whatever little cover you might have left."

Scotty stared at him. "You did *what?*"

"I told him everything. How you were a silly little cub reporter who, when your paper wouldn't go along with you, left your job—got canned, actually—to work on an unsubstantiated rumor; how you beat your brains out and found nothing; how you'll probably cave in before long and go back to Atlanta with your tail between your legs."

"The hell I will."

"Yeah, but I'd rather Bo thinks you will. It might help keep you . . . both of us, alive."

Scotty's eyebrows went up. "I see, I see. Good move. What can it hurt?"

"Us, if you get cocky. I'm not at all sure Bo bought it. The best thing we can do for ourselves is act as though he didn't."

"I get your point. Now, what did you deduce today?"

"Actually, I got lucky. There wasn't much deduction to it." Howell spread out the ledger sheets. "I figured out what LSCA is."

Scotty hunched over his shoulder. "What? What?"

"Well, SCA is Sutherland County Airport."

"What? I didn't even know there was a Sutherland County Airport."

"There almost isn't. It's a grass strip less than a mile from here, just past the Kelly place. There are a couple of light aircraft up there that don't look much used. There's a disused shack—apparently there used to be a local flying club—a wind sock and, most important, runway lights."

"Landing, Sutherland County Airport," Scotty read out, looking at the sheets. "LSCA."

"What else?"

"And we know what day and what time," she shouted gleefully.

"We do, unless it's changed," Howell said. "That's why I told all to Bo; I don't want him getting nervous and making new arrangements. Still, you better keep a sharp eye on the teletype, okay?"

"Sure thing. And I want to go up there and take a look at the landing field."

"Absolutely not. I don't want you anywhere near the place. We don't know who's in this with Bo. He might have the place staked out for days ahead of time. I only hope nobody saw me poking around."

Scotty nodded. "I see what you mean. Well, do we have enough to go to the GBI or the feds now?"

"Yeah, we might have, but I don't think we'd better do that just yet."

"How come? We're going to need a stakeout at the airfield on the night. I don't much fancy trying to arrest Bo ourselves; like you say, we don't know how many others are involved."

"Don't worry, we're not going to try that. But I don't think we can just telephone the law, either. Bo's getting his schedule on a statewide law-enforcement teletype. His messages could be coming from any state, county, local, or federal office hooked up to it. If we yell cop now, there's no telling who might hear us. If somebody cancels the landing, then what have we got?"

"A phony passport charge. Apart from that, zip."

"Right. So I think our best bet is to go up to the landing strip that night and get some substantiation of our charges. If we can prove it's happening and, maybe, place Bo there, then the law will have to move on it. Certainly the newspaper will."

"Oh, yeah," Scotty crowed, "they'll jump a mile high when I come in with this."

"Well, if you want them to jump that high, you'd better come in with some pictures, I think. You've got a camera up here, haven't you?"

"A Nikon and five lenses."

"Good. I called a fellow I know, and he's sending us half a dozen rolls of some extremely light-sensitive film. We'll be able to get faces and numbers on an aircraft in nothing more than starlight." Howell turned and pulled her around to face him. "Now look, Scotty, we've only got a few days to go. Don't get too eager around the office, okay? If we blow this, somebody could get hurt, and it would almost certainly be us."

"I'll be cool, I promise," she said.

"And I want the gun. Now."

Scotty pulled back. "I don't know . . ."

"Listen, the heat's off with Bo. You can only get yourself into trouble with that gun."

She turned her eyes to the floor for a moment and thought. "Oh, shit, all right," she said finally. She went to her handbag and fished out the little revolver.

Howell unloaded it and put it and the bullets in his desk drawer. He felt better now, but they had only three days, and he had the feeling that if he didn't resolve the O'Coineen question by that time, he might never have the chance again. He had a lot to do in the meantime.

30

Bo left the office and drove slowly through the town. He had been relieved when John Howell had come clean about Scotty, but now something felt wrong. He knew from reading Howell's investigative stuff and his book that he was a clever and tenacious reporter, and Bo felt himself getting off a little too easily where Howell was concerned. His description of Scotty as a green cub rang true, and he now felt little fear of her, but Howell was another matter. Bo was worried.

He had nearly a million in Switzerland, and if he was going to stick it out here, what was the point of taking this risk for another eighty thousand bucks? He was greedy, but he wasn't stupid. Alarm bells he didn't even understand were going off, and he was listening.

He reached the parking lot outside Minnie Wilson's grocery store a couple of minutes before the hour and sat in the car for a bit. When there was half a minute left, he got out of the car, went to the pay phone in the parking lot, dialed a number, fed the phone some quarters, and waited. The phone was answered before the first ring was complete.

"Okay, I got your message."

"We've got problems; I'm canceling."

"What problems?"

"There's a reporter up here sniffing around." Bo didn't feel it necessary to mention that the reporter had been working in his office for more than three months. "Apparently there have been some rumors."

"Does he know what, where, and when?"

"No, but—"

"No buts. We're on."

Bo began to sweat. "*I* say whether we're on or not. It's off."

"Scully, let me tell you something. This delivery has been in the works for nearly a year. The stuff has been stockpiling in a jungle for that long. What we've been bringing in in light planes the last couple of years is nothing compared to this. A lot of time and a lot of money have been invested, and the people who invested it are expecting a big return. Why do you think your end is eighty?"

"Now, listen—"

"Ours is the third of three aircraft to be used to keep the feds off the track. We're on a tight schedule; we have to pick up on time, and we have to deliver on time. My plane left this morning; it picks up tomorrow; it delivers when you were told it would. If you've got problems on your end, solve them. You understand me? Listen, because I'm telling you this like a friend. You confirmed a week ago. Everything is in motion now. If that load doesn't deliver and distribute when we said it would, you will be the only reason. The people we're dealing with won't let you live an hour. You think there's no backup at your end? They'll be there. That plane lands, unloads, and takes off on schedule, or you're a dead man. There, on the spot. Is that plain enough for you?"

Sweat was rolling out of Bo's armpits and down his body. "Yeah, I guess so."

"No guessing. We're on as confirmed, right?"

"Yeah, okay."

"Say it. Confirmed."

"Confirmed."

"I'll tell them you said so." The connection was broken.

Bo hung up and pressed his forehead against the cool glass of the phone booth. He had never thought they'd have anybody on the ground here. Maybe that was a bluff, but probably not. If what his contact had said about the load was true, backup on the ground made a lot of sense. It was the sort of thing he'd do himself, if he were running things. He took a couple of deep breaths and resigned himself to what was coming. He'd just have to make sure it went smoothly.

Bo got back into the car. As he started to pull into traffic, he glanced down the road and saw something that interested him. A few hundred yards away, in the little hilltop cemetery, were two men. One was on his hands and knees, doing something to some shrubbery, the other stood over him, watching him work. Bo put on the emergency brake and reached into the glove compartment for his binoculars.

The man tending the Scully family plot was the filling station attendant, Benny Pope. The man reaching into his pocket for money and paying him was Enda McAuliffe.

He watched as McAuliffe walked back to his car and drove toward town. Bo put the car into gear and followed. The lawyer parked in front of his office, put some money into the parking meter, and walked down the street to Bubba's. Bo parked and followed him in.

"How you doin', Mac?" Bo asked as he slid into the booth opposite the lawyer.

"Not bad, Bo."

Bo ordered coffee and stirred in some sugar. "Mac," he said, gazing out the window into the middle distance, "I was out at the old cemetery the other day—first time in a real long time—and I couldn't help but notice that my family's plot was very nicely taken care of, even had some fresh flowers. I was surprised, because I never did anything to the plot myself, and everybody who's related to me around here is buried in it."

Bo stopped for a reaction. There was none. McAuliffe sat looking at the table, drinking his coffee.

Bo continued. "I was especially surprised because just about all the other plots, your family's included, were rough and grown over. And yet, just a few minutes ago, I saw you out there, paying Benny Pope to work on my family's plot. Now, I don't want you to think I don't appreciate your thoughtfulness, but I sure am curious as to why you would do something like that for my folks when you wouldn't do it for yours?"

McAuliffe took a sip of his coffee and put down the cup. "I'm sorry, Bo, but I can't talk to you about that."

Bo looked at the lawyer in amazement. "Why not?"

McAuliffe put a half-dollar on the table and got up. "Coffee's on me, Bo, but I can't talk to you about the cemetery. Please don't ask me again." He turned and walked out of Bubba's.

Bo sank back into the booth and watched the lawyer leave. He sat there drinking coffee for nearly an hour, letting his mind drift around the problem, and finally something occurred to him—just a fleeting idea. As he considered it, it began to make sense; all the known circumstances fit, and if there was anything at all to what he thought, he had a new reason to sit tight in Sutherland County, and the hell with Switzerland.

A crunch was coming, he could feel it. And, he reflected, in a crunch Bo Scully had a way of protecting himself. He had learned a long time ago about his instinct for self-preservation—in Korea and afterward—and he had no doubt that, when the time came, he would again do whatever was necessary to survive. It wouldn't matter who got hurt. It hadn't mattered before, although he still sometimes dreamed about it, and it wouldn't matter this time, either. He would do what had to be done.

Enda McAuliffe let himself into his office, hung up his coat, and flopped heavily onto his new sofa. He wondered how he had let himself land in the middle of all this. He got up and opened his new safe, got out the file, and read through the document again. He didn't want to know all this stuff. If he'd had any idea what had happened so many years ago, he might never have gotten mixed up in this, but now he knew nearly everything and suspected more. He stared at the other envelope in his safe, Bo's signed and witnessed document. With some difficulty, he resisted the urge to rip it open and read the contents.

He knew that Howell was on to something, too. Father Harry had told him about his visit to Howell's cabin and the questions asked. He hoped the lecture he had given the old man had put a stop to any more idle chatter from him. And to think it was he himself who had first put the flea in Howell's ear. What a stupid, mischievous thing to do; but he hadn't known that at the time. He had been out just to annoy Eric Sutherland, to pick at his scabs. If only he'd known more at the beginning. If only Sutherland had told him the truth sooner.

The genie wasn't going back into the bottle, he could feel that. Maybe he could, somehow, limit the damage. He didn't see what else he could do.

31

Howell was as nervous as a cat. It was the morning of the ninth; Bo Scully's shipment was due to arrive at three thirty the following morning, and nothing was going right. He wished he had a few more days, another week maybe, to bring it all together. The goddamned film hadn't even arrived, and without it, Scotty wasn't going to get any photographic evidence; in the circumstances, she could hardly use a flash. He had called Atlanta twice and had been assured it was on the way.

But what worried him even more was that he was stuck on the O'Coineen mystery, absolutely stuck. He had thought that somehow he could bring that to a head along with Scotty's evidence against Bo, but it wasn't happening. He was losing, he could feel it.

There were a couple of things he needed to know, but he didn't know how to find them out. He had been to see the priest, Father Harry, but the old man had clammed up tight, after accepting a bottle of good Irish whiskey. He suddenly didn't want to talk about the O'Coineens again. Somebody had gotten to him, Howell thought.

He walked up to the mailbox and found a special delivery notice. At least the film had arrived; that lazy bastard of a postman might have brought it to the house. Special delivery, my ass, Howell thought. Still, he didn't mind going into town; he was too nervous to work. There was also a letter, forwarded from Atlanta: a *New York Times* envelope, hand addressed, the name "Allen" written in the upper left-hand corner. His old boss. Not like him to send personal notes, Howell thought. He ripped it open. "Dear John," it said. "Don't know what you're doing with yourself these days. Nairobi's opening up next month. You want it?" No closing; it was signed "Bob."

Howell crumpled the letter and threw it as far as he could. Nairobi! It had been a running joke between them for years as the place in the whole world he would least like to work. You could always go back to the *Times* once, they said. This was that sadistic bastard Allen's way of saying if he wanted to go back, he'd have to crawl. The letter wasn't even worth replying to; Allen could go fuck himself. That sort of aggravation was all he needed today, with everything else on his mind.

The station wagon wouldn't start. Howell tried repeatedly before he was able to admit to himself that he had let it run out of gas. He pounded silently on the steering wheel a few times, then he called Ed Parker's filling station; Ed promised to send out some gas right away.

After a few minutes, Benny Pope pulled up in Ed Parker's pickup truck and unloaded a five-gallon can from the back. He grinned at Howell. "You run right out, did you? Well, that's what we're here for."

Howell watched Benny empty the can into the fuel tank. He got behind the wheel and, after a few tries, the engine came to life again.

"Well, I'll be getting back," Benny said, and turned to go to the truck.

"Hang on a minute, Benny," Howell said.

Benny stopped and came back, his usual grin in place. "Yessir, anything else I can do for you?"

"Benny, you don't like it around here, do you?"

Benny looked puzzled. "Why, sure," he said. "I've never lived anywhere else. I was born and raised right here. I like it fine."

"No, I mean right here, around this cabin, around this part of the lake."

Benny's grin disappeared.

Howell kept his voice friendly and gentle. "I remember a while back, you said you didn't want to come up here at night, and the day you brought the outboard out here, you wouldn't go out on the water. Why was that?"

"Well . . . the cove just makes me nervous, that's all."

"Something happen to you here, Benny, in the cove?"

"Yessir," Benny said with no further hesitation, "you could say I've had a couple of experiences around here I wouldn't want to go through again."

"Something to do with the O'Coineens?"

Benny looked surprised. "You know about the O'Coineens?"

"Not as much as I'd like to. Tell me about your experiences."

Benny leaned against the fender of the pickup and pointed out over the lake. "Well, I was out there one night, right out there, fishing, and I seen under the lake."

"Benny," Howell said, "I know it's early, but let me buy you a drink."

They went into the house and Howell poured them both a generous bourbon. Half an hour later Howell knew that he and Benny Pope had been sharing a vision; only for Benny, it had been the real thing.

"I know you're sure it was Eric Sutherland's car, Benny, but are you sure he was driving it?"

Benny screwed his face up tight with the remembering. "Well, now you mention it, I can't say that I am. It was Mr. Sutherland's car; I just reckoned it was him driving it."

Howell leaned forward in his chair. "Now, Benny, what happened after the car drove away? Do you remember that?"

"Well, sir, you understand I was a little bit worse for wear that night. I'd been at some shine for quite a little while. I used to come up here to the picnic place some nights and have a few."

"Do you remember anything at all after the car drove away?"

"Just a noise. It was like a loud noise from a long way off. I guess I dozed off after that; I didn't wake up until after daylight."

"Did you look at the O'Coineen house again when you woke up?"

"Yessir, I did. Leastways I looked where it used to be. It was under the lake."

Howell picked up the film at the post office and signed for the package. Then he began to drive south through the town. There were only two people who could tell him what he wanted to know about that night in 1951. One of them had already lied to him about it; now it was time to go and see the other one.

It would have only caused trouble to approach Eric Sutherland before, but now the Lurton Pitts autobiography was nearly finished; even if Sutherland got mad it couldn't matter much. It occurred to Howell that if Sutherland had got rid of the O'Coineens, he might feel no compunction about getting rid of a nosy reporter. He felt it might be prudent to tell Sutherland that he had shared his suspicions with people in Atlanta. That would give him some sort of insurance. Confronting Sutherland might be an incautious thing to do, but Howell had the very strong feeling that it was now or never, that he was running out of time.

He pulled into the circular drive of the big house and parked at the front door. The atmosphere was peaceful; the sun shone, flowers bloomed. Howell wondered whether it would be so peaceful after he had bearded the lion in his den.

He got out of the car and walked to the front door, which was ajar. He pressed the doorbell and heard the chimes clearly from inside. No one came to the door. Where was old Alfred? Off doing the grocery shopping? Wasn't there a cook, too?

Howell pushed the door open a foot and stuck his head in. "Hello!" he called out. "Anybody home?" He found himself hoping there wouldn't be. He was still a little afraid of Sutherland. And he would dearly love a few minutes alone in his house.

"Mr. Sutherland?" He pushed the door open farther and stepped into the entrance hall. There was a small echo as his heel met the gleaming mahogany floor. "Hello? Anybody home?" He walked boldly down the hall, straight through to the door opening onto the broad rear veranda, with its commanding view of the lake. There was no one out back, either. He walked down the back lawn to the little office building he had once broken into. No one there; the door was locked, and he didn't have a Neiman's charge card this time.

He walked quickly back to the house and called out again a couple of times. He was apparently alone in the house, for however short a time, and it was tempting. He had already had a thorough look in Sutherland's office; now he wondered what might be in the study. Making no effort to be quiet, just in case someone was in the house, he walked toward the study. As he approached it, he could see his own reflection in one glass door of the shotgun case. The other door was open. The next thing he saw was a bare foot.

He stopped in his tracks and regarded it for a moment. It was a large foot, long and narrow, very white. The toes seemed particularly long. The foot of a tall man. Howell took another step. The other foot was there too, resting at an odd angle to its companion. Those, Howell said to himself, are the feet of a tall, white, dead man.

He took two more steps into the room and made himself look at the rest. The body, clad in silk pajamas and dressing gown, lay as if it had slipped off the sofa, propped halfway up against the arm. The wall behind the sofa held a smashed hunting print, hanging at a crazy angle, and a substantial portion of Eric Sutherland's brains. Howell looked back at the body. All that remained of the head was the lower jaw, attached to a partly scooped-out shell that had been the back of the skull. It still had ears.

Howell stood still and tried to breathe normally. He had seen his share of corpses, but never one quite like this. And he had never been the first on the scene. He looked slowly and carefully around the room. A beautifully engraved shotgun lay near the body; alongside it was a yellow pencil. The desk seemed undisturbed. A small safe next to it was closed. Nothing else seemed out of place. He stepped to the desk, being careful not to trip over anything or step in anything. He took a ballpoint pen from his pocket, stuck it through the handle of the middle drawer, and opened it. He poked around with the pen. Nothing unusual; paper clips, rubber bands, a checkbook. He opened the other drawers: a bundle of bank statements, some stationery, stamps. The sort of stuff he'd expect to find in anybody's desk.

Howell inserted the tip of the pen under the desk blotter and lifted it. Nothing. Eric Sutherland didn't appear to have left a note. Not at the scene, anyway. Howell squatted and looked at the safe next to the desk. He knew nothing about cracking safes, but he knew something about human nature. On his knees, he opened the desk drawers again with his pen and looked underneath each. Nothing. He stood up and pulled out the stenographer's shelf on the right. There was a piece of paper taped to the shelf containing a list of phone numbers: the sheriff's office, the bank, a couple of banks in Atlanta, Enda McAuliffe. He pushed the shelf back in and pulled out its mate on the left side. The face of the shelf was clean, but Howell spotted a piece of cellophane tape on the edge, protruding slightly. He pulled the shelf out to its limit. The combination to the safe was taped to its inner edge.

Howell looked at his watch. He reckoned he had been at the house for less than five minutes, in the study for half that time. He ran to the door and had a look around the front of the house. Still deserted. He ran back to the study and slipped out of his shoes and socks. Quickly, he pulled the socks onto his hands, knelt, and dialed the combination of the safe. It didn't work. He tried again more carefully, and this time the handle moved and the door swung open.

The safe was crammed with all sorts of papers. Evidently, Eric Sutherland had been the sort of man who preferred to keep important things locked away, instead of in unlocked desk drawers where people like Howell might find them. Howell flipped quickly through the contents. He was breathing fast now, terrified that someone would walk in on him. There were a lot of deeds in the safe—the farmland under the lake, Howell suspected; a bundle of cash, twenties, fifties, and hundreds; some ledgers; no time for any of that stuff. A heavy, bright blue envelope caught his eye. It looked new. He fumbled with the string closure with his stocking fingers and finally got it open. The document was headed "Last Will and Testament." Howell flipped quickly through it, noting small bequests to the butler, cook, and gardener. There were some small charitable bequests, not many. When he got to the bequest of the residue of Sutherland's estate, he was brought up short. He re-read the first paragraph twice, to be sure he absolutely understood its meaning, then he pressed on for two more pages, reading as fast as he could and still retain what they said. The will was witnessed by Enda McAuliffe and two other people whose names he did not recognize. But it was what came after the will that riveted him to the spot. He read on. He was totally rapt now; a platoon of police storming into the room would not have disturbed him.

He finished and looked about him. Eric Sutherland had a copying machine, but it wasn't here. Where had he seen it? Of course, in the office building out back. He looked at his watch. He had been in the house for a good eight minutes, maybe longer. He tried to think how long it might take him to get out there, jimmy the door, wait for the machine to warm up, and copy the will. Five or six minutes, and he couldn't afford to make a mess of the door. There had been no keys in Sutherland's desk. Since the body was wearing pajamas, they were probably upstairs in his bedroom with the normal contents of the man's pockets.

No. Too much time, too much risk. He couldn't afford to end up in jail, not today. He put the will back into the envelope, got the string wound around the closure, and replaced it in the safe. He closed it, worked the handle, and spun the lock.

He pulled the socks off his hands, then picked up the phone and dialed the sheriff's office. Scotty answered.

"Is Bo there?"

"Yes," she said in a hushed voice. "Why? What's up?"

"Let me speak to him."

"Why? What's going on, John?"

"Let me speak to him right now, Scotty." He heard her call out to Bo.

"Hey, John, how's it going?"

Howell glanced at his watch. "I make it four minutes to eleven, Bo. What time have you got?"

"Four and a half to. You want to compare watches? I'll show you mine if you'll show me yours."

"Please make a note of the time, Bo. I'm at Eric Sutherland's house.

Sutherland's dead. Looks like suicide. You want to get out here very fast, please?"

There was a strange noise behind Howell. He spun around to find Alfred, the butler, standing there in his hat and coat, holding a small suitcase. Alfred was staring at Eric Sutherland's body. He made the noise again, then crumpled and fell sideways, bounced off a chair, and landed heavily on the floor.

"John? What's going on?"

"Hang on." Howell bent over the butler and peeled back an eyelid; the pupil contracted immediately. He felt for a pulse; strong and rapid. He took a pillow off a chair and placed it under the man's feet, then picked up the phone again.

"Looks like Alfred just got home from somewhere. He's fainted, but I think he's okay."

"You wait there with Alfred and don't touch anything, you hear me?"

"Sure."

"I'll be there in two minutes."

Howell sat down on a chair and put on his socks and shoes. He hoped to God Alfred hadn't noticed he was barefoot.

32

Howell heard the sheriff's car from the moment Bo left the office. After a minute, the butler began to stir and wanted to get up. Howell helped him to his feet and walked him to a living room sofa as the siren grew louder and louder. He had just settled Alfred there when Bo strode through the open front door.

"Where?" he asked.

Howell pointed to the study and followed him in.

"Jesus Christ," Bo said.

"Yeah."

Bo stood and looked at the corpse for a long moment. "Well," he said finally, "we had our differences, I guess, but I sure wouldn't have wanted him to end up that way."

Howell wondered how Bo would have liked for Sutherland to end up. "You see the pencil," he said. "I reckon he took off his slippers, there, put the pencil through the trigger guard, holding it in his toes, and pushed it against the trigger with both feet."

"Yeah, maybe," Bo said, still rooted to the spot. "He couldn't have put the barrel in his mouth and still reached the trigger with his hand." He was quiet again for another moment, then he took a breath and shook himself. He picked up the phone and dialed. "Scotty, give me Mike. . . . Mike? Get on the horn and get everybody over to Sutherland's house. . . . Yeah, he's dead. . . . I don't know yet, just hold your horses and listen. Call Dr. Murphy and ask him to get out here right away. Call Herman McWilliam and tell him to get over here with his wagon; we're going to have to take the body to Gainesville for a proper postmortem. Then you round up the fingerprint kit, a lot of evidence bags, and the Polaroid and the thirty-five millimeter—every-

thing we could possibly need to work a scene—and get over here. Tell
Scotty and Sally to handle the radio and the office, and not to leave until
they hear from me. I don't think anybody knows about this yet, so tell
them to keep things as normal as possible, okay? Tell the guys to park
around back, then stand at each entrance to the drive. Nobody gets in
unless I invited them. I'll want you inside with me. Got that? Any
questions? . . . Okay, move it."

He hung up the phone and turned to Howell. "All right, John, what
were you doing here?"

Howell had thought about that one. "I dropped by to ask Mr. Sutherland some questions about local history."

"Why didn't you go to the library?"

"They were questions I thought only Mr. Sutherland could answer.
Or would."

Bo glared at him. "You're still after that, are you?"

Howell looked him in the eye. "You bet."

Bo shrugged. "All right, give me this morning from the top."

Howell ran through the events of his morning: seeing Scotty off to
work, running out of gas, Benny Pope's visit, stopping at the post office,
and his arrival at the house. He stretched the time a little to cover his
search of the study. Bo made copious notes as he talked.

"What did you touch?"

"The phone, the cushions to make Alfred comfortable . . . that's it,
I think."

"Not the doorknobs?"

"Let's see. The front door was ajar; I touched the door, but not the
knob. I touched the back doorknobs, inside and out, when I went out
there. The study door was open, and one side of the shotgun case was
open; I remember I saw my reflection in just the one door."

The sheriff looked at him sharply. "John, I know you well enough to
know that you didn't just stand here when you found the body. Did you
touch the desk or the safe or the filing cabinets or anything else at all?"

Howell felt tiny sweat beads breaking on his forehead. He hoped Bo
didn't notice. "I stood here in my tracks and looked at the room real
hard for about, I guess, a minute. My first thought was that there might
be a note."

"Was there a note? Did you find anything like that?"

"No. The room is exactly the way I found it." It was, too. Everything
in its place.

"John, listen to me. Nobody else is here yet. I haven't even read you your rights. If there's anything else you want to tell me, anything you might just have forgotten or overlooked, anything you might have done, now's the time to tell me, unofficially, if you want. In a minute this place is going to be swarming with people, and it'll be too late for me to help you."

Howell blinked. "Help me? I don't need any help. Jesus, Bo, you don't think for a moment this is anything but a suicide, do you? Come on, you're not going to play me like a suspect."

"All right, all right, it looks like a suicide, but you know I've got to be thorough." He looked again at what was left of Eric Sutherland's body. "More thorough than I've ever been in my life." He looked back at Howell. "Did you go upstairs or into any of the other rooms?"

"No, I made it a suicide right away. I reckoned if there'd been anybody in the house, they'd have heard it. If I'd thought there was a murderer hiding upstairs, I'm not so sure I'd have looked, anyway."

"When was the last time you saw Eric Sutherland alive?"

"At his party. Not since."

"Not anywhere? Not here, not in the town, not anywhere?"

"Nope. In fact, I only ever spoke to Sutherland twice; the day I arrived in town, when I saw him and stopped to introduce myself, and the day of the party. That was it."

"You ever have harsh words with him?"

"Nope. He was a little cool when I met him the first time, but at the party he was all charm."

"Apart from the time you broke into Sutherland's office, did you ever come to this house when he wasn't here?"

Howell waited for a moment before answering. "I think you must be referring to the time when Scotty lost her credit card at Sutherland's party, and Sutherland thought somebody had broken into his office. I have never visited this house when Sutherland was not here. Do I make myself absolutely clear on that point?"

"Yeah, okay, we'll forget about the credit card. You've explained that well enough, and I think it's best forgotten."

"Fine. I know you've got a doctor on the way, Bo, but for what it's worth, this looks hours old to me. The blood and the other stuff are partly dried."

"Yeah, I think you're right." Bo looked up as a car came to a halt outside the house. "Look, John, I'd appreciate it if you wouldn't go phoning this in to any of your newspaper buddies, and if you'd keep

Scotty from doing that, too. I want to have this thing covered from every angle before the press gets on to it, okay?"

"Sure, Bo."

Mike came into the study carrying two briefcases, saw Sutherland's body, put down the cases, and fled to the driveway. They could hear him retching.

"He's going to be a lot of help," Bo said wryly.

Howell laughed. "He'll get used to it. First time's the worst."

"Well, John, we've got a lot of work to do around here. I'll call you if I have any more questions."

"Okay, I'll let you get on with it." Howell turned and started for the door.

"Oh, John," Bo called out.

Howell stopped. "Yeah?"

"Like they say in the movies, don't leave town."

33

Driving back toward the town, Howell reflected that there was a certain symmetry emerging in all this that seemed more than coincidental. He had a couple of things to confirm, then he would know. Maybe.

He glanced at his watch; the timing was about right. He parked in front of the courthouse, and, sure enough, right on schedule, the battle-ax, Mrs. O'Neal, left for lunch. Howell bounded up the steps. This wouldn't take long; he just wanted to confirm his own memory. He was in and out of the records office in minutes.

As he got back into the car, another thought hit him, right from left field. Curious, he drove to the shopping center, parked in front of the drugstore, and went in. He stood staring at the shelf.

"May I help you, sir?" A girl in a white jacket stood at his elbow.

"Oh, no thanks, I was just looking," Howell replied, and tried to smile at the girl.

She looked askance at the shelf of female products and back at him.

"Uh, just looking," he said lamely, and left quickly. Howell felt very strange as he got back into the car. All this had suddenly become a little too much. His first reaction was that he wanted a drink. With some effort, he scaled the desire back to a beer, then headed for Bubba's.

He was on his second beer when Enda McAuliffe came in. Howell was, at first, surprised that McAuliffe wasn't out at Eric Sutherland's house, then it occurred to him that the lawyer probably didn't know yet. It had been no more than half an hour since Howell had found the body.

"Mind if I join you, John?" The lawyer was a lot friendlier than the last time they had met.

"Please do, Mac. I was about to come to see you, anyway."

"Listen, John, I'm sorry I popped off at you out at Sutherland's. I'd had a lot to drink, and I wasn't at my best that day."

"Not at all, Mac. You were protecting your client. I understand."

McAuliffe ordered lunch. "Why were you coming to see me?"

"I think I might need a lawyer pretty soon."

"Well, I don't know, John . . ."

"I can promise you that any legal advice you give me won't conflict with Eric Sutherland's interests, Mac. In fact, I can guarantee it."

"Well, okay. How can I help you?" He looked around. "I used to do most of my work in this place, anyway, if you don't mind talking here."

"Couple of things," Howell said, sipping his beer. "One's a long-term sort of thing that I'd like you to handle locally for me. I'll talk to you about that in a day or two, I think."

"And the other?"

"There's a fair chance I might be arrested before the day is out. I'll try to avoid it, but if I get picked up, I don't want to spend the night in jail."

"What's the charge going to be?"

Smart lawyer, Howell thought. Not "What did you do?" "It could be almost anything, but probably material witness. Maybe murder."

"You thinking of killing somebody?"

"Whatever it turns out to be, you can rest assured I didn't do it."

"That's good enough for me."

"If you need some muscle, call Denham White in Atlanta. He's still my brother-in-law, after all."

"John, are you sure there isn't something you want to tell me?"

"Yes, but first, I want to ask you a personal question."

"Okay, shoot."

"Why did you never marry, Mac?"

The lawyer said nothing, just looked at Howell without expression.

"Could it have been for the same reason Bo Scully never got married?"

McAuliffe continued to look at Howell for a moment. "Which one of my half-dozen stock answers would you like?"

"Never mind, Mac. I'm sorry."

"John, perhaps you shouldn't count on me to represent you."

"Sorry, Mac, you're stuck with me. I know you'll do a good job. Look, a lot is going to happen around here during the next twenty-four hours, and I want you to remember that some of it may not be what it seems to be." And that, Howell thought, was a direct quote.

"You're getting pretty mysterious, John. What's going to happen?"

"Well, I don't know all of it, maybe not even most of it, but it's already started. Eric Sutherland is dead."

McAuliffe sat up. "Are you serious?"

"Apparent suicide. I found the body this morning."

McAuliffe looked stunned. "Where?"

"At his house. In the study. Shotgun in the face."

"You found him? What were you doing out there?"

"I went to ask him some questions about the O'Coineens."

"Oh, shit."

"Yeah, that would have been a touchy point with him, wouldn't it? When things have quieted down a little, I think you and I should get together and compare notes."

"I think I'd better get out to Sutherland's," McAuliffe said, getting up. "Why don't you and I have lunch tomorrow?"

"That's good; we should both know more by then. Tell me, Mac, does Bo know what's in Sutherland's will?"

McAuliffe looked at him narrowly. "I don't know, but I think he may suspect." He turned and left.

Howell went to the pay phone at the back of Bubba's and called the sheriff's office. Scotty answered.

"Bo still out at Sutherland's?"

"Yes. What happened out there, John?"

"I'll tell you later. Now listen to me. Say 'Oh, no!' as if you mean it."

"Oh, no!" Scotty changed her voice to a whisper. "What's going on?"

"All right, now hang up and tell Sally your father is sick and you have to drive to Atlanta right now."

"I can't do that. It's going to be crazy here when Bo gets back."

"Just do as I tell you. Leave, but don't go home, and don't go to the cabin. Go out to the Kelly place, and when you get there, park your car behind the house so it won't be seen from the road. I'll be waiting for you. Got that?"

"All right; whatever you say."

Howell hung up and started for the Kelly house. He drove fast, and when he turned into the drive he continued until his car was out of sight, behind the house. Leonie came out the back door to meet him.

"What is it?" she asked, and she didn't sound very hospitable.

"A lot has happened," Howell said, "and a whole lot more is going to happen." He took her arm and walked her into the kitchen. "First of all, I'm sorry about the scene at the shopping center. I apologize. I think I understand, and I want to help."

"I don't need your help," she said icily.

"Yes, you do," he said, "but let's not argue about that now. Eric Sutherland is dead, and I have a feeling Bo Scully may be looking for me before the day is out. Can I stay here until after dark? I don't think he'll come here."

She looked as shocked as he had expected her to. "Well, all right, sure. What's—"

"Later. First, there's something I need to know, and I hope you can help me. Do you know why Bo's engagement to Joyce O'Coineen was broken?"

She shook her head. "No."

"Do you know why the younger girl, Kathleen, was taken out of school?"

"No. I was only about eight when all that happened. There was a lot of whispering going on in the house, but I never understood what was happening."

"Then I've got to talk with your mother."

Leonie shook her head. "You can't, she's asleep, and I don't want to wake her. She's in a bad way, John."

"I know that, but I think this may be more important to her than to me."

"Leonie?" The call came, weakly, from the direction of Mama Kelly's room.

"Just a minute," Leonie said. She went to her mother.

Howell fidgeted in the kitchen. A moment later, Leonie came back.

"All right, you can go in, but just for a minute. And please don't get her excited."

"I hope I won't. Listen, I think you know about Scotty—she's going to be here in a minute. I hope you don't mind if she stays awhile too."

Leonie shrugged. "Oh, hell, why not?"

Howell took a deep breath and headed for Mama Kelly.

34

Howell placed Lorna Kelly's thin hand back on the bed and watched her for a moment. Her breathing was shallow, but peaceful. There was something like a smile on her face. It was odd; every time he had been to see her he had been looking for some sort of supernatural revelation, and finally, what she had given him was a simple piece of information—something she had known all along and hadn't thought important—that had tied the whole thing together for him.

When he walked into the living room, Scotty was there. She and Leonie sat on opposite sides of the room.

"Your mother is sleeping quietly," he said, and looked from one woman to the other. "I take it you two have met."

"Did you find out what you needed to know?" Leonie asked.

Howell smiled. "She says so. You know how she is. I've still got some things to figure out. She also says this is her last day on earth."

Leonie nodded. "Then it is," she said. "I'd better ring Father Harry."

Scotty suddenly spoke up. "Why am I here? What's going on?"

"I think Bo is going to want us out of circulation tonight, and he has an excuse now." He told them about his visit to Eric Sutherland's house that morning. "Since I found the body, and since you and I are associated, he could hold us for questioning. I think he'll wait until evening, then try to pick us up. I hope he believes you're on your way to Atlanta. Tomorrow, when he's all done with his private business, he'd release us. Suppose he's planning to quit after this one? Then it would be just about impossible to pin anything on him after tonight."

"He's really going to be annoyed when he comes back and finds me gone," Scotty said. "That office is jumping. People have been calling in

for the last hour wanting to know what's happening out at Sutherland's."

Howell laughed. "Jesus, Scotty, I think you're worried about getting
fired! Well, you've worked your last day for the Sutherland County
Sheriff's Department, whatever happens."

Scotty brightened. "Yeah, I guess you're right."

"I'm afraid I don't understand what's going on here," Leonie said.

Howell explained who Scotty was and what she was doing in Sutherland. "We think Bo's going to be up to something at the county airport
tonight, and if we can catch him at it, then Scotty has her story, and
Sutherland County will get a new sheriff. By the way, can we get to the
landing strip from here through the woods?"

Leonie nodded. "Sure, but it might be slow going. There's no path. I
suppose it's about half a mile. Maybe less."

"Good. I don't think we can risk it in a car."

"What time will you go up there?"

"I think just before dark."

"Then you'll have supper with us."

"Sure. Thanks."

"Well, I'd better look in on Mama, then I've got some things to do in
the kitchen." Leonie left them.

"Listen," Scotty said, "if we go up there before dark, aren't we more
likely to be seen, if there's somebody there already?"

"Maybe. But we're also more likely to see anybody else, and I don't
want to be thrashing around a patch of strange woods at night, making
a lot of noise and waving a flashlight around." Howell saw Leonie leave
her mother's room and head toward the kitchen. Now seemed like a
good time. "Excuse me, I've got to talk to Leonie about her mother."

Howell walked to the kitchen and found Leonie shelling peas. He sat
down at the kitchen table next to her and picked up a handful. "I'll give
you a hand."

"I expect you're wanted out there," she said coolly, nodding toward
the living room.

Howell ignored the gibe. "I've found out a lot of things today," he
said, cracking open a pod and emptying the peas into a bowl along with
hers. "I found out, for instance, why you were shoplifting."

Leonie flushed. "Can't you just forget about that?"

"I guess a single girl in a town this size can't just walk into the
drugstore and buy a pregnancy-testing kit. Might as well advertise in
the local paper. It was positive, wasn't it?"

She continued shelling peas in silence.

"No, I can't forget about it," he said.

"It's not your responsibility," she said, her voice softer. "It was my decision. You had nothing to do with it. Well, not very much, anyway."

"It's my responsibility too. I understand now why you thought it was the only way."

"It *is* the only way," she said. "Who'd marry me?" She looked him in the eye. "You?"

"I'm already married," Howell said, and they both knew it was an evasive answer.

She didn't call him on it. "I don't want anything more from you. I've got what I want, what I've wanted for a long time. I'm content."

"Are you sure you ought to be content? You're entitled to a life of your own, you know. Why don't you get out of here when your mother's gone? Make a new start somewhere."

"I have responsibilities," she said. "Brian and Mary depend on me. I can't just lock them away someplace. Dermot's different, he's an independent soul. But I can't abandon the twins."

"I see," he said.

"I'm not sure you do see," she came back quickly. "People like you are footloose; you go where you want to, when you want to. You don't let yourselves get tied down with things as ordinary as family."

Now it was Howell's turn to flush.

"I don't think you understand that other people are born into situations—or just accept them, live with them and do the best they can."

"Sure, I understand that."

"No, not really, John. It's something you've never learned. Maybe it's the reporter in you; you dig into something, get what you want out of it, then move on. When you've finished whatever it is you want to do here, you'll leave, and you won't come back. You'll put yourself first, and I guess that's the right thing for someone like you to do."

"Look, I want to help you. I . . ."

"No." She put her hand on his arm. "Don't make commitments you may not be able to keep. You'll just have that much more guilt to bear when you don't keep them. I meant what I said. I trapped you. It was my decision, and I knew what I was doing. I didn't do it lightly, and I know how to bear the responsibility I've taken on. You owe me nothing. That's the way I want it."

"All right," Howell said, pushing back from the table, "if that's what you want." He left her and went into the living room. Scotty was asleep on the sofa. Dermot and the twins were sitting on the front porch. Dermot was picking at his mandolin. Howell sat down in a comfortable chair and picked up the photograph he had seen on his first visit to the house.

Kathleen O'Coineen stared back at him with huge eyes. The priest had been right; she was startlingly beautiful. She couldn't have been more than eight or nine in the picture. There was still that familiarity about her. He thought, for a moment, that he knew why, but then the sound of a car engine distracted him. He parted the curtains slightly and looked out. A sheriff's car was pulling into the Kelly driveway. Howell stepped away from the window. Bo had moved faster than he had expected. There was no place to run. He'd have to go along and hope McAuliffe could get him out in time.

He peeked carefully through the curtains again. The car had stopped in the drive. The reflection on the windshield concealed the driver; Howell thought he must be taking a careful look at the house, and he was glad that he and Scotty had parked out back. Then the car backed into the road and drove away toward town.

Howell sank back into the armchair and let his pulse return to normal. Then he leaned back and let himself doze. What had he been thinking about before? He was too sleepy to care. He had wrestled with too much today. His mind needed to gather itself for what was ahead.

When Howell woke up, the priest was coming out of Lorna Kelly's bedroom. He nodded to Howell.

"Father Harry, how are you?"

"I'm fine, m'boy, fine."

Howell pointed toward the bedroom and raised his eyebrows.

"She's asleep, bless her heart," Father Harry said, "and you look as though you could use a few more winks yourself." He waved and went toward the kitchen.

At six o'clock Scotty woke him, and they went in to supper. All of them dined quietly in the old-fashioned kitchen on fried chicken, fresh corn and peas, cornbread muffins, and iced tea. Father Harry seemed to have been sipping something else. Howell remembered meals like this from his childhood, at the homes of family friends whose people were dying, except at those meals the food had been brought by sympathetic neighbors. Apart from her family, there was no one to attend Lorna Kelly's death but an alcoholic priest and two fugitives.

They lingered over coffee until the sun was nearly on the horizon. Scotty got her camera gear from her car, and Howell gave her the film. He went back into the house.

"Can I borrow a flashlight?" he asked Leonie.

"Sure." She went to a cupboard and brought back a large, six-volt model. "Listen," she said tentatively. "I'd like to see this again." She looked up at him. "And I'd like it delivered in person."

He smiled at her and touched her cheek. "I'll be careful. There's not much to this; we're just going to go up there and perch in the woods and take some pictures and come back."

"See that you do. The baby might want to meet his father one of these days." She handed him a thermos of coffee and a paper bag. "You might get hungry."

Howell nodded and turned to join Scotty. They left the Kellys' backyard and entered the woods, picking their way through the trees and brush. The sun was below the treetops, and dusk was nearly upon them. They tried to hurry, to be in position before it got dark. They were climbing slightly.

Twenty minutes later the ground leveled off, and they came to the edge of the airfield and stopped, still well into the trees. Howell looked at the windsock. He pointed to the little shack next to a couple of small aircraft near the end of the runway. "Let's work our way down there. Any airplane is going to land in that direction, and it seems like a natural sort of meeting place, anyway."

In the fading light, they circled a quarter of the way around the airfield, walking as quietly as possible and not using the flashlight. They saw no one, no cars, nothing that hadn't been there when they arrived. In the trees near the end of the runway, perhaps thirty yards from the shed, they found a depression in the ground, well padded with pine needles.

"This looks good," Howell said, masking the flashlight with his hand and playing it briefly over the ground. It was something like a sandtrap on a golf course. The ground seemed to fall away rapidly from there. In the last moments of light, Howell could see tops of trees below them, and, in the distance, the lake. "The pine needles won't make much noise when we move around. A lot better than leaves. What's the longest lens you've got?"

"A one-fifty to two-fifty zoom, but it's not very fast."

"My friend says it doesn't have to be. That film will make it look like daylight."

"Good." She sighted through the camera toward the shed. "Jesus, I can't see much. It's just as well the film can. We've got six rolls. I'll use the motor drive; we'll practically have movies of this event."

"I hope to God there *is* an event," he said.

"They're going to be here at three thirty," Scotty said firmly. "That's what the teletype said, and I believe it."

Howell looked at his illuminated watch. "Just past nine," he said. "A long wait."

The wind whistled through the trees and rustled the pine straw around them. Scotty snuggled up close and Howell put his arm around her.

"Tomorrow," she said, "I'm going to take this film back to Atlanta, write a big lead story, and hold up the *Atlanta Constitution* for the biggest raise in the history of the newspaper business."

Howell laughed. "And what if they won't sit still for it?"

"Then I'll just call up AP or UPI or maybe the Atlanta bureau chief of the *New York Times.*"

Howell had once held that job himself. "They'd go for it, all right."

"You think this story could get me on the *Times?*"

"It might. I think you'd be better off going back to the *Constitution* with it, though. Then, after you've won your Pulitzer, you can accept the *Times'* offer."

She dug him in the ribs. "Listen, I'm serious about all this!"

"Jesus, don't I know it!" he said, laughing. "I hope it comes off just the way you want it to."

"Johnny, what do you want? What are you going to do after you finish the book?" She sounded as if she really wanted to know, so he told her.

"I don't know," he said. "But I think maybe I've reached a point in my life where I should go back and figure out what's happened to me, instead of always chasing what's going to happen next."

"Hey, there's a country song in there somewhere. I think you ought to fool around with that a little and send it to Willie Nelson."

"Aw, shut up."

"Why don't you go back to the *Times?*" she asked. "You said everybody could go back once."

"Funny you should mention that. I got an offer from the *Times* today. Nairobi."

"Are you kidding? That's great! You're going to take it, aren't you?"

"Are *you* kidding? Do you know what Nairobi means? It isn't just the Serengeti Plain and the game parks, you know. You cover the whole continent. It's Africa. The asshole of the planet. It's flying to hell and back on poorly maintained, forty-year-old C-47s flown by half-trained African pilots; getting hassled by the police in South Africa; interviewing insane master sergeants who are suddenly running countries; having to look at the swollen bellies and pitiful eyes of starving kids; bribing customs officials in backwoods airports; having beggars hanging all over you every time you walk down a street; and finally, getting a bullet in the back of the head from some jungle corporal with a superiority complex and not enough reading skills to understand your press credentials. Thanks, but no thanks."

"Gee, you sound really interested."

"Interested? Do you know the sadistic sons of bitches would probably make me learn *Swahili?* They're sticklers for their boys knowing the local language."

"I think it sounds fascinating."

"That's because you're young and stupid."

"I think you ought to take it."

"They'd be stunned if I did, I can promise you that. This is just their way of saying I had my chance. I'm not going to Nairobi, and they know it." Howell was tiring of this conversation. "Listen, why don't you get some sleep; nothing's going to happen for a while yet."

"Mmmmmmm," she said, and snuggled closer. Within moments she was breathing slowly.

Howell leaned his head against hers and closed his eyes. He was bone tired. Nairobi. Christ! Over the next hours he stirred himself every few minutes to have a look around him, but nothing happened. Around midnight he laid the sleeping Scotty on her side and had some coffee from the thermos and a slice of pie from the paper bag. Then, feeling full and contented, he drifted off into a deep sleep.

The noise was familiar, almost too much so to be disturbing. Then Howell was wide awake, trying to remember the sound, to place its direction. A car door, that was it; he had heard a car door slam. Now there was another noise, a sound of metal scraping on metal. He turned to follow its direction.

There was only starlight to see by, but near the shed a car had parked, and its occupant, a large shape, was unlocking a padlock on the shed door. Cursing himself for sleeping so deeply, Howell put a hand over Scotty's mouth and shook her awake. Holding a finger to his lips, he pointed toward the shed, some thirty yards away. They sat up on their knees, and Scotty began taking pictures.

"Is it Bo?" she whispered.

"I don't know. He's big enough. Easy on the film. Don't use it up too soon."

Scotty had squeezed off a dozen or more frames with the camera's machine drive. She stopped. The man, who seemed to be wearing coveralls and a baseball cap, leaned against the fender of his car and waited. Howell and Scotty waited with him. The luminous hands of Howell's watch read just past three.

For ten minutes they sat there, then there was a flash of headlights in the distance, and a very large truck began driving toward them along the road that paralleled the runway. It made a wide circle, then pulled up next to the shack, a few feet off the edge of the grass landing strip. It was a moving van, and Howell thought he could read the name of a nationwide moving company painted on the side. Just before the headlights went out, they briefly illuminated Bo Scully, who shook hands with the driver and another man as they got down from the truck.

The three men immediately went to the rear of the van, unlocked the doors, and unloaded half a dozen pieces of furniture. Scotty looked at Howell with raised eyebrows, then shot another dozen frames. At twenty-five minutes past three, Bo went into the shack, and a moment later the runway lights came on, little spots of blue reaching away down both sides of the grass strip. Then, a minute or two past the half hour, there was a distant hum, and Howell looked up to see a pair of white landing lights drifting toward the strip. Scotty finished a roll of film, handed it to Howell, and quickly reloaded.

The plane landed at what seemed so great a speed that Howell thought it would never stop, that it would crash through the shack and end up in the trees, on top of them. But it came noisily to a stop and began turning around at the very end of the strip. He was surprised to see that it had four engines and that, illuminated by Bo's headlights, which had suddenly come on, it bore the insignia of the Georgia Air National Guard. Howell pointed at the plane; Scotty nodded and photographed the insignia, zooming in on it. It would have done little good to speak, because the roar of the four engines overpowered everything, and the propellers kicked up a hurricane of wind and pine straw. As the lighter ground debris blew away, they were able to see better.

The rear door of the airplane flew open and somebody began kicking out what looked like small bales of cotton, wrapped in burlap. The two men from the truck and Bo quickly loaded them into the furniture van. Scotty handed Howell another roll of film, reloaded, and started to shoot again. Now the man on the plane was handing out what looked like four ordinary suitcases, then, finally, a canvas briefcase. Bo unzipped the briefcase and inspected the contents, apparently counting.

Bo gave the man on the plane a thumbs-up sign, and at that moment somebody kicked Howell hard in the ass.

Howell turned angrily around to find a flashlight in his face, and, ahead of that, the barrel of a rifle, pointing at his head. His anger immediately turned to fear. The man behind the rifle was shouting, but Howell couldn't make out what he was saying. He cupped a hand behind his ear to indicate this. The man leaned forward until the rifle barrel was nearly touching Howell's forehead and shouted again.

"Get you hands up and throw that camera over here!"

Scotty seemed to have no trouble hearing him. She pushed the camera toward him, hard, like a basketball. It struck the flashlight, and Howell took the opportunity to grab for the rifle barrel and push it aside. As he did, a single shot went past his ear. The skin on the side of his head seemingly on fire, Howell kicked toward the other end of the rifle as hard as he could and thought he connected with the man's belly.

The man fell backward, leaving the rifle with Howell, and, in the reflected glow of the car's headlights, Howell could see the man struggling to one knee, clutching his middle. He got a better grip on the barrel with both hands and swung it as hard as he could, like a baseball bat, catching the man flush on the ear with the stock. He spun about, landed face down, and didn't move.

Howell checked the weapon. It was an M-16 assault rifle with a long banana clip; he had qualified on it in the army. He felt for the automatic-fire switch and looked back toward the group at the end of the runway. Even over the continuing roar of the airplane, the shot had been heard. The two men from the truck were running toward him. He pointed over their heads and fired a short burst. The two men immediately reversed course and began running for the truck.

Howell picked up the camera and shoved it at Scotty. He grabbed her and brought her ear close to his mouth. "Get back down to the Kellys' and call the highway patrol station at Gainesville," he yelled over the roar of the plane's engines. "Tell them what's happening!"

"I can't leave you here!" she shouted back.

He held up the assault rifle. "Don't worry, I've got them outgunned with this thing." He handed her the flashlight. "Don't use this unless you have to. Now run!"

Scotty ran, and Howell turned back toward the airplane. Dirt flew in his face, and he realized that it wasn't the wash from the propellers; somebody was shooting at him. He ran a few feet to his left, raised the automatic weapon, and got off a short burst, aimed at nothing in particular. To his surprise, one side of the furniture van suddenly dropped a few inches. He had hit the double tires at the right rear of the truck.

He ducked and ran back to his right, then took a moment to catch his breath. What the hell, if he could hit the truck, he ought to be able to hit the plane. He popped his head up for a look.

The rear door of the plane slammed shut, and it started to move.

Howell fired a burst and saw sparks fly off the runway under the plane. Too low. He raised his aim and held the trigger down. The weapon fired for two or three seconds, then stopped. Howell cocked it and tried to fire again. Nothing. He had emptied the clip. He ran back to the unconscious man and felt around him for another clip, but there was none.

Howell glanced back toward the runway and saw the airplane moving down the grass strip. His eyes widened; there was a lick of flame on the right wing. Dirt and leaves kicked up around him. They were firing again, and this time he couldn't fire back. He dropped the rifle and started to run.

He headed straight downhill, ninety degrees from the direction in which Scotty had run. Her chances would be better if he led them that way. He managed to cover thirty or forty yards before he tripped on something and fell headlong down the hill, which was steepening with every yard. He fetched up hard against a tree. He couldn't breathe for a moment, then a breath came, and he tried to struggle to his feet. The woods around him were suddenly illuminated, and, a moment later, a huge noise and a rush of hot air told him the plane had exploded.

He glanced behind him just long enough to see a large orange fireball rising above the trees, then he started to move down the hill again, taking care this time not to run blindly. His ribs ached from the collision with the tree, and the skin on the side of his head was still afire with the powder burn, but he was up and moving, and he reckoned that Bo and his friends were far too busy getting the drugs and the furniture van out of there to come after him.

He half ran, half walked down the steep hill, until he came to a stream. He stopped behind a tree and looked back up the hill. The glow from the burning airplane would backlight anybody coming after him. He saw no one. Suddenly, he was exhausted. He sat down beside the little stream and splashed water on his powder burns. It didn't seem to help much. He drank some of the water, then some more. That helped.

After what he thought was ten or fifteen minutes, he got to his feet and looked at his watch. It was a quarter past four. The plane had landed just after three thirty. Surely Scotty was at the Kellys' by now, and the Georgia State Patrol was on its way. As if to confirm this, the distant scream of a siren reached him. It sounded as if it were closing on Sutherland County Airport.

He thought about returning to the airfield, but he was hurting, and it was uphill. He decided to follow the stream; he thought he knew where it met the main lakeside road. A few minutes later, he found he was right. The stream gurgled under a stone bridge and ran on down to the lake. Howell struggled up the embankment and made the road, clutching his arm to his side to keep his ribs from moving around. He'd give a lot for an elastic bandage, he thought.

He set himself as good a pace as he could manage and hiked down the road toward Sutherland. No cars passed, and the glow from the direction of the airfield had subsided. He made the crossroads in less than fifteen minutes and turned down the road toward the cabin. As he walked the last few yards and came around the bend, he was relieved to see Scotty's car parked outside and a light on in the cabin.

He started up the steps and stopped. Suddenly cautious, he climbed softly, staying near the edge of the steps. At the top, he leaned over the rail and looked through the window at the side of the landing, which gave him a view of the living room. Scotty was sitting at his desk at the other end of the room, her head resting on her folded arms, asleep.

Howell was nearly overwhelmed with relief. She had made it. He opened the cabin door and crossed toward her. When he was halfway to the desk, a board creaked under his feet and Scotty sat up and turned. Her face was puffy and red on one side, and her left wrist was handcuffed to the chair.

"What took you so long?" someone behind him asked.

Howell sagged at the sound of the familiar voice. He turned slowly around to find Bo Scully leaning against the wall behind the door. In one hand he was holding an open bottle of Jack Daniel's; with the other, he was pointing a riot shotgun, the same sort Howell had used to save Bo's life at Minnie Wilson's grocery store.

36

Howell took as deep a breath as he could and let it out. "Well, Bo, I'm glad to see you. I was hoping you and I could have a talk before they take you away."

Bo chuckled. "Now who's going to take me away, John?" He seemed a little drunk. The Jack Daniel's bottle had a big dent in it.

Howell looked at Scotty. She shook her head. "He caught me just as I got to the Kellys'. I woke up here." She held up the handcuffed wrist.

"But I heard the siren . . ."

Bo chimed in. "That was the Sutherland fire department. Police cars don't have sirens anymore. We use whoopers these days."

Howell suddenly knew that Bo was drunk because, sober, he couldn't do what he planned to do. Howell tried not to show how afraid he was. "Come on, Bo, there's no way you can get out of this."

"Oh, sure there is," Bo said amiably. "Try and look at it objectively, John. The boys got one of the tires on the van changed, and they're gone; just a load of somebody's furniture on the way to God-knows-where. My car's parked in the woods down the road; the fellow you hit with the rifle recovered enough to do that for me, and then be on his way. He even picked up the shell casings before he went." Bo chuckled. "Matter of fact, I had a hard time getting him to go. He wanted to hang around and remove your liver."

"You could never explain the plane, Bo. That's just too big a mess."

"Oh, it's a mess, all right. An Air National Guard plane crashes and burns on a training exercise, probably trying to make an emergency landing on our little strip. The woods will be swarming with state patrolmen and FAA inspectors by noon. Course, there's nobody left alive to identify me."

"That plane's got a few bullet holes in it. Somebody'll notice."

"I wouldn't be surprised if they did. Imagine, some crazy person taking a shot at an airplane. I predict they'll never find him. And Scotty's pictures are over there."

Howell followed Bo's glance to the fireplace, where something was smoking. There were still two rolls in Howell's pocket, though. Bo didn't know about those.

"And where are you right now, Bo? Why isn't the sheriff up there at that plane crash?"

"Oh, I'm asleep in a motel over at Gainesville. I went over there with Eric Sutherland's body this afternoon and waited for the autopsy results. The medical examiner and the coroner agree with your judgment, by the way; clear-cut suicide. Then, I was just so tuckered out, I checked into the Holiday Inn and went right to bed with instructions not to be disturbed." Bo grinned ruefully. "Have I left out anything, John? Anything I forgot?"

Howell felt numb. He knew now that Bo was going to get away with it, with everything.

"I'm real sorry, John," Bo said, "but I'm afraid we're going to have a murder and a suicide up here. The way you're holding your ribs there, and the way Scotty's face is, it's going to look like a real knock-down, drag-out, too."

"You're getting real good at suicides, aren't you, Bo?" This was just a stab, but Howell didn't know what to do except keep talking.

Bo's eyebrows went up. "Now that really interests me," he said. "I'd really appreciate it if you'd tell me how you figured that. I thought it looked real good."

"It did look good, Bo. The pencil was a particularly nice touch. And then I read Eric Sutherland's will and an affidavit he'd attached. That got me thinking that you had a first-rate motive to blow Sutherland away." Howell tried to talk as slowly as he could. He needed the time to think. "Then I began to think that if Sutherland had put the shotgun into his mouth, only the back of his head would have been gone, not most of the front as well. It occurred to me that if I were going to kill myself with a shotgun, I wouldn't look right down the barrel, as Sutherland apparently did. On the other hand, if I were going to kill somebody in the heat of the moment, I probably wouldn't take the time to stick it in his mouth. I'd just point it at his head and pull the trigger. Which is what I reckon you did."

Bo nodded thoughtfully. "And just how did you happen to read Eric's will?"

"He kept the combination taped to the edge of a stenographer's shelf in his desk. Who the hell could ever remember the combination to a safe? And when I read that will, a lot of things began to make sense. What I don't understand is why you went through with that business at the airport. If you hadn't, you'd be free and clear now, with all of Sutherland's money."

Bo nodded. "I'm afraid my business associates insisted."

"Excuse me," Scotty said, sounding irritated. "I'm awfully sorry to interrupt, but this doesn't make any sense to me at all. Would you please tell me what you're talking about?"

"It's a long story," Howell said. He looked at Bo. "Have we got time?"

"Oh, sure," Bo said. "I'd like to hear this myself. Go right ahead." He held up the bottle. "You want a drink?"

"Don't mind if I do," Howell replied. He watched closely as Bo poured a slug of bourbon into a dirty glass on the table at the end of the sofa and handed it to Howell. Bo was very careful about it.

"Well," Howell said, knocking back some of the bourbon, "where to begin? A long time ago, I think. The middle of the last century. When the original settlers of the valley started putting down roots here, they had an idea that they were establishing something permanent, something that would live on. They expected to proliferate. They were Irish, after all. But every time their numbers began to build, something would happen to set them back again—war, disease, that sort of thing. Father Harry brought me up to date on that. Well, nearly up to date, anyway. Do you mind if I sit down, Bo? These ribs are giving me hell."

Howell moved around to the sofa and sat down. Bo didn't stop him, but moved around with him, leaving his back to the fireplace. Howell was hoping Scotty would remember that her pistol was in his desk drawer, but, maddeningly, she rolled the office chair toward the sofa, away from the desk, clearly fascinated by his story. When she moved, though, he saw on the desk behind her the red glow of the On light of his tape recorder. Good girl, he thought.

Howell continued. "The Irish in the valley were staunch Catholics, of course, and they wouldn't intermarry with the locals hereabouts, who were all Baptists and Methodists and other such heathens. And, unlike the Mormons, they didn't have instructions from an angel of God to practice polygamy, so—God knows how it began—somehow, they came around to incest. Father with daughter, brother with sister, that sort of thing."

"Jesus Christ," Scotty said.

"Well you might say," Howell said, "and you might wonder why they didn't themselves, and why the Church didn't keep them from it. They were Christians, after all, and the Faith clearly prohibits incest. On the other hand, it prohibits a number of other things that good Christians often quite proudly do and advocate. Well, who knows exactly how they rationalized it, but they managed. And since they were choosing their priests from among their own number every generation or so, they were able to send young men to the seminary in Ireland who had grown up with the local idea, who understood, who felt an obligation to their families and friends to help perpetuate their community, no matter how they had to do it. Which is how poor Father Harry came to grief."

"He married Lorna Kelly and her brother in the Church," Scotty said.

"Right," Howell replied, "and a great many more besides, I suspect. He was a priest for a long time around here, after all. But the Kellys didn't live in the valley; they didn't have the protective insularity of the community. Eric Sutherland was outraged, and he blew the whistle on Father Harry."

"How did you find out all this?" Scotty asked.

"Some from Father Harry, some from Eric Sutherland's will, and, most important, some from Mama Kelly. A piece here and a piece there," Howell replied, "but Sutherland's affidavit was the most interesting. He went to some lengths to justify himself."

"What made him get involved?" Scotty asked. "I mean, if this had been going on for a hundred years or more, why go after the priest?"

"Aha!" Howell exclaimed, raising a forefinger. "Now you're getting at the heart of things. You see, in 1930, Eric Sutherland fell in love. He met a lovely young Irish lass from the valley, and he went head over heels, perhaps more so than she. She was unhappy with the way things were going in the valley, as were some others in the community. Once in a while, a girl would break away and find herself a beau from the outside; at least, long enough to get pregnant." Howell knew about this from personal experience. He glanced at Bo, who was staring, glassy-eyed, into the middle distance. He still gripped the shotgun, though.

"As you might imagine, a few generations of interbreeding were having their effect on the community. This girl had already borne a retarded child by her brother, and she wanted a healthy baby. Then, as soon as she knew for sure she was pregnant, she broke it off with Sutherland. He was devastated. For a long time he didn't understand what had happened, but when he finally did, he determined to bring what was going on in the valley to a halt. He was in a position to do it. He started with Father Harry."

Howell eased his feet onto the sofa and leaned back, apparently to make his sore ribs more comfortable. The move also brought one arm closer to Bo Scully's shotgun.

"Sutherland was, as we all know, a very straitlaced sort, and the last thing he wanted was a huge scandal in his neck of the woods, getting in the newspapers and all that, especially when he was so personally involved. So, because the Kellys didn't live in the valley, he used them to discredit the priest. He went to the archbishop, told him that Father Harry had married this couple, brother and sister. The archbishop, horrified, called in Father Harry, who admitted it, but nothing more, I suspect, and in short order the priest was officially 'silenced'—that is, he could no longer say Mass or perform marriages—and was quietly pensioned off. That was a blow to the families in the valley, but, of course, Sutherland wasn't finished. He had a civil engineering degree, and he saw the possibilities for a lake where the valley was. A lake would suit his moral purpose as well as his business ones. He went to work buying up the land. You understand, he didn't put every word of this into his affidavit; I'm filling in the cracks. How'm I doing, Bo?"

"Not bad," Bo replied absently.

Howell continued. "And then Eric Sutherland ran smack up against Donal O'Coineen. O'Coineen was an independent sort, one of the ones in the valley who was horrified by what interbreeding was doing to the community. He had a blind daughter, Joyce, whose affliction may have been related to her ancestry. He wanted to farm his land, dig wells on the side for cash money, and raise his children in the valley like a normal human being. He made a point of sending the girls to the town school instead of the one in the valley. He wanted them both to eventually make marriages with young men who were untainted by the valley's interbreeding."

"Wasn't Joyce the one who was engaged to Bo?" Scotty asked.

"That's right, and Donal O'Coineen objected violently to the match. Bo was, in O'Coineen's eyes, tainted. He was from a valley family. That right, Bo?"

Bo nodded. He seemed almost in another place. "He made Joyce break our engagement. He ran me off."

"And then everything came to a head," Howell said slowly. "Sutherland had bought all the land in the valley, except Donal O'Coineen's. Sutherland had built the dam and closed it; the water was rising—the road past the O'Coineen place was all that was holding it back. O'Coineen had pulled Kathleen out of school, but not because of a siege mentality. He had still been trying to make it work, for his children to have a normal life. No, he had another reason for bringing Kathleen home."

"What?" Scotty demanded. "What reason?"

Howell ignored her. "The screws were tightening on everybody; on Sutherland, on O'Coineen, and . . ." He paused. "On Deputy Sheriff Christopher Francis Scully, known to one and all as Bo."

Howell was flying by the seat of his pants now. He had played nearly all his cards, told nearly all he knew, and, if he was to learn any more, he would have to get Bo Scully into the game.

"Here was a young man who was deeply ashamed of his family history, an ambitious young man who had come back from serving his country in Korea and, with the help of Eric Sutherland, was working his way out of the valley into the sunlight of a normal, respectable life. And now the valley, with its dying gasp, had come back to haunt him. He couldn't have the girl he loved, because he was tainted with the valley's sin." Howell looked at Bo expectantly. He was laying it on thick now; he had to get Bo to play.

"And then," Howell said, "a few weeks after Donal O'Coineen had denied him the marriage he wanted, at the very height of all the tension surrounding the building of the lake, young Bo Scully went out to the O'Coineen place, the place he had been driven from." Howell made his voice as soft and gentle as he could. "You know what day it is, Bo?" he asked. "It's September 10, 1976; it's twenty-five years to the day since you went out there to get Donal O'Coineen's signature on a deed of transfer."

Howell held his breath. Bo either played now, or it was all over. Howell nor anyone else would ever know what had happened at the O'Coineen place, and, before dawn, both he and Scotty would be under the lake.

Bo turned and looked at Howell for the first time since he had begun his story. "How did you know I went out there? Eric always told everybody he went."

"Because you witnessed the deed of transfer," Howell said, still softly. "I saw it at the courthouse. I double-checked the date this afternoon. How did you get Donal O'Coineen to sign it, Bo?"

Bo was staring into the middle distance again, lost.

"You killed them, didn't you, Bo? You forged Donal O'Coineen's signature, and then you killed them all, the whole family." He held his breath again.

Bo turned and focused on Howell. "No," he said. "No, I didn't. You don't understand how it was."

Howell was stunned. This wasn't going the way he thought it would. Now, just when he thought he had it all figured out, Bo had surprised him. He let his breath out slowly. "Tell me," he said. And then he knew Bo Scully was going to play.

When I came back from Korea, Joyce and I got engaged. We knew Donal objected to us getting married, but I was doing all right and expected to do even better. Eric Sutherland had taken an interest in me when I was in high school, and when I got out of the Marines he fixed up the deputy sheriff's job and told me that one of these days I'd be sheriff. But Uncle Martin had shot Mama by this time, and that reminded Donal that I was valley and always would be. Still, he let me see Joyce, and just about every night we were out on the front porch swing necking, but necking was all she'd do, and I was about to go crazy. I was engaged to a girl who wasn't going to do anything until we were married, and her papa didn't want her to marry me. That's when Kathleen came into it.

When I left for Korea, she was just a skinny little girl, but when I got back, it had all happened. God, she was something! She was a tiny thing, but even at twelve she had a shape. She'd sit in my lap and move around and, believe me, she knew what she was doing. I've never known anybody so . . . completely sexual. She couldn't turn her head without it being a come-on. She'd come riding with me in the patrol car when I was making rounds, and she'd have her hand in my lap. Pretty soon, we were spending more time in the back seat than in the front. Nobody ever made me feel the way she did . . . nobody. She could look at me and I'd be on fire, and she knew it. She could pull my string, and I'd jump.

I wanted the thing with Kathleen to be over, but I couldn't stop; Kathleen wouldn't let me. Oh, hell, I guess I didn't want it to stop all that bad, but I reckoned when Joyce and I were married Kathleen would find a boyfriend to drive crazy and let me alone. Then Donal pulled her out of school, and when I came out to the house Kathleen wouldn't be there. She'd be sick upstairs or something, always something. This went on for a long time, and I thought Donal had found out about us and was trying to keep her away from me.

One day Donal sat me down and told me he didn't want me to marry Joyce. Said he'd always liked me, but I was valley, and that was that. I asked Joyce straight out, and she said that was the way she wanted it. Donal had finally gotten to her.

I left there, and I've never been so wrecked, before or since. My life was ruined—I couldn't marry Joyce, and she was valley; if she wouldn't have me, then nobody would. In school, the kids had shunned us, and now the only valley girl I wanted wouldn't have me. I didn't know what to do. And then I started getting phone calls from Kathleen.

She'd talk about the things we'd done to each other in the back of that patrol car. She said she loved me, and she wanted me to take her away. We'd go to California or someplace where nobody knew us. She looked older than her age, she said; we could do it. She really was getting to me. I began to think that if I couldn't have one O'Coineen girl, I might have the other one. I began to think about leaving everything—my job and the idea of being sheriff, Eric Sutherland's help—everything. I was tempted, but I knew it was a crazy idea. I liked hearing from Kathleen, though, so I never told her I wouldn't take her away.

The thing between Eric Sutherland and Donal O'Coineen had heated up pretty good by then. Donal wouldn't budge, and the water was rising. I knew Eric wouldn't flood him out, but Donal didn't know that. They were at an absolute stalemate, and I knew that before long, something had to give.

Then one night Kathleen called me.

"Hey, Bo."

It was the way she knew how to say that. Bo's guts turned to water.

"Listen," he whispered, already breathing hard, "I can't talk right now, the sheriff'll hear me. I'm fixing to go out on patrol, anyway."

"You don't have to say anything," she said. "Just listen. I talked Daddy into selling."

This was some sort of trick, Bo thought immediately. She just wanted to get him out there.

"No," she said, anticipating his thoughts. "Daddy really said he would sell. He's already signed that paper Mr. Sutherland sent out here. He says for you to come out here and get the paper and take it to Mr.

Sutherland. He wants Mr. Sutherland to put the money in his bank account in the morning."

"Let me talk to Donal," Bo said.

"He doesn't want to talk," Kathleen replied. "He's already packing everything up. He means to leave here tonight and take us all somewhere else."

Bo hesitated, trying to think.

"You better come out here quick, Bo, before he changes his mind. Mr. Sutherland would be awful mad if you gave Daddy a chance to change his mind."

"All right," Bo said at last. "I'll be out there in about half an hour." He hung up, told the dispatcher he was going on patrol, and left the station. In the car, though, he had second thoughts. Instead of heading for the valley, he made a U-turn and drove to Eric Sutherland's house.

"You mean it?" Sutherland asked, pacing his study. "You think he's finally decided to sell?"

"That's what Kathleen said on the phone," Bo replied. "I think you ought to go out there."

"No, no," Sutherland said quickly. "Donal hates the sight of me by now, and, anyway, he said for you to come. We'll do as he says. You go out there, get the paper, and tell him I'll deposit the money in his account in the morning, just as he wants."

"But, Eric, I'm on patrol tonight," Bo pleaded. "I can't go running out there in a patrol car; the sheriff'll have my skin." Sutherland dug into a pocket. "Here," he said, tossing Bo some keys. "Take my car. Don't worry. I'll fix any problems with the sheriff that might come up. Just get out there and get those papers." He kept pacing. "I can't believe it; Donal's finally caved in. We can start filling the lake again tomorrow!" He stopped and looked at Bo. "Well, don't sit there, boy. Get going!"

Bo left the house and got into Sutherland's old Lincoln Continental convertible. He put the top up so nobody would see him in his uniform in the car, then started for the north valley road. He turned left at the crossroads and started down into the valley. It was a glorious night. Ahead of him, down the road, the house was lit up like a Christmas tree. The moon flooded the valley, casting a glow over the surface fog that covered the lake, right up to the roadway that held the water from Donal O'Coineen's farm. Bo thought it looked like the floor of Heaven. Bo swung the car through the gate and drew up next to the front porch. Donal's truck must be behind the house; he was loading it there, Bo thought. Kathleen met him at the door, slipping her arms around his waist, moving against him. He plucked at her arms, moved her away. "Are you crazy?" he whispered.

"It's all right," she said. "They're all upstairs, packing." She led him toward the table in the front hall. "Here," she said, handing him a pen and placing a paper in front of him. "Daddy wants you to witness it. There's a place there for a witness to sign."

Bo looked at the paper. Donal O'Coineen's name was written at the bottom. Bo signed it. Kathleen hugged him again.

"Now it's done," she said. "Take it back to Mr. Sutherland, and then we can go anywhere we like, you and me."

He held her back. Something was wrong. It was dead quiet in the house, not a sound. There was always some sound, he remembered, Joyce playing the piano or Donal and Mary listening to the radio, but it was strangely quiet. "Where's your folks?" he asked. "Where's Joyce?"

"They're all upstairs packing," Kathleen said, taking his hand and leading him toward the front door. "Now you take the paper to Mr. Sutherland, then come back for me. I'll be all ready to go."

Bo held her by the shoulders and looked at her. "Don't talk crazy, Kathleen," he said. "Something's wrong here." He was beginning to be frightened. He started toward the stairs. "Donal!" he called out.

Kathleen grabbed at his sleeve and pulled, but Bo swept on down the hallway toward the stairs. "No, Bo, don't go up. He doesn't want to see you, I told you."

"Donal!" he called again as he put a foot on the stairs.

"Bo, let's go now," Kathleen cajoled, climbing the steps beside him, tugging at him.

He shook her off. "Joyce!" he yelled, louder now. He turned at the landing and continued upward, Kathleen still begging. "Joyce!" he called as he reached the top of the stairs, and the name died in his throat. Halfway down the hallway, at the door to her room, Joyce lay sprawled in an unnatural position, her legs crossed oddly. Her chest was a mass of blood, and most of her face was gone. She had been shot at least twice with a shotgun, up close, a part of Bo registered, the deputy part. The dark glasses she always wore lay twisted near her head. Her golden hair was scarlet now, spilling over a pool of her own blood.

Bo's mouth worked, but nothing would come out. He made himself continue down the hallway, toward Donal and Mary's room. Kathleen was quiet now. She had stopped begging. Bo came to the door, which was slightly ajar. He pushed it and it swung freely with a loud squeak. Donal and Mary were in bed, sitting up, or, at least, they had been. Donal was twisted sideways, both his arms flung to the same side of his body. Mary's head, what was left of it, lay across his leg, and a great deal of her blood had soaked his trousers. The wall behind the bed held gobs of red and gray matter; bits of hair were stuck to it.

There was a pump shotgun on the floor beside the bed. Bo picked it up and worked the action. Empty.

Kathleen spoke for the first time since they had reached the top of the stairs. "I took the plug out," she said matter-of-factly.

The gun would have held eight shells without the plug, Bo thought. He tried to reconstruct what had happened.

"Daddy and Mama were in bed listening to the radio," Kathleen said, in the same calm voice. "I shot them first, twice each. I heard Joyce call out, and I went into the hall and shot her twice when she came out of her room. Then I came back in here and shot the rest of the times at them." She paused. "Then I turned off the radio."

Bo dropped the shotgun, walked back down the hallway past Joyce's body, and sat down on the top step. He was very tired, it seemed; he felt numb, almost drowsy, and the feeling didn't square with the beating of his heart, which was rapid and hard.

Kathleen sat down beside him and put her head in his lap. "You see," she said. "It's all right now." She stroked his thigh the way she had done in the car so many times. "I practiced Daddy's signature from his canceled checks for a long time, then I signed the paper." Her voice was soothing. "Nobody in the world would think it wasn't his signature, believe me."

Bo held her wrist to stop the stroking. It astonished him that he was becoming excited, even now, after what he had just seen. Her power over him was that great.

"Now here's what we do," Kathleen said, still in her soothing voice. "There's some dynamite out in the shed. Daddy used it in the well digging. What you do, is you put some dynamite under the road. We'll get my things into the car—I'm all packed—and when we drive off you'll blow up the road. You did that stuff in Korea, so you'll know how to do it. Then the lake will come in, and the house will go under." She raised her head. "Oh, I nearly forgot. We'll put Daddy and Mama and Joyce in the well. There's some cement bags in the shed, too. We'll put the cement in the well on top of them; that way, when the lake comes in they won't float up. Bo, you're hurting my wrist."

Bo was surprised that he was gripping her wrist so tightly. He tried to hold it more gently. It was hard.

"We'll take Daddy's typewriter with us," Kathleen continued, resting her head in his lap again, nuzzling his crotch. "I'll write letters to people from him saying we've all moved away. I always typed his letters, I'll know what to say. We'll take his checkbook, too. I can write the checks just the way he did. And I'll write letters to people from Joyce, too. I've always written her letters for her, nobody will think that's funny. Remember how I used to write letters to you from her when you were in Korea? It was me who put in the sexy parts. Bet you didn't know that, bet you thought it was Joyce all the time."

Bo nodded dumbly. He had thought it was Joyce, but when he thought about it, it made sense; it would have been Kathleen saying those things, wouldn't it? It made sense. He had to make some sense now. He had to.

"We're going to be so happy, Bo," Kathleen said, rubbing her ear against his crotch. "We'll get us a nice house on a beach out there. There's lots of beaches in California. At night, we'll take a blanket out on the beach and lie out there naked, and I'll do nice things to you, really nice things."

"Kathleen," Bo managed to say. He had to make some sense.

"I'll do things you never even dreamed about. I'll . . ."

"Kathleen, shut up," Bo said. He put his hand on her neck and held her still. "And stop doing that. I've got to talk to you, and I can't talk to you if you're doing that."

"All right, Bo," she said quietly. "Talk to me."

"This is all completely crazy," Bo said, keeping his hand on her neck, holding her head still. "Nobody will believe any of this, and there isn't enough money. Houses and things cost a lot more in California than they cost here. The money would be gone in no time, it just isn't all that much."

"I'll figure it all out, Bo," she said. "Don't you worry, it'll be wonderful."

"No, you can't figure it out," Bo replied. "It can't be figured out. I can't disappear on the same night that your whole family does. They'll come looking for us, and they'll find us, and they'll bring us back."

They were both quiet for several minutes. Then Kathleen tried to move her head, but Bo tightened his grip a little and held her still.

"Bo," she said, "we have to go away tonight. We have to do it just like I figured it out. If we don't, they'll put you in the electric chair."

"What?" he said. "No, that's not what will happen. They'll send you away for a few years; you're only thirteen, they won't put you in the electric chair."

"Not me, Bo," she said. "You."

Even before she spoke, Bo knew what was coming. He made a small whimpering noise.

"I'll tell them you did it, Bo," she said, and her voice took on an edge he had never heard. "You better take me to California, or I'll tell them you did it, and they'll believe me. I'll make them believe me, you know I can do it."

Bo felt a great sadness. He knew she could do it, this little slip of a girl, she'd tell them every sort of lie, and they'd believe her. She'd sit in a courtroom and deny she'd ever called him and asked him to come out there. She'd say he'd made her do the things they'd done in the patrol car. She'd say it, and they'd believe her.

"You know what I could tell them, Bo," Kathleen said.

He knew. He knew the fix he was in and what he had to do to get out of it. After all, she had laid the whole thing out for him. Not the money, of course; he couldn't do anything about the money. But the rest of it made perfect sense.

"Bo?" she said. It was her last word.

He tightened his grip, put his other hand on the back of her neck to help. He took a deep breath and did it. It didn't take long, only an instant. She didn't feel much, no more than a chicken felt when you wrung its neck. The crunching of bone transmitted itself up his wrists and then she was limp, gone. He sat there and stroked her hair for a few minutes, running through it all in his mind. Then he got up and did the things that Kathleen had told him to do.

A little under an hour later, he stopped the car near the top of the hill, got out, and waited. He had timed it nicely. There was a *whump!*, not much of a noise really, and a flash, and the fog moved on the water as it ran through the gap in the roadbed. Soon the gap widened, and a rushing noise reached him. After a few minutes, the rooftops had vanished. Donal O'Coineen and his family were under the lake.

For a long moment, it was quiet enough to hear the crickets. Then Howell spoke.

"All of them, Bo?" he asked. He took a deep breath and asked the question he had been waiting all night to ask. "What about the baby?"

Bo winced as though he had been struck.

Scotty came to life. "What baby?"

"Kathleen O'Coineen was pregnant," Howell said. "That's why Donal pulled her out of school."

"How the hell did you figure that out?" she asked, dumbfounded.

"Lorna Kelly told me; she and Mary O'Coineen were sisters, remember. Kathleen had her baby a couple of weeks before the family disappeared. What happened to the baby, Bo?"

Bo made a vague gesture. "I didn't know about the baby," he said heavily. "Honest to God I didn't, not until after Kathleen was dead."

"Tell us about the baby, Bo," Howell urged. "It can't hurt to tell us now."

Bo looked defeated. "I'd finished at the well and set the charge at the road, but I damn near forgot to get the transfer deed. I went back into the house for it, and the baby started to cry. I went upstairs. It was in a crib in the room that Joyce and Kathleen shared. It was crying, and I didn't know what to do."

"What did you do, Bo?"

"At first, I was going to throw it down the well," Bo said, "but I couldn't. It was a *baby,* and it was mine; I knew it was mine."

"For Christ's sake, Bo," Scotty nearly shouted. "What did you do with it?"

"I thought about leaving it on somebody's doorstep, but that would have only caused a lot of talk, made the newspapers and all. Then I remembered; when I came back from Korea, I flew from San Francisco to Atlanta and took a cab to the bus station. On the way we passed the Georgia Baptist Children's Home in Hapeville, out by the airport. It was the only orphanage in the state that I knew about. I called Eric and told him that everything was okay, but that I was tired and wanted to go home, that I'd bring his car and the deed to him in the morning. Then I put the baby in a box, and I drove it to Atlanta in Eric Sutherland's car. It was the middle of the night, and there was no traffic. I gave the baby a bottle I found in the kitchen, and it was real good all the way to Atlanta; it didn't cry or anything, it just slept. I guess I got there about four in the morning, before daylight anyway. I left the box on the steps of what looked like the kitchen door and rang the bell. Then I got the hell out of there. I was back in Sutherland before Eric got up."

Scotty, wide-eyed, was the first to speak. "What kind of box did you put the baby in?" she asked Bo.

Bo turned to her. "I didn't even know whether it was a boy or a girl, until . . ."

"What kind of box was it, Bo?" Scotty demanded.

Bo hung his head. "It was a dynamite box," he said, his face contorted with guilt. "I'm awful sorry, Scotty. I just didn't know."

The three of them stood in the room, silent, Howell looking back and forth from Scotty to Bo, baffled. "Hang on just a minute," he said finally. "What's all this about a box?"

Scotty was staring incredulously at Bo, apparently unable to speak. Then, never taking her eyes from Bo, she said, "I'm adopted. My parents got me from the Georgia Baptist Children's Home, in Hapeville, in September of 1951. I had been left on the doorstep there in a dynamite box. My father used to tell the story all the time. 'Dynamite comes in small packages,' he likes to say." She continued to stare at Bo as if she were seeing some fascinating creature for the first time. Tears began to spill from her eyes.

"Holy shit," Howell said, looking worriedly at Scotty. She was flushed and breathing rapidly.

"This can't be happening," Scotty said, still staring at Bo. "I've lived all my life wondering who the hell I was, and now I find out." She suppressed a sob, then went on. "Let's see, my paternal grandfather was Eric Sutherland, right?" She went on without waiting for confirmation. "My maternal grandfather was Donal O'Coineen. My mother was

Kathleen O'Coineen, who, it turns out, was a mass murderer and who still comes to visit from time to time."

"Huh?" Bo said.

"And you . . ." She pointed a finger at Bo. *"You* are my father? Christ, I've been trying to put you in jail for three months!" She sat back in her chair and shook her head violently. "I know this is a weird time to think of this, but whatever happened to my journalistic objectivity and detachment? I'm up to my ass, I'm *trapped* in my own story! What editor would ever believe this? What *reader* would believe it?" She began sobbing. *"I* don't believe it!"

"I'm real sorry about everything, Scotty," Bo said. "I just didn't know until you told me that time about being found in the box. I want you to believe that."

Scotty managed to get control of herself for a moment. "I believe you, Bo," she said. "I'll try to forget about it if you will." She started to sob again.

Howell was baffled. "Forget it? Forget *what?* He's your father, for Christ's sake!"

"Thanks, John," Scotty said through her tears. "I believe I've got the picture."

Howell's eyebrows shot up; he snapped his fingers. *"That's* what Mama Kelly has been on about, then. She kept saying, 'Little Kathleen is in danger.' Jesus Christ, *you're* little Kathleen!"

"I guess I am. And I'm in danger," Scotty said, nodding at Bo and his shotgun.

Howell had nearly forgotten about that. Fascinated by Bo's story, he had forgotten that he had meant to grab for the shotgun the first chance he got. "Listen, Bo . . ."

"Just shut up for a minute, John," Bo said, waving the shotgun. "I've got to think for a minute."

Howell stopped talking, stopped breathing, but not because of Bo. He had heard something, or rather, didn't hear something. The crickets had stopped. Something was happening.

"Look, Bo," he said. "You can't kill us. You can't kill Scotty, she's—"

"You think I haven't thought about that? If you'd just stayed away from the airport tonight, everything would have been all right. That was the last delivery here, ever."

"No, Bo," Howell said, shaking his head, "nothing would have been all right. You murdered Eric Sutherland. You've killed your *father,* for

God's sake. You've killed the mother of your child. Do you think killing your daughter will make it all right? Do you think anything could ever be all right again?"

"Yes, I killed the sonofabitch," Bo shouted. "He played me along all my life; he never told me. If he'd told me, not when I was a kid, but even as late as when I came back from Korea, then I could have married Joyce. I wasn't tainted, but I didn't know that. None of this would have ever happened if he'd only told me, can't you see? It wasn't until I figured it out on my own, when I found out he'd been having my mother's grave tended all these years, that he admitted it. Then he tried to buy me off, showed me his will and how everything was left to me; *that's* when I killed him."

"He didn't tell you, just like you didn't tell Scotty," Howell said.

"Hardly," Scotty chimed in.

"Everything would have been all right if you hadn't been at the airport tonight, don't you see? With Sutherland's money, I could have taken care of Scotty for the rest of her life. Hell, I was already planning it."

"It's got nothing to do with our being at the airport, Bo," Howell fired back. "It's got to do with *you,* and the way you always try to overcome your own weakness by killing somebody. You were weak enough to let yourself be seduced by a twelve-year-old girl, then you killed your way out of it. You were weak enough to let Eric Sutherland run your life, and you killed your way out of that. Then, with all you had going for you here, you were weak enough to take drug money, and now you're going to kill your way out of that, too?"

Bo turned a violent red, and Howell knew he had gone too far. "You stupid bastard," Bo shouted. "I own this town now, I own this lake, I own everything Eric Sutherland owned! Do you think I'm going to let you walk out of here and take that away from me?" He swung the shotgun toward Scotty. "You're goddamned right, I'm going to kill my way out of it, and right now!" He pumped the shotgun and started to bring it to his shoulder.

Howell was struggling past the pain of his inflamed ribs, trying to get to his feet before the gun went off, but instead of a shotgun, what he heard was a loud click from across the room. Bo swung the shotgun in that direction and froze. The player piano was starting to play.

"I'll Take You Home Again, Kathleen" rolled from the machine at a loud volume.

Bo stared open-mouthed at the piano; then, an animal noise rising in his throat, he fired at it. Bits of wood flew everywhere, but the piano played madly on. He fired again, then spun to his left. Howell turned to follow his stare.

She looked different, more womanly. The childish overalls were gone, and she wore a simple, virginal, white dress, tied at her small waist with a narrow sash. Her dark hair fell in long waves around her shoulders, and there was a suggestion of lipstick, stark against her white skin. Two buttons undone revealed the swell of her full breasts, straining against the tight fabric. Her huge, dark eyes were fixed on Bo Scully; a little smile played about her lips. Then she turned and looked at Scotty for the first time, frankly, with curiosity; then, it seemed, with something like approval.

Scotty stood transfixed by her first sight of her true mother. Howell remembered a photograph he had seen at the Kellys', a family group on a front porch, a little girl of four or five. Now he knew why the child had looked familiar; she had looked like Scotty. Now the resemblance was less strong, but it was there. They were mother and daughter, Kathleen and Scotty.

Bo pumped the shotgun again. He was now emitting a continuous noise made up of a growl and a scream. He raised the gun, took aim, and, to Howell's helpless horror, fired at Kathleen. He was astonished when she seemed unaffected. Her expression never changed, but a large section of the French doors behind her exploded into fragments.

Three shots, Howell managed to count to himself, in spite of what was happening; five more to go.

Kathleen O'Coineen stood, smiling indulgently, as Bo emptied the shotgun at her, affecting only what lay behind her.

Howell hurled himself across the room toward the desk, clawed the drawer open, and found Scotty's pistol, its shells lying next to it. Frantically, he began loading the gun. He had two shells into the chambers, when Kathleen turned gracefully, glanced beckoningly at Bo, and walked out of the house, onto the deck. Bo threw the shotgun through what was left of the French doors and ran after her. Howell saw him stop on the deck, staring out at the lake. Howell finished loading the pistol and went after him, then stopped as he reached the door. Scotty was right behind him, dragging the chair to which she was handcuffed.

Bo gazed, wide-eyed, out over the valley. Howell gazed with him. It was just as in the dream, the house ablaze with light, the fog on the rising lake, and all of it lit by a large moon.

Bo said something, not quite a word, and started moving down the steps from the deck.

"Wait a minute, Bo!" Howell said, and pointed the gun at him. Bo glanced back, then continued down the steps. "Stop, Bo!" Howell said, louder this time. Bo had reached the bottom of the steps and was moving toward the road to the valley. Howell lowered the gun and screamed as loudly as he could. "Bo, don't go down there! For Christ's sake, come back!"

Howell moved to follow him, but Scotty had squeezed her chair through the door and grabbed at him, getting hold of his belt. "No, no, Johnny, don't follow him!"

Howell struggled on down the steps, dragging Scotty after him, she dragging the chair. They reached the bottom and moved a few steps toward the road before Scotty was able to stop him.

"You can't follow him, you can't!"

Howell realized she was right, and stopped. They stood in front of the cabin and watched Bo run down the road toward the house, as fast as his legs could move him. Occasionally he shouted something, but they couldn't make it out. They saw him reach the house and run through the front door.

Suddenly the valley was gone, and the lake was back at their feet. They stood silently, unable to react. Then, as they watched, a soundless explosion of light came from under the lake, rising to a brightness that hurt their eyes, then, pulsating erratically, faded slowly into darkness, until they were left staring once again at dark and peaceful waters. There was no moon. The crickets began to chirp again.

A touch of dawn had begun to light the sky. Howell turned to lead Scotty back into the cabin and stumbled over Denham White's double-barreled shotgun, lying at the lake's edge.

"Where did that come from?" Scotty asked.

Howell picked up the weapon and broke it to inspect the chambers. Empty. "It's something I misplaced," he said.

"Tell me again how this tape recorder works." The Georgia State Patrol captain's voice came down somewhere between skepticism and outright incredulity.

"It's voice-activated," Howell explained again. "Once it's turned on, it records only when it hears something, and it automatically controls the recording level. Miss MacDonald managed to turn it on when I arrived at the cabin, when Scully was occupied with me."

"Okay, I'll take your word for that," the captain said. The late afternoon sunlight reflected off his collar insignia. "And you say that right after this shooting on the tape, Sheriff Scully threw down the shotgun, ran out onto the deck, ran down the steps out there, and jumped in the lake."

"Jumped in and started swimming away," Howell said. "I tried to stop him, but he wouldn't listen to me; he just kept going."

"We found his body nearly a mile along the lake," the captain said, shaking his head. "I expect we'll get a suicide-by-drowning verdict from the coroner. Wasn't a mark on him."

"He seemed to hear the piano and see something outside on the deck before he started firing," Howell said. "I think he must have been hallucinating. He'd had a lot of bourbon."

"Well, there's no piano on the tape," the captain said. "I guess maybe he must have been. I'll tell you, though, I'd have said that Bo Scully was just about as level-headed a fellow as I ever knew. This sure don't fit him."

"I guess every man has his breaking point," Howell said. "He'd been under a lot of pressure, I think, what with having killed Sutherland and having the drug delivery aborted."

"I wouldn't say exactly aborted," the captain came back. "We're still looking for that furniture van. The GBI have picked up an Air National Guard lieutenant colonel down at Dobbins Air Force Base, though. Maybe they'll get something out of him."

"I'd be willing to bet that his training logs jibe with the schedule from Scully's files."

The captain put his hands on his knees and stood up. "Well, Counselor," he said to Enda McAuliffe, "I can't see any reason to detain your clients. Everything they've told me seems to be backed up by the evidence we have." He put on his Stetson hat and squared it carefully. "I don't mind telling you, though, this is the damnedest thing I've investigated in nineteen years on the job."

"I don't doubt it," McAuliffe said, shaking the man's hand.

"Just as long as they're available if we need to know anything else," the captain said, and took his leave.

McAuliffe came back to the fireplace and flopped into a chair. "I think we did the best thing," he said to Howell and Scotty. "If you'd told him what you told me, we'd never hear the end of it, not for the rest of our lives." He still looked skeptical.

"I think you're right," Howell said. "I'd be hard pressed to tell the truth about what happened; I'm still not sure what the truth is."

"I don't have any speculation to offer," McAuliffe said, "but I do have Bo's will." He reached into his coat pocket and withdrew a heavy blue envelope. "He typed this out himself and brought it to my office to be witnessed a few days ago. Following Bo's instructions at the time, I opened it and read it when you called me and told me he was dead."

"I remember his working on something all one morning at the office and saying he was going over to your place," Scotty said.

McAuliffe nodded. "It's pretty straightforward. He leaves everything to his only living relative, Heather M. MacDonald, also known as Scotty Miller."

"Is it legal?" Howell asked.

"Airtight," the lawyer replied, then took another, plain envelope from his pocket and handed it to Scotty. "He left this for you."

Scotty opened the envelope and read the sheets inside while Howell and McAuliffe waited. Finally she looked up. "It's a short version of what he told us last night," she said, "and the number of the Swiss bank account."

"That's a bunch of money, Scotty," Howell said.

"I don't want it," she said unhesitatingly. "It's dirty money. I liked him, in spite of everything, and I'd rather forget that part of him." She turned to McAuliffe. "Can I give it away?"

"Well," the lawyer said, "there'll have to be some negotiations with the Internal Revenue Service; you can give away what's left. In any case, you don't need the money. Bo was Eric Sutherland's heir, and you're Bo's heir. I can't give you a figure off the top of my head, but you're a very wealthy young woman."

Scotty nodded. "That occurred to me. I don't know what the hell I'll do with it."

"There's a fair amount of liquid stuff—stocks and bonds, plus his house—but the main thing is the lake. You're the majority stockholder in the power company—the banks have a chunk."

Scotty looked at him and grinned. "Does that mean I can hand out lakefront lots around here?"

"Yep. You're the boss, or will be, when the will is probated."

"Okay, Johnny," she said, turning to Howell. "Take your pick. Find a lot you like, and it's yours. It's the very least I can do for you."

"Thanks, Scotty. I'll take you up on it. I think a place on another part of the lake, though. It gets a little hairy around here."

"There's something else, Scotty," McAuliffe said. "It seems pretty clear that you're entitled to the money that Sutherland thought he paid Donal O'Coineen, plus the interest that's been building up for the last twenty-five years. I'll make a claim with the bank, if you like. Strictly speaking, the transaction never took place, since Kathleen forged Donal's signature on the transfer deed, but it hardly matters, I think, because you're O'Coineen's heir as well as Sutherland's. They were both your grandfathers. I can straighten out the legal end of it with the bank."

Scotty put her hands to her cheeks. "This is getting to be too much for me to handle."

"Can I make a suggestion, Scotty?" Howell asked.

"Sure. I could use a suggestion."

"Before you start thinking too much about your inheritance, why don't you let Mac sort things out for you here? Just go back to Atlanta, write your story, and be a reporter. I think you'd be very unhappy doing anything else for quite a while, speaking as somebody who left the profession before he should have."

"That's good advice," Scotty replied. "Mac, you want to be my law-yer?"

McAuliffe grinned. "Sure. I'm already working for the power company, anyway, for my sins." He closed his briefcase and stood up. "Well, I've got things to do. We'll talk later." He left Howell and Scotty alone.

Scotty came and put her arms around Howell.

He winced. "Ouch."

"Sorry, I forgot about the ribs. Listen, why don't you come back to Atlanta with me? I've gotten sort of used to having you around."

Howell put his hands on her shoulders. "That's very tempting, but you and I have different fish to fry for a while. When this story breaks, you're going to have to spend some time dealing with fame, not to mention fortune. Me . . . well, I think I've got a shot at recapturing something I thought I had lost. I'm not sure I could do it if anyone were watching."

"I guess you're right," she replied, and kissed him lightly. "I'll miss you, though."

"That's nice to hear," Howell said. "Listen, Scotty, there was something going on between you and Bo last night that I never got a handle on. What was it?"

Scotty grinned ruefully. "Well, that was something between father and daughter, I guess you'd have to say. Maybe I'll tell you about it one of these days." She sighed. "I'm going to have him buried in his family plot, next to his mother. There's nobody else to do it, and I guess it's my job."

Howell nodded. "You might think about putting Eric Sutherland alongside them. The three of them never found much peace together in life, but somehow, it seems right."

"That makes sense. I'll get Mac to make the arrangements."

There was a knock at the cabin door. Howell went to answer it and found Leonie Kelly standing there. He turned to Scotty. "Will you excuse us for a few minutes?" He walked her out onto the deck.

"I heard about Bo," she said. "It's all over the town. But what happened here?" she asked, picking her way through the broken glass.

Howell told her about his and Scotty's experiences of the night before. "You're the only person I know, apart from your mother, who would believe it," he said. "I don't think Mac does, and we gave a laundered version to the state patrol."

"Mama died early this morning," Leonie said. "Just before dawn."

"I'm sorry. She was quite a lady."

"It was a relief. She took a long time about it. She was waiting for things to be resolved here." Leonie looked out over the lake.

"It's a peculiar thing," Howell reflected, following her gaze. "The symmetry of everything that's happened here is remarkable. The same things kept repeating in each generation: what went on in the valley; the steps two women—Bo's mother and you—took independently to avoid it; murder—Bo's mother, the O'Coineen family, Sutherland; and now, within the past forty-eight hours, three of the principals—Sutherland, Bo, and your mother—have died, two of them leaving written accounts in a last-minute attempt to set things straight."

"Mama wouldn't have found that remarkable," Leonie said. "She would have regarded a lot of what happened as evil, but all of it as natural, as human nature; and she would have regarded the outcome as the most natural thing of all—perfect justice. In fact, she said something like that just before she died."

"What did she say?"

"She looked at us—we were all in her room—and smiled, and said, 'I can go now, it's all been put right.' "

"Not quite," Howell said, "but it will be put right before the day's out. I've already talked with Enda McAuliffe about setting something up for the baby."

"I've told you . . ."

"By the way, was Denham White once in love with you?"

She nodded. "His family wouldn't let us marry. I don't blame them, really. I don't blame Denham, either. I suppose I was trying to use him to find a way out of here. That was before I realized that this is where I belong. I still have a family to take care of. But I don't need your—"

"No. Listen to me. You were right last night; I've always found it too easy to move on and let other people sort out my responsibilities. It's time I stopped that. In a few days I'm coming into a bunch of money for a job I'm doing, and it's going to Mac's office to help the child later on. Mac knows it's my baby, and I've told him I don't care who else knows. I may not be able to be a perfect father to him, but I can give him my name and find ways to help him get through his life." He took her shoulders and turned her to him. "I want to do that, do you understand?" He didn't want Lurton Pitts's money anymore, and doing this for Leonie made him feel less ashamed of the way he had earned it.

She nodded and put her arms around his waist.

He yelped in pain. "Watch it. I think I've cracked something in there."

She put a hand on his ribs, at the center of the pain. "Yes, you have," she said. She put her arms around him again and held him gently to her body.

Howell felt once again the amazing warmth he had felt when she healed his back. A moment later, she stood back and looked at him.

"I think you can take off the bandage now." She smiled and kissed him on the cheek.

Howell took a tentative breath, then another, deeper one. "I think you're right," he said, but she was already walking down the steps and turning toward the truck. He watched her drive away, then went back into the cabin.

"I've been on the phone to the paper," Scotty said triumphantly. "Would you believe they're sending a chopper up here for me and the film? We've only got the first two rolls I shot, but that's got just about everything on it."

"Good for you," Howell laughed, and hugged her.

"I'd better get into town and get my stuff together," she said. "They'll be at the airport in an hour."

Howell kissed her. "Get going then."

"Listen, we'll see each other in Atlanta, won't we?"

"From time to time, no doubt."

"That's not often enough," she said, punching him playfully in the ribs. "Jesus, I'm sorry. I forgot."

Howell pulled out his shirttail. "Undo this, will you?"

Scotty unclipped the bandage and unwound it from his rib cage. "Shouldn't you leave this on?"

Howell took several deep breaths. "Don't need it," he crowed.

"There isn't even any bruising!" she said. "There sure was when I wrapped you up this morning. I thought you'd be weeks . . ." Then she stopped. "Oh, I see. Mama Kelly."

"Well, sort of. By long distance, I guess. She died this morning, just about the time Bo did, I suspect."

"Oh, I'm sorry," Scotty said. "I never even met her, but I could sure feel her in that house yesterday." She cocked her head to one side. "Listen, what was going on between you and Leonie? There was *something* going on there, I know it."

"I'll tell you about it sometime," he said, grinning. "And you ought to get to know her better, when you're back up here. She's your cousin, you know."

"I guess she is, at that."

"So are Dermot and Brian and Mary," he said, more soberly. "When you get used to the idea of being a wealthy woman, you ought to think about doing something for them. After all, if it hadn't been for their mother, you wouldn't be the filthy capitalist you are now."

"I'll do that," she said. "Listen, I don't want to get all maudlin, but I'm awfully grateful to you for getting me through this alive. I'll call you for lunch next week and thank you properly, okay?"

"I'd better call you," Howell said. "I'm not sure just where I'll be."

"I think I know," she said. "But let me hear from you." Then she grabbed her two precious rolls of film and fled.

A couple of days later, Howell threw the last of his gear into the back of the station wagon and shut the tailgate. He went back into the cabin, picked up the phone, and dialed a number.

"Bob Allen, please." There was a click and some ringing.

"Allen."

"Hello, Bob. It's John Howell."

"Well, I'll be damned. A voice from the past. You got my note, huh?"

"Sounded more like a death threat to me."

"You want it?"

"Maybe. We can talk about it. We'll have to get some things straight, like what happens after Nairobi."

"What did you have in mind?"

"London."

"I expect we might find a slot there in about three years."

"I won't stay in Africa a minute more than eighteen months."

"Two years, and I'll see what I can do about London. When can you get up here?"

"I've got a few things to sort out in Atlanta. A week from Monday?"

"Okay, you're on. Uh, listen, you'll have to learn Swahili, you know."

Howell could hear him grinning. "You bastard," he said. "That's going to cost you an extremely expensive lunch." He hung up.

Howell picked up the completed manuscript of Lurton Pitts's autobiography from the desk, and looked around the cabin. It was strangely dark, with its boarded-up windows. It seemed dead; just a lot of lumber and furniture.

He still wasn't entirely sure of what had happened to him here, and he doubted if he ever would be. But he felt ready to go back and work at his life, instead of just wandering through it; to go back to what he did best and try to do it better.

He walked over to the battered player piano. It was missing chunks of veneer and spattered with buckshot, but still, somehow, whole. He flipped the switch. A flood of music poured out.

George Gershwin was playing "I've Got Rhythm." Howell waited until it was finished, then he flipped off the switch. He laughed all the way to the car.

ACKNOWLEDGMENTS

I must begin at the beginning, by thanking Elton Drake, who, twenty-five years ago, invited me to a mountain lake and told me a ghost story, one I never forgot.

I also want to thank Eric Swenson for his early reading of the manuscript and his most helpful suggestions; my agent, Morton Janklow, and Anne Sibbald of his office; everyone at Simon & Schuster for their extraordinarily high level of enthusiasm for this book, but particularly Joni Evans and Michael Korda, busy people, who took such a deep interest; Scott Corngold, who kept the wheels oiled; and most of all, my editor, Laurie Lister, who did all that had to be done, and more.

Finally, I must thank Elaine Kaufman for running the sort of place where a writer can meet an editor, and Gay Talese for seeing that it happened.

Stuart Woods is the author of four novels, including *Chiefs*—which received the Mystery Writers of America Edgar Award and was made into a successful television miniseries—and the international best-selling espionage thriller *Deep Lie*. He has also written two nonfiction books and is currently at work on a screenplay. Woods divides his time between Atlanta, Georgia, and the Isle of Wight in England.